THE REAL DEAL

THE REAL DEAL

Marty Shevelove

Rock 'n' Rant

ISBNs
Paperback: 978-1-7642011-0-0
eBook: 978-1-7642011-1-7

Published by Rock 'n' Rant Publishing

Printed by IngramSpark

Front cover: Alamy D733YE
Rear cover: Shutterstock 2393885769 & 1960476814
Title page: Shutterstock 111707318

About the AUTHOR

Former little leaguer, sports journalist, radio host and humourist Marty Shevelove, a money maker for GPs and specialists up and down the east coast of Australia and Tasmania, gave a lot of thought to his latest project. And what better place to pen a novel about baseball than the expanses of northwest Tasmania where the site of a baseball diamond is as rare as a 27° day. By all accounts, actually just his own, the die-hard New York Mets tragic, has knocked it out of the park.

The author can be reached via email: martymelbourne@gmail.com

Chapter 1

THE HAND-STITCHED Rawlings baseball rose quickly, sailed over the chest-high outfield fence, bounced several times as it struck the asphalt-covered parking lot and wound up in the back of a white ute travelling eastbound towards the coast.

"I want that freakin' kid drug tested," New South Wales head coach Clem Davenport screamed from the front steps of the home team's dugout while Victoria's Billy Jenkins circled the bases in the fourth inning of the grand final of the Under 12 National Baseball Championships in Newcastle, NSW.

"That's right, drug tested," he barked to the home plate umpire. "That ball is halfway to the moon and still going. How old is he anyways? He shaves more often than I do."

Had the 11-year-old been drug tested, the substances detected would have been Weet-Bix, Uncle Tobys Oats, apples – he was partial to Royal Galas – and oranges.

After striking out the last NSW batter of the game on three straight pitches, Jenkins was carried off the field by his teammates. At the awards ceremony that night he was named tournament MVP and given yet another trophy.

"Anybody got a spare bag? How am I going to get all this stuff home?" he joked when he returned to his table.

Billy Jenkins was not only the best junior player to ever wear an Aspendale Aces uniform but the finest young ballplayer in Victoria. With his sky-blue Aces cap perched on his head, he was recognised more often than the Shire's unpopular mayor, Mitch Ford. Billy was asked several times a day to pose for selfies and even sign autographs.

"Shit, when was the last time someone asked me to take a photo with them?" Mayor Ford asked his wife Meg over breakfast as he scanned the sport pages of the *Cheltenham Post.*

"Well, there was that time when you were picked up for drink driving on Nepean Highway and those nice constables drove you home," Meg cheekily said.

Ford dropped the weekly newspaper on the dining room table and glared at his wife of 16 years. "For fuck's sake Meg, can you stop bringing that up? If that ever got out, I'd be through."

Billy Jenkins' 12th birthday was still six months away. There was talk going around the clubrooms of the Aspendale Baseball Club of retiring Billy's number 16 jumper. "Let's ease off on that for a bit," club president Dan Weedman told those pushing for it. "He's 11 years old, a little leaguer, not Babe Ruth."

Billy Jenkins had played for Victoria at national tournaments each summer since he was nine years old. He was a unanimous state selection that year and the next two. But his heroics in Newcastle took his game to a whole new level.

Nearly a head taller and 5-10 kilos heavier than any of his Victorian teammates, the soft-spoken youngster led the Vics to six straight wins to reach the grand final and tossed a no-hitter as the Vics whitewashed New South Wales 7-0 to claim the national crown.

His home run, his sixth of the 10-day tournament, was estimated to have travelled an unheard of 350 metres before it was unwittingly hauled away by the ute and never seen again.

Six weeks after his remarkable performance in Newcastle, Billy was named the *Cheltenham Post*'s Sports Star of the Year. He was given a handsome plaque and a $500 cheque by Channel 12 sports presenter Harry Halfpipe, the event's compere, during a dinner at Mama Calzone's Italian Restaurant and Function Centre in Mordialloc in Melbourne's southeast.

He thanked his proud parents for driving him to practices and games throughout the city and regional Victoria, his two older sisters for their love and support, and his coaches and teammates.

The evening's guest speaker was Caulfield Cup winning part-owner Gary Delaney, formerly of *Turf News*, who was well lit when he followed Billy onto the stage.

"My advice to you sports stars here tonight – the winners and nominees, young and old – is to leave school or quit your job, and buy a share in a racehorse. There was a long pause before he added "and get yourself a versatile wife or girlfriend."

"Thank you, Gary for those illuminating remarks," Halfpipe said as he snatched the mic from his hands and quickly ushered him off the stage.

"Who the fuck booked that arsehole?" *Cheltenham Post* general manager Sid Fields screamed between bites of his tiramisu. He turned to the weekly newspaper's marketing man, Marshall Thurgood, one of nine others at his table of 10. "Was it you Marshall or that four-eyed failure assistant of yours?"

"He'll be gone by the morning Sid."

"And where is he anyways? Why isn't he here?"

"He said he had a prior engagement."

"A prior engagement? With who? The guys in that gay choir he sings showtunes with?"

Thurgood quickly scanned the room of 200. Nobody appeared upset with Delaney's remarks.

"It will pass," Thurgood assured Fields.

"Oh, it will pass alright. Like a fucking kidney stone. This is a fucking nightmare. There are young kids here for goodness sake. Thurgood, get into the kitchen and tell the staff to serve all the tiramisu and whatever other shit they have back there to our guests. Maybe everyone will forget all about it. And if any of them ask for their money back it is coming out of your pay packet."

Delaney and Halfpipe later wound up at Braeside brothel Satisfaction where they were greeted at the door by manager Susie Lee Wong. Susie was 35 going on 60 and had been around the block more times than a Kenyan marathon runner. Wong introduced the well-soused Delaney and Halfpipe to her six working girls. "Stand up," Wong told her half-naked employees. "Let these fine gentlemen get a good look at you."

Wong's girls – all but two of whom were Asian – put down their phones and posed for the two. Delaney took a long look, walked up to a potted plant, and loudly said "she'll do."

Halfpipe nearly pissed his pants from laughing. "My mate has had a few," he explained.

Halfpipe had a difficult time deciding who he would spend his $250 on.

"Why not Sally?" Wong asked. "Look at the body on her. She's just 20, they're real, and she's versatile."

"Versatile? Listen closely because I am only going to say this once. I do not want someone who cooks, irons and vacuums, or a decathlete, I just want to get laid," Halfpipe said.

BILLY JENKINS' first taste of fame came three years earlier when as a nine-year-old Little Leaguer he foiled a burglary at his Cheltenham home.

It was a few minutes before 3am on an overcast Tuesday night and Jumbo Dickey and Yogi Larson were looking for an easy target on one of the few quiet streets left in the southeast Melbourne suburb.

Unlike some other hoods their age, the 20-year-olds had no desire to knock down the front door of a home, wake the frightened occupants and demand – sometimes at gunpoint – car keys and wallets. Dickey and Larson were looking for an unlocked back door to gain entry to one of the double-storey family homes Cheltenham used to be known for. In the past four or five years, large apartment buildings had sprouted up like weeds in the highly sought-after suburb known for its championship golf courses, Southland Shopping Centre, the train line to Melbourne's CBD and its proximity to Port Phillip Bay.

A couple of mugs like Dickey and Larson did not have enough brain cells between the two of them to disable modern security systems and break into one of the new buildings or even to gain access to their underground garages. So, they stuck to family homes.

If they found at least one unlocked back door, Dickey and Larson planned to spend no more than four or five minutes quietly gathering whatever valuables they could their hands on. Laptops, big screen name brand TVs, iPads and smart phones topped their list.

Dickey and Larson's fence, an overweight, single chap named Harmon Ruffing, paid them 15 cents on the dollar for whatever they brought to his aging Moorabbin home. Ruffing liked to call himself a collector of antiques and even had business cards to hand out if he was ever asked what he did for a living. The problem was nobody ever asked. The 45-year-old had three teams of burglars working for him, and three and four times a week in the early hours of the morning, they dropped off shitloads of stolen merchandise, got paid and blew the cash on drugs, booze, cigarettes, bad haircuts, sex workers and tattoos.

None of the three teams had come close to getting caught in the four months they had been working for him, so Ruffing's garage was beginning to resemble a Harvey Norman showroom.

Dickey and Larson parked their beat-up ute underneath a malfunctioning streetlight on Harrelson Lane and with small torches in their hands and dark green shopping bags stuffed in their back pockets, began to scale backyard fences. They tried numerous back doors on DiMaggio Court, but every single one was locked.

"I'd rather not break in," Dickey told his mate.

"We might not have to. Let's try a few more," Larson said

Dickey agreed.

The third house they tried on Steinbrenner Lane also had its back door locked. But Dickey had his eye on a doggie door just to the right of the back door.

"I can get in there," Dickey said.

Despite his nickname, Jumbo was not a particularly big man.

Larson had his doubts. "You seriously think you can get through there? And how are you going to get a TV through that thing?"

"Simple. I'll open the door and walk out with it."

Larson thought it over for a moment. "Give it a go mate. But what about the dog? What if it barks or starts chewing on your arse?"

Dickey pulled a sealed baggie from his jacket pocket and held it up for his dim partner to see. It contained a frozen soup bone.

"I'm way ahead of you mate. While the dog is chewing on this, we'll be cleaning his owners out."

The two exchanged high fives.

Dickey got on his knees and without much difficulty got his shoulders through the doggie door and pulled himself completely through. He landed on the hardwood floor with a thump and woke the family dog, who had been sleeping in his bed less than 10 feet away.

Before Dickey was able to stand up, he found himself face-to-face with some sort of Labrador mix. The dog bared his teeth and growled. Dickey reached into his pocket and carefully placed the bone in front of the animal. He had a few sniffs, carefully removed the bone from Dickey's hand and went back to his bed with the unexpected late-night treat.

Jumbo opened the back door to let his mate in and both went to work scouring the contents of the living room and kitchen. The bedrooms were upstairs and off-limits. They grabbed an iPad and an iPhone from the coffee table in the living room and started to unscrew a year-old 60-inch Sony TV which was mounted to the main wall. Halfway through the operation, Dickey dropped his screwdriver which landed with a thud on the floor, rolled and came to a stop in front of the dog. He gave it a sniff and went back to his bone. Dickey and Larson waited a few moments to see if anyone had awakened, and sensing that no one had, went back to work.

Billy Jenkins preferred to sleep with the door to his room open and even though he was upstairs, the sound of the screwdriver hitting the floor below was loud enough to wake him. Grabbing a baseball from his bedside table, Billy crept downstairs in his bare feet to investigate. He ducked past the kitchen and slowly made his way to the living room. He nearly yelled when he saw two figures in the living room taking the TV off the wall; the same TV he and his dad watched ballgames from the states on. Instead, Billy switched on the lights. Dickey and Larson momentarily froze, then turned and saw the lad. Larson headed for the door while Dickey undid the last screw on the TV and tucked it under his arm. As he moved to the open back door, Billy flipped the baseball in his hand and sized up his target. He reared back and let go with an A-Grade heater which caught Dickey flush on the back of the head. Dickey fell backwards and was unconscious by the time he hit the floor. The television landed on Dickey's soft stomach unharmed. Nearly done with his bone, Sparky walked over to Dickey and began to lick his face. "You weren't much help, were you boy?" Billy told the dog.

Billy ran upstairs, woke his parents, and told them what happened. Charlie Jenkins grabbed a baseball bat from the hall closet and ran downstairs, aggravating a calf injury which had kept him from playing for the Aspendale Aces senior side the previous Sunday.

Charlie Jenkins laughed when he saw the intruder lying unconscious in the living room. A baseball was a foot or two away from his head.

Cassie Jenkins rang 000 and checked to see what was missing. She picked up a shopping bag laying on the floor and removed her iPad and iPhone from it.

"You nailed him son," Charlie told Billy as he ruffled his hair.

"He's not dead, is he dad?"

Charlie got down on his knees and checked to see if the man lying flat on his back in his living room at 3.15 on a spring morning was breathing. He was.

"He's not dead son. He's just sleeping. Did you use your fastball?"

"The two-seamer."

"Good man. Always go with your best pitch when you find yourself in a tight jam."

A few moments later a squad car pulled into the Jenkins's driveway. Senior Constables Harvey Conway and Tim Korman knocked on the front door.

"Thank you for getting here so quickly," Cassie Jenkins told them. She led them into the living room where Dickey was still laid out. Conway squatted and lightly slapped the burglar's face until he came too. Conway then rolled him over onto his stomach and slapped a pair of cuffs on him. "How are you feeling mate?" Conway asked.

Dickey groaned. On the back of his nearly clean-shaven head was a lump the size of a golf ball. "What happened?"

"Looks like you got hit by a pitch son. A HBP for those who like to keep score."

"I got hit by a what?"

"Never mind. Get on your feet mate. You have anyone with you?"

"Yogi, where the fuck is Yogi?"

"Hey, watch your language young man. There's a woman and a young child present," Constable Korman warned.

"Sorry."

"How'd you two get in?"

"I came through the doggy door."

"You're kidding, aren't you?"

"No sir. I squeezed through and then opened the back door for Yogi."

Cassie Jenkins shook her head. "Why couldn't we have gotten a fish tank?"

"The kids wanted a dog," Charlie Jenkins said in his defence.

"What if they had come upstairs Charlie? What about the girls?"

He put his arm around his wife's shoulders to comfort her.

"We'll sort everything out sweetheart. I never thought anyone would be able to crawl through that thing. I'll board it up in the morning and get better locks for the back door too. Okay?"

"Okay. But what about Sparky?"

"I'll let him out before I go to bed, and he'll just have to hold it in the rest of the night. It's only six or seven hours. He'll be able to do it. I think.

"Say how about that star baseball player of ours?" Charlie said changing the subject.

"What about him?" Cassie asked.

"Billy knocked the guy out. He threw a baseball at him and got him square in the bonce."

"You're kidding?"

"Nope."

"Billy. Come here and show your mother how you beaned that guy."

"I was standing right here mum," Billy Jenkins calmly said. "I flicked on the lights, saw the two guys and aimed for that guy's head," he said pointing at Dickey, who was being stood up by Conway and walked outside to a waiting paddy wagon.

Korman took down every word Billy said and put it in his official report. The next day Korman called the reporter who did the police rounds for the *Cheltenham Post*, the local weekly.

"I've got a peach of a story for you Chris."

"Good, I can use one. I've gotta sell more subscriptions or the suits will be all over my arse."

"You'll sell some subscriptions with this one; don't you worry about that mate."

Korman gave Chris Bachman all the details.

"This is gold Tim, gold. You think we can get a photo of the kid?"

"Yeah, the perp is harmless. We caught his mate too. He nearly shat his pants when we collared him. A couple of real lightweights."

"Were they working on their own?"

"I doubt it. But they ain't talking."

Dickey and Larson never told the cops they were working for Harmon Ruffing. And it's a good thing they hadn't because Ruffing never gave a squealer a second chance. The last bloke who yacked to the cops, a high school classmate of Dickey and Larson's named Denny Lewis, led police to a storage unit in Braeside where more than $25,000 dollars of merchandise was recovered.

When Ruffing found out it was Lewis who opened his mouth, Lewis was pulled from his rented unit in Mordialloc late one evening, stuffed into the boot of a car and was never seen again.

"Give the lad's mum and dad a ring and see if they're keen," Korman told Bachman.

Three days later, on page 5 of the *Post*, a pearler of a picture of Billy Jenkins in his Aspendale Aces Under 9 jersey tossing a baseball in his hand appeared under the large headline *Billy Bags Burglar*.

AMONG THE first items put into the crib of Billy Jenkins were a foam baseball, a tiny baseball glove and a plastic baseball bat. A colourful mobile – a gift from his Aunt Sally – hung just above him, and stuffed toy animals surrounded him. But from day one, all Billy wanted to do was get his tiny hands on the glove, ball and bat.

Billy Jenkins could throw, catch and hit a baseball while he was still in diapers. Clad in a blue and white Aspendale Aces jersey still several sizes too big and a cap which covered his blond curls, blue eyes and nearly his entire head, he was a regular visitor to the home of the Aspendale Aces on Edithvale Rd where his dad played for the club's seconds.

When he was four-and-a-half, Billy became the batboy for his dad's team. His job was to bring a hitter's bat back to the dugout if he made contact and took off for first base. Billy nearly got cleaned up one day at home plate by one of his dad's teammates trying to score on a base hit. After that scare, young Billy was told by his dad to have a good look at who was on the base paths before bending down to pick up a bat. He needed to be told just once.

On many nights in the small backyard of their overpriced, heavily mortgaged Cheltenham home, Charlie played catch with his young son after dinner. They started tossing around a tennis ball and graduated to a much harder regulation sized baseball when Charlie was nearly five. Charlie bought a light wooden bat for Billy and tossed balls to his son for hours on end. Anyone could see that the young lad had superior hand and eye co-ordination. Not many balls got by him, so Charlie increased the speed of his deliveries, first with tennis balls and then with baseballs and put more distance between himself and Billy, tossing pitches from the Little League distance of 45 feet.

After Billy sweetly connected with a pitch and sent it rocketing into Charlie's ribs, they went back to using tennis balls which Sparky routinely retrieved. The baseballs were saved for the Edithvale Rd batting cages.

By the time he was five, Billy was excelling at T-ball where youngsters hit a ball off a tee instead of facing live pitching. Billy was light years ahead of his teammates in ability and at the age of seven, two years younger than nearly everyone else but just as tall, he was chosen to play for one of Aspendale's Under 9 sides.

Billy was assigned to play the outfield, but after several games his coaches realised his talents were being wasted and moved him to shortstop. He handled every ground ball flawlessly and his throws to first base were always on target. He even pitched in a few games and was touched up just once. A Sandringham youngster, who was twice Billy's size, hit two long, fence-clearing home runs off him. No one else managed to get a ball out of the infield.

"Don't worry about it," Charlie told his son after the Sunday morning game, a rare Aspendale loss. "A lad that size should be knocking the cover off the ball. In another year or two, you'll be the one hitting home runs."

Charlie wasn't so keen on stats being kept for a group of Under 9 players, but when he was handed a stat sheet one day halfway through the season, he looked at it. Billy was leading the team in hitting with an average of .600, meaning he either singled, doubled, tripled or homered six of every ten times he came to the plate. The next best hitter on the team, Kevin Warren, a nine-year-old, was batting .350.

Billy had made only one error in his team's first nine games. Most teams regularly made five or six errors a game; dropped fly balls, bad throws and balls going between legs were the most common. Billy's error came on a wild throw in a tie game when with a man on first he fielded a grounder, stepped on second base to record the force out, and in his haste to complete an unassisted double play, threw the ball just past the reach of first baseman Jake "Stretch" Goldman. Jake was tall for a lad his age but needed a ladder to grab Billy's throw. Billy was so annoyed with the throw, which allowed the Bonbeach batter to reach second, that he threw his glove down into the infield dirt. His coach, Bert Axelrod, called time and walked onto the field to have a word with his shortstop.

In the stands, which were filled with parents and family members, Charlie Jenkins stood up and caught his son's eye. With his hands, he motioned for Billy to settle down. He mouthed the words "take it easy". Billy acknowledged his dad by nodding his head and waited for Axelrod to reach him.

"We all make mistakes Billy, yes even you. But when you make an error, just walk back to your position. Okay?"

With his head down, Billy told Axelrod that he understood.

Axelrod called his infielders and catcher to the mound for a word before he left the playing field. "Okay guys, remember, there's two outs. Two. If the ball is hit on the ground the play is to first. Okay?"

In unison, the six players gathered at the mound yelled out "yes coach."

It was the top of the fifth inning of the six-inning game and the score was tied 4-4. Aspendale pitcher Randy McNally walked the next two batters to load the bases. "Settle down Randy. Just throw strikes mate," Axelrod yelled to his pitcher over the crowd noise.

"Think we should give him the hook?" assistant coach John Powell asked Axelrod.

"Nah, taking him out now would shatter his confidence."

Aspendale catcher Tommy Cuellar took off his mask as the next Bonbeach batter walked to the plate and called out to his teammates. "Remember, there's a force on at every base."

"The kid is on the ball," Axelrod told Powell. "He's nine years old for goodness sake. He must watch more baseball than I do."

The Bonbeach baserunners each kept a foot on the base they occupied as McNally sent his first pitch to the plate. It bounced in the dirt, but Cuellar stopped it with his chest protector. Bonbeach hitter Harry Walker took the next pitch which was a called strike. The Aspendale players were shouting words of encouragement to McNally as Walker dug in at the plate. Walker fouled the next pitch out of play leaving Aspendale just a strike away from getting out of the inning without losing the lead.

McNally went into his wind-up and delivered a pitch on the outside part of the plate. Walker strode into it and lined a one-hopper up the middle past McNally. It looked like at least two runs would score. But Billy Jenkins reacted quickly, moved two steps to his left and dove for the ball. He snared it in the webbing of his glove and while on his stomach flipped the ball to second baseman Tim "Choo Choo" Coleman, who stepped on second base to get the force out.

"Holy shit. Did you see that?" Axelrod screamed at Powell. "The kid is seven years old. Derek Jeter couldn't have made that play."

"He's something special, no doubt about that," Powell noted.

Jenkins' teammates mobbed him when he returned to the dugout. Billy looked up in the stands for his dad when the congratulations subsided. Charlie Jenkins locked eyes with his son, smiled and lifted his right thumb.

By night-time, the clip of Jenkins' defensive gem had been viewed more than 300 times on YouTube thanks to video shot by catcher Tommy Cuellar's dad.

During dinner time the next evening, several hundred thousand people watched the clip on Harry Halfpipe's sportscast which was named Channel 12's Play of the Day. It wasn't on a par with Tiger Woods's appearance on the Tonight Show with Johnny Carson when Tiger was barely out of diapers, but it made the seven-year-old a household name for a few hours.

Billy was the third child of Charlie and Cassie Jenkins. Susie was three and Vicky five when Billy was born.

Charlie Jenkins, now 37, earned a decent living as a purchasing agent for a major supermarket chain and was the third baseman for the Aspendale Baseball Club's seconds. Up until two years ago Charlie played for the firsts and helped the Aces win several flags in Baseball Victoria's top division. But age took away his power at the plate, his speed on the bases and the sharp reflexes needed to play the hot corner.

Charlie knew it was time to let a younger player have a go one steamy Sunday summer afternoon during a game at Waverley. In the top of the third inning, he was thrown out at first base on a ball collected on two hops by Waverley's right fielder. Anyone with decent wheels would have easily reached first safely with a base hit.

Two innings later his head was nearly taken off by a line drive which rocketed down the third base line. A few years earlier Charlie would have made the catch with one eye closed.

So, he willingly moved down to the twos where a combination of older players and young lads showed up each Sunday to play a two-hour timed game beginning at 1pm. First pitch in the top grade had been 3:30 for as long as Charlie could remember. He usually hung around for a couple of innings of the nightcap before heading home to Cassie and the girls.

Parental duties came first when Susie and Vicky were born, although Cassie knew how important it was for her husband to spend a few hours training at the club during the week and playing on Sundays.

As the demands of his job grew, baseball was forced even further into the background.

Charlie's job started to take him out of the office more than he liked. There were farms and growers to visit and prices to negotiate up and down the east coast along with trips to Tasmania which meant leaving Cassie and the girls on their own a couple of nights a week. Cassie's younger sister, Evie, a year 12 student at Kilbreda College in Mentone, came over on those nights to help prepare dinner and put the girls to bed.

4

BY THE time Billy Jenkins was 16, he stood six-foot-two, weighed 80 kilograms and was the starting shortstop for the Aspendale firsts in Baseball Victoria's top grade.

He was being chased by more girls than John, Paul, George and Ringo – yes, even Ringo got his fair share of tail – and was the hottest prospect not just in Melbourne, but in Australia. He was also a top student much to the delight of his parents who worried that all his success on the field would come between him and his studies. Charlie and Cassie Jenkins expected their son to graduate high school – he had just Year 12 to complete – before he began his pro career which was a certainty. As an international player who had never attended a school in the United States, Billy was ineligible for the Major League draft. However, he could be signed by any Major League team as a free agent regardless of his age. Major League scouts had known about him for nearly two years but not one had yet visited Australia to see him play in person. That was about to change.

On the other side of the world, the New York Stars were coming off their third straight losing season and had finished with the worst record in the Major Leagues. To make things worse, the New York Bombers had been to two of the last three World Series, owned the back pages of the city's two tabloids and dominated the conversation on *WRBI*, the city's sports talk radio station.

The Stars needed to do something to bring fans back to their home ground and needed to give a manager a reason to take the job of turning around the worst team in baseball. Expensive free agents like outfielder Bobby Batista had caused the team payroll for 2025 to swell to well over $200 million. With an $18 million one-year guaranteed contract tucked into his back pocket, Batista barely broke a sweat on game night and had about as much enthusiasm for his job as a teenager working the late shift at McDonald's.

"Do we really have to pay the son of a bitch? He's not even trying," Stars general manager Dicky Moore asked the club's top attorney after his 0-for-4 outing against Cincinnati in late August. "He was booed off the fucking field for goodness sake. Can we release him?"

"We could, but we still have to pay him the whole $18 million," David Lindsay said. "On the bright side, he's only signed until the end of the season."

"October 1st can't come soon enough," Moore said.

The Stars put out a press release on October 2 in which they announced that Moore and field manager Casey Montgomery would not be re-hired and that Batista and his mate "Stubby" Hendricks would not be re-signed. A right-handed pitcher, Hendricks was a $32 million-dollar bust. Over the course of his two years in New York he had a won-loss record of 12-30, a poor earned run average of 5.79 and had nine lawsuits filed against him for various degrees of sexual assault. He also fathered four children with four different women.

Two weeks after the Los Angeles Legends beat the Bombers four games to three in the World Series, the New York Stars announced that Dan McLain, the head of their talent-rich farm system, had been given a three-year deal as general manager. His appointment was well-received by the New York media. "He's the one guy who can turn the whole thing around," *WRBI*'s Bud McAllister told his faithful afternoon drive listeners.

While the media speculated on who would be named field manager, McLain flew down to Texas to chat with former Baltimore Crabcakes manager Darren Betts, who had been out of the game for six months after getting into a shouting match with Baltimore general manager Stu Palmer before a mid-season home game with the Boston Bean Eaters. It had been widely rumoured that Betts, a former Army man, had broken three of Palmer's ribs with a crisp right hand to his midsection. "Shit, I didn't spend three years in fucking Afghanistan so I could stand here and listen to your bullshit," he told Palmer, who was sprawled on the carpet of Betts's office gasping for air. "These high-priced fuckers you call ballplayers need discipline, not a fucking babysitter."

Palmer spat out two words – "you're fired" – before he lapsed into semi-consciousness. Still dressed in his uniform, Betts grabbed his things and left the stadium in his Hummer. He collected his gear from the fully paid and furnished apartment the Crabcakes had set him up with and was on the road to his home in Texas before the first pitch of that night's game was thrown. Palmer was found by clubhouse attendant Elmo Fredrickson, who frantically rang team doctor Julio Barrosa. The barely competent Dr Barrosa, who had gotten his diploma from a Caribbean medical school which advertised in the back of *MAD* magazine, drove Palmer to Baltimore General Hospital where X-rays revealed three broken ribs on his left side.

"Still got the urge to manage Darren?" McLain asked the former Army captain over a couple of beers on Betts's five-acre property 20 miles outside Fort Worth. "We need someone to kick a little ass in New York. How does $15 million over two years with all the usual perks sound? We got a good young farm system, the number one pick in the draft and we've gotten rid of those damn freeloaders who had the nerve to call themselves ballplayers."

"Do I get a say in who the club drafts with that number one pick and who it signs as free agents?"

"Absolutely. But I have the final say along with the bean counters."

"I'll take the job under one condition."

"And that is?"

That we send the best scout there is – Duke Carlisle – to Australia to check out this 16-year-old kid who my sources tell me may be the best player to come along since Steve Soto. Soto being the outfielder for the Los Angeles Caballeros who signed a 15-year US$765 million contract in 2024.

"Isn't Carlisle under contract with Atlanta?" McLain asked.

"Was. His deal ran out on October 1. All I need to do is make one call and he'll be the top scout for the Stars."

"How much would he want?"

"Half a million per plus $350 per diem when he's on the road to cover his hotel, meals and car rental."

"That's a lotta coin Darren."

"Not if you consider the $50 million spent on dogs like Batista and Hendricks."

"Good point. Word around the traps is that Carlisle has a bit of a drinking problem."

"Had Dan. Had. He's all but given up the booze. He's gone from downing a bottle a night to just a drink or two. During the day he lives on coffee and cigarettes. But I'll tell you this Dan, there is no better man out there judging young talent. Nobody. Sign Duke and I'll come aboard."

McLain downed the rest of his beer and extended his hand to Betts. "I believe we have a deal."

"We do. And I'll tell you this, if I don't have the team playing .500 ball or better on July 4 of my second year, I'll donate my salary to charity."

A WEEK after signing his contract with the Stars and renewing his passport – it was due to expire in four months – Duke Carlisle was ready to leave Atlanta and head to Australia.

"Five hours to LA, 15 more to Australia. This is going to be the longest fucking road trip in baseball history," the 52-year-old said as he stashed several cartons of Marlboro cigarettes in his carry-on bag, and wheeled his large suitcase to the front door of the two-bedroom condo that he shared with live-in girlfriend Cindy Bartkowski.

Ms Bartkowski was not overly enthusiastic when Carlisle first told her of his new job and his first assignment.

"What are you going to do in Australia? Sign a fucking kangaroo"

"He can't be any worse than what the Stars sent onto the field this year."

"Seriously Duke, how long are you going to be gone for?", the stunning 44-year-old real estate agent asked.

"I'm guessing about four to six weeks. The Stars want me to take a good look at this kid in Melbourne."

"Damn it, Duke. You're on the road half the year as it is. And now when we have a chance to be together under the same roof for a few months you're taking off? What the fuck am I supposed to do when you're gone?"

"You could come with me."

"I can't leave the office at the drop of a hat. Our vacations are plotted out six months in advance."

"It's six weeks tops Cindy. We'll still have a few months together before I go back on the road. The Stars offered me half a million a year for goodness sake. I couldn't say no. With that sort of money, I'll be able to retire before I turn sixty. This will set us up for life."

"It might set you up for life Duke. But I'm through moving. I'm not moving to fucking New York."

"I'm not either love, but I will be spending a few months a year up there."

Cindy Bartkowski was not the kind of gal prone to emotional outbursts. Even when a million-dollar deal fell through which cost her a commission of $50,000, she was able to keep her cool. Not this time. The petite blue-eyed blonde picked up a half-empty beer bottle and hurled it towards Carlisle's head. He ducked out of the way and watched the bottle crash against a living room wall. Shards of glass flew in every direction. What was left of the beer slowly flowed down the wall onto the wall-to-wall carpeting.

"You could've at least waited till I got the radar gun out hun. That's a hell of an arm you got there."

Cindy stormed off to their bedroom and slammed the door shut.

Well, that didn't go exactly as planned, Duke thought. *I'll camp in the spare bedroom tonight.*

Duke spent the next five nights alone. He tried to patch things up with Cindy but she was done talking. On the morning he left for Hartsfield Airport, he tried one last time.

"Can we talk Cindy? Please?"

After a few moments of silence, Cindy opened the door to the master bedroom and spoke up.

"I'm sorry Duke, but it's over between us. I'm tired of spending my nights alone, tired of your drinking and tired of kissing a damn ashtray. I won't be here when you get back, whenever that is."

"You won't?"

"No. I'm getting my own place."

"Okay. But if you change your mind ..."

Without saying a word, Cindy Bartkowski shut the bedroom door in his face.

Carlisle tossed his hands into the air, walked to the front door and gathered his bags.

"I'll wait outside for the taxi Cindy," he hollered.

There was no reply. Not even a "have a nice flight".

Carlisle spent the night in a Los Angeles hotel room adjacent to LAX, watching planes take-off and land from his window. His marathon flight to Melbourne was due to depart at 11am the following morning. He checked his phone. There was nothing from Cindy. *Should I call her? Text her?* he wondered. *Maybe it's better to wait a couple of days.*

Groggy from a lack of sleep and more than a little pissed-off after taking 90 minutes to get through customs, Carlisle made his way to the baggage carousel at Tullamarine Airport with his carry-on bag flung over his right shoulder. He grabbed his large navy-blue suitcase and strode outside into the mild Melbourne air. He opened his suitcase, took out a pack of cigarettes, stuck a Marlboro in his gob, lit it and inhaled for the first time in nearly 17 hours. *Now,* he wondered, *how the fuck do I get out of here?*

As Carlisle was assessing his options, a large red and white double-decker bus pulled up to the curb 10 metres from where he was standing. Carlisle bought a ticket and joined the queue for the *Skybus* into the city. He figured a taxi into town would have been twice as dear as the $19 *Skybus* fare. *No sense tossing money away.*

On top of his $350 per diem, which grew to about $475 thanks to the generous exchange rate, the Stars had booked a hotel for him in the heart of the city for a week. Carlisle had done a bit of research on Melbourne before leaving Atlanta and after a couple of days familiarising himself with the city of four million people, he rented a car late on a Thursday afternoon and drove an hour to the eastern bayside suburb of Edithvale, where Aspendale played its home games and practiced.

The *Melways*, which Carlisle bought from the rental agency as a backup in case Google Maps failed, was on the passenger seat. Apart from driving on the left-hand side of the road, which took some getting used to, Melbourne was just like any large city back home near peak hour. Inpatient drivers going well above the posted speed limit passed him on the left and right; car dealerships, small businesses, apartment buildings and the same fast-food joints as back home dotted both sides of the highway.

Carlisle checked the car's dashboard as he passed through the swanky suburb of Brighton. It was 5:20pm and a pleasant 22° or 72° Fahrenheit outside.

The Aces had a practice session at Edithvale Rd starting at 6pm which would be the first time Carlisle would see Billy Jenkins in the flesh. He'd seen plenty of the 17-year-old on tape, but as any good scout worth his weight in Doritos will tell you, it's a whole new ballgame seeing a prospect in person. Neither Carlisle nor the Stars front office had been in touch with the Aces. If anyone at the ground asked who he was, he'd say he was visiting friends in the area and stopped in to have a look.

6

THE BASEBALL Victoria summer season was heading into its third week, and the Aces were 3-0 and in sole possession of first place in their division. The players and coaches would be much more relaxed than the group 25 minutes away at Sandringham which was off to a miserable 0-3 start.

Jenkins had started all three games at shortstop, including a 4-2 mid-week victory over Essendon eight days ago at a venue called Melbourne Ballpark at the other end of the city, and was flying. He was batting .450 with two home runs and 10 runs batted in. He had also not made an error in the field.

Arriving in Aspendale, it took Carlisle another 20 minutes to find the ground, which was in Edithvale, a few hundred metres from the Edithvale Wetlands; home to thousands of different birds. One species – the red-bellied Putin – came all the way from Russia to spend the northern winter at the wetlands. It had more frequent flyer miles than Carlisle and were easier to cash in.

At first glance Carlisle thought Aspendale's home ground was on a par with many of the better suburban high school fields he'd been visiting for the past 25 years.

Carlisle was an outfielder during his high school days in Pioneer County, Kentucky and was good enough to play minor league ball for the St Louis Spirit.

In his third year with the Spirit organisation, the 21-year-old was promoted to their Class A advanced side in Clearwater, Florida, where it became apparent to all some 20 games into the season that Carlisle could not hit the curveballs thrown by the league's better pitchers. Late one afternoon in May of 1989, he was called into manager Duffy Dougherty's office. General manager Spike McCauley was there as well. As soon as he saw McCauley, Carlisle knew his time as a player in the Spirit organisation was over.

"We love your work ethic Duke; your enthusiasm, the way you help out with some of the younger kids, but we're going to release you. If you were only able to hit a damn curveball," Dougherty said.

"No other club wants me?" Carlisle asked.

"Not with a .220 batting average," McCauley said.

Carlisle lowered his head. *All I ever wanted to do was play pro ball. Shit. What am I going to do now?* he thought.

"But like I said Duke, we like the way you go about things. You're one of the first at the ground, one of the last to leave. Would you be willing to take a coaching job with the organisation?" McCauley asked.

Carlisle quickly lifted his head. He looked at McCauley and then Dougherty, who nodded. "Take it," he mouthed.

"Where would I be coaching?" Carlisle asked.

"At Jackson City with the Rookie League team. Being just a few years older than the players there we feel they would be able to relate to you."

"Jackson City, Tennessee? Where I started? The Appalachian League"

"The same place. Your old manager, Ron Bauer, is still there."

"I liked playing under him. He's a class guy."

"It's a two-year deal," McCauley said. "Twenty thousand per plus per diem money when you're on the road. If you need some time to think it over ..."

"I don't need any time. I'll take it."

Carlisle signed the contract the next day in McCauley's office and five days later, on May 23, he packed all his belongings into his battered Pontiac and left Clearwater bound for east Tennessee. The Spirit gave him

$1000 cash to help him relocate. What he didn't spend on petrol went to the landlord of a one-bedroom furnished unit six blocks from the home ground of the Rookie League club.

Jackson City was three weeks away from starting its two-and-a-half-month, 80-game season so there was plenty of time for Carlisle to familiarise himself with the side's players. Only two coaches remained from his time there as a player: pitching coach Buzz McNally and hitting coach Rob Powell. In Carlisle's first year with Jackson City, he worked with the side's outfielders during training camp and coached first base once the season began.

He got along well with manager Bauer and the following year became his third base coach, a job he held for the next four years.

After five seasons of coaching, which included one pennant, the Spirit asked him if he'd be interested in joining their scouting department. He was offered $36,000 a year along with per diem money when he was on the road, which would be quite often. He took it and stayed with the Spirit for eight more years. He signed several players who went on to be all-stars and numerous others who became solid big-league players. Other clubs took notice, including the Atlanta Knights who needed young, talented players. They tripled what the Spirit were paying him to become one of their top scouts. His job was to find another Tom Glavine or Chipper Jones. Despite his loyalty to the Spirit, he couldn't turn down the kind of money the Knights put on the table.

Carlisle's new patch was the south, from Florida up through the Carolinas, an improvement weather wise over the mid-west and northeast where spring didn't arrive until mid-May; two thirds through the high school season.

He scouted and signed hundreds of ballplayers for the Knights over the next dozen years, many of whom made it to the major leagues. Several even went into broadcasting after they retired.

But starting today, Thursday, October 16, 2024 he was working for the NY Stars.

Carlisle parked the rental car, put on his Atlanta Knights ballcap, grabbed a folding chair from the boot of the car – which he had "borrowed" from his hotel – and his backpack, and made himself at home down the right field line.

He had the tools of his trade with him; binoculars, speed gun, notebook, pen, a thermos of hot coffee and two packs of cigarettes.

He looked for Jenkins and found him milling around the batting cage waiting to take his swings. For a 17-year-old kid he had a well-developed upper body despite rarely having set foot in a gym. "Get him in a weight room a couple of days a week and he'll have arms like Popeye," Carlisle said to himself.

After a few minutes Jenkins took his place in the cage and knocked the batting practice deliveries thrown to him all over the field. Carlisle looked on through his binoculars. He'd later write in his notebook; "textbook swing, makes solid contact, sprays the ball wherever he wants and with good power."

Jenkins then took his spot at shortstop and easily scooped up every ground ball hit his way. "The kid's got a rifle for an arm," Carlisle said as he watched Jenkins throw balls to first base. "I know where'll I'll be on Sunday – right here. I hope this Williamstown club he's going to face has a good pitcher or two who can test him."

An hour later, as the field became entirely covered in shadows, Carlisle gathered up his things and marched back to his rental car. Not one person had approached him which is the way he liked to operate. Nerves could make even the best ballplayer look like a member of the 1962 New York Mets if he knew he was being watched.

7

CARLISLE STOPPED for dinner at a pizza joint in Cheltenham and then with dusk settling in took a wrong turn at a roundabout while trying to follow the spoken directions given by the Google Maps lady to get back on Nepean Highway.

"What the hell is a roundabout?" he asked as he pulled over on Keys Rd in Moorabbin to consult his Melways.

He found where he wanted to go and how to get there, circled the route in ink and was about to put the Toyota back in gear when he noticed four scantily clad young women heading into the building he was parked in front of. One of the four waved at him, another smiled. *What's this all about?* he wondered. He found the answer when he looked at the glowing neon sign on the front of the building, Playmates.

Since he hadn't heard a peep from a certain real estate agent back in Atlanta, Georgia, Carlisle decided to go in and have a look. "I'm practically single," he said. "Cindy said we were through. What harm could come from going in? Who the hell is going to know? I'll use cash."

When he stepped through the doors Carlisle thought he was in the home of Santo Mendoza, a third baseman he signed on a quick jaunt to Havana, Cuba in 2009. Mendoza was on a guaranteed $16 million a year and had spent a shitload of the money turning his main living room into what he was now looking at.

There were about a dozen gorgeous women seated on plush couches and chairs. A massive chandelier hung from the high ceiling. The walls were painted blue. The room's carpeting was deeper than the rough at Shinnecock Hills Golf Club in New York which he had played several times with fellow scout Pete Giacomin and agents Subway Stemkowksi and Saul Bernstein. Stemmer's legendary foot-long pecker would have ripped a hole through his trousers if he was looking at the women Carlisle was gazing at.

Chinese, Vietnamese, Thai, Aussie, a dark-skinned woman Carlisle thought was Brazilian. *This a better than the fucking smorgasbord at Caesar's Palace.*

Carlisle approached the counter where a stunning blonde of about 40 asked him if he had been to Playmates before.

"No mam. I'm here on vacation," he said, overplaying his southern accent. He looked around. "You mean, this is all legal here?" he asked.

"One hundred percent legitimate. Pick whoever you like. You can have her for half an hour or a full hour. You and she negotiate what you want when you get to her room. She gets half, Playmates gets half. All the girls are regularly tested for STDs so there's no need to worry about catching anything. Even so, condoms are a must."

"Let's say I want the full monty, for an hour. How much would that run me?"

"Three hundred and fifty bucks hun. You in?"

Carlisle peeled off seven brand new fifty-dollar Australian notes from his bankroll and handed it to the hostess.

"The ball is in your court, pick whoever you like," she said.

Growing up outside of Lexington, Kentucky, Carlisle went to a high school that was 100 percent white. The small towns he played ball in, including Jackson City, were also predominantly white as were his two ex-wives.

His eyes immediately focused on an exotic dark-skinned woman he later found out was Colombian. He reached his hand out to her. She took it, stood up and wobbled slightly on her five-inch heels. Carlisle's eyes nearly popped out of their sockets when he got a look at her. She had the body of an Olympic hurdler. Her legs were longer than the Pacific Coast Highway, her stomach flatter than the Nullarbor, her nipples were so hard and pointy you could hang laundry on them and she had an arse that was sweeter than a Georgia peach.

Carlisle was an inch shy of six-foot and only came up to her chin. "My friends call me Duke, what's your name?" he asked.

"Isobel," she said softly. "Isobel."

"Beautiful name for a beautiful woman," Carlisle said.

Isobel took Carlisle by the hand and led him to her place of business; a room which looked to have been decorated by the same person who did Santo Mendoza's mansion.

The room was bathed in soft red light, smelled of expensive perfume, had a nightstand, a small closet filled with racy lingerie one would never find in Jackson City, Tennessee and a bed the size of Yankee Stadium.

Isobel took care of every one of Carlisle's desires and after the hour was up, led him back to the main room.

"Well, the blonde said. "Enjoy yourself?"

Carlisle nodded.

She handed Carlisle a tissue. "Wipe the drool off your chin hun," she said. "And come back again."

"If I can find the strength I will," Carlisle said as he exited.

"I need a damn ice bath," Carlisle said as he eased his aching body into the rental car. "Okay," he said. "What's wrong with this picture?" he asked himself.

"THE STEERING WHEEL IS ON THE OTHER FUCKING SIDE," he screamed. "SHIT."

Carlisle changed seats, drove off, found Nepean Highway without much trouble and made it back to his hotel by 9:30. He went straight to the bar, downed two shots of Jack Daniel's and took his time finishing off a beer. Halfway through his beer, a young lovely sat down next to him. "Up for a good time?" she asked.

"Hun. I'll be lucky to make it back to my room," he said. "I'm aching in muscles I never even knew I had. But thanks anyway."

If anyone had looked at Carlisle slowly walking to the lift, they would have thought he was a bull rider who had repeatedly been tossed on his bottom.

He took a warm shower, swallowed three Panadol and slept for the next 11 hours.

While taking a long piss two mornings later, Carlisle screamed in horror when he saw his pecker. It was covered in welts and turning a shade of green. "ISOBEL", he yelled.

He showered, dressed, had a cup of coffee in his room and googled *doctors in Melbourne*. It was Saturday so many clinics were closed. He found a place on Swanson St which was open until noon, hailed a cab and was sitting in the waiting room within 20 minutes. He filled out a form and explained that he was visiting from the US and did not have a Medicare card.

"I've got cash and credit cards," he told the receptionist. "I'll pay you upfront if you want."

"No that's okay. Just take a seat and fill out the form. The doctor will call your name when he's free. There were three others in the waiting room, and they gave Carlisle funny looks when he kept rubbing his crotch.

Carlisle handed back the form, adjusted his merchandise and sat back in the same seat.

Ten minutes later his name was called by Dr Mohammed Khazbekistanski. He followed him into an examining room and sat down. There were pictures of the Pakistani cricket team on one wall and a diploma hung on another next to a huge poster of the human body.

"What seems to be the problem today, Mr Carlisle?"

"Well doctor, it's a little embarrassing. I went to a brothel two nights ago and had sex with this Colombian woman and this morning my pecker has a rainbow of colours on it."

"Take off your trousers please, and your underpants and let's have a look," Dr Khazbekistanski said.

While Carlisle dropped his drawers, Khazbekistanski put on a pair of latex gloves, shined a light on the multi-coloured appendage and sighed.

"Oh boy. Oh boy. Very serious indeed, very serious," he said.

"How serious?" Carlisle replied.

"I've only seen one other case like this, and amputation is the only way to stop the infection from spreading."

"AMPUTATION? YOU WANT TO CUT MY COCK OFF?" Carlisle screamed.

He hitched up his pants and said, "if you don't mind Doc, I'm going to get a second opinion."

Back on the street, Carlisle flagged down a cab.

"Where to mate?" the turban wearing driver asked.

"The nearest hospital."

Several moments later Virat Singh pulled his taxi up to the emergency room doors of St Vincent's Hospital.

Carlisle handed him a twenty-dollar note and strode inside.

He glanced around the near empty room and headed to the triage desk.

"How can we help you sir?" the nurse asked.

"I think I've got a bad case of venereal disease."

He told the nurse what Dr Khazbekistanski wanted to do and that he wanted a second opinion ... from a real doctor.

After filling out another lot of forms, Carlisle was told by a different nurse to follow her to one of the ED's examining rooms.

"You're lucky. It's a quiet morning," nurse Tamara Aiken said as she took his blood pressure and temperature. "Put this gown on please and relax, one of our doctors will be with you shortly."

Just as Nurse Aiken pulled back the curtain, Dr Dick Long arrived.

"You're having a problem with your penis?" Dr Long asked.

"Something like that," Carlisle said.

"Okay, let's have a look."

Dr Long put on a pair of gloves, shined a light on Carlisle's pecker and examined it thoroughly without saying a word.

"You're not going to amputate, are you doctor?"

"Amputation? No, no, no."

Carlisle breathed a sigh of relief.

"In three, four days it will fall off by itself," Dr Long said.

After Carlisle was revived, Nurse Aiken again took his vitals and handed him two tubes of medication.

"I've applied the first dose. In four hours apply enough cream from the second tube to cover the entire length of the affected area."

"You mean, it's not going to fall off? You're not going to have to amputate?"

"No. Dr Long was just having a little fun with you."

"Fun? I'd like to insert something in him. Like a baseball bat – sideways."

Aiken laughed.

"Use the entire contents of both tubes. And try and keep your penis dry when you shower. Put one of these sheaths over it," she said as he handed him a small box.

"Okay. When will I be able to, you know, use the appendage again?"

"I'd give it a rest for about three weeks. And next time you have sex make sure you use a condom."

"I'm sure Isobel, or whatever her damn name is, put a condom on me."

"If might have been a cheap knock off, and either ripped or broke."

"Jesus. I'm not even here a week and I thought I lost my pecker."

"You can get dressed now," Mr Carlisle. "Visit the cashier on your way out."

"Thank you, I will."

A very relieved Carlisle got dressed, walked to the cashier and paid his $565 bill by credit card.

"That's the most expensive fuck in the history of Pioneer County, Kentucky," he said to himself.

He hailed a taxi and went back to his hotel for some rest. The next afternoon he would be back in Edithvale watching Billy Jenkins.

Chapter 8

AFTER A large lunch in Chinatown and a bit of sightseeing on a picture-perfect spring afternoon, Carlisle drove back to Edithvale to have his first look at Billy Jenkins in game conditions.

He got there just as the reserves game was winding up, ambled down to the same spot he was three days ago and set up camp.

He asked to see the line-up cards from the scorer and quickly wrote the names down in his notebook.

"You with the local paper?" the woman scorer asked.

"Something like that," he answered. "Do you know anything about this pitcher Williamstown is throwing?"

"Just that he's been out a year with a knee injury he got from playing footy."

"Footy?"

"Yeah. Footy. Aussie Rules. Who do you barrack for?"

Barrack for? What's she going on about? Carlisle wondered.

"I follow Collingwood myself."

Carlisle remembered reading something about them in one of the papers and about a team called Carlton, which apparently was one of the worst teams in the AFL.

"The Pies are a good side, but I go for Carlton."

"Sorry to hear that mate, chin up," she said.

"Cheers," Carlisle replied

Cheers was one of the few Aussie expressions Carlisle had picked up in the last week. Without even thinking about it, he was also calling people mate and saying fair dinkum as often as he said hello.

Carlisle typed the name of Williamstown left-handed pitcher Patrick Kennedy into his phone and within a few moments, thanks to Google, he had the kid's life story on his screen.

Twenty-one years old; a likely AFL draft pick until he tore his anterior cruciate ligament in a TAC Cup match playing for Calder. Gave up footy and returned to baseball after a long rehab; back with Williamstown's top side after spending a season in the reserves playing first base and working on rebuilding his arm strength. Kennedy had pitched for the Victorian Under 16 and 18 teams until his knee injury and had gotten a few nibbles from US scouts. Once he got hurt, he hadn't heard a peep from any of them.

Carlisle got up from his seat, grabbed his radar gun from his bag and wandered further down the right field line where Kennedy was warming up. He nodded to Kennedy when he was spotted and took a spot behind the catcher Kennedy was throwing to. The sound of the ball landing in catcher Terry Harding's mitt made a loud pop which got louder with each pitch he threw.

Jesus. I reckon he's hitting 85, 86 miles an hour, Carlisle thought. *In the fucking bullpen.*

Carlisle held up his speed gun, looked at the number from Kennedy's last pitch and looked again. *Eighty-eight? Are you fucking kidding me?*

The next three deliveries registered eighty-seven, eighty-eight and eighty-six.

"That's enough Paddy. Save it for the game," Harding yelled out after five more pitches landed in his mitt.

Kennedy took off his cap, wiped his brow and walked back to the Williamstown bench which was behind a protective fence.

Harding turned to Carlisle and took off his catcher's mask. "We haven't had any scouts around for a couple of years mate. The Knights send you down here Carlisle?"

"The Stars."

"The Stars? Good luck mate."

Carlisle laughed and held out his hand.

"Duke Carlisle."

"Terry Harding. I'm the playing manager for Willy. If you want to talk to Paddy just wait until after the game, okay?"

"Done. What can you tell me about this kid Jenkins?"

"He's never faced a 90 mile-an-hour heater like Paddy has. Don't get me wrong. He's a super talent, but his first real test is today."

Carlisle nodded in agreement, and then as Harding turned to go back to the dugout, asked him how he knew his name.

"Everyone knows who the scouts are mate."

"But I've never been down here."

Harding laughed. "Enjoy the game mate – and let me know if Paddy hits 90."

Willy batted first and put two men on base against an Aspendale righty who threw with just a little more pace than a Major League batting practice pitcher. The home crowd of a couple of hundred sensed it could be in for a long afternoon. But a decent curveball totally bamboozled Willy's clean-up hitter for the second out of the inning.

The next batter made solid contact and sent a two-hopper to shortstop where Jenkins fielded the ball cleanly and threw to first to get the batter by two strides.

As the Aces came off the field, Carlisle scratched the words "above average arm" in his notebook. He left his chair and bag where they were and took up a position behind the backstop about 20 feet behind home plate.

Patrick Kennedy completed his warm-up tosses, adjusted his cap, got the sign from Harding, and delivered his first pitch of the afternoon to Aspendale lead-off man Tucker Jefferson. It whizzed past him for a called strike. "Shit, he throws hard," Jefferson said. He was not wrong. Carlisle's radar gun clocked Kennedy's first delivery at 91 miles per hour, his second at 93 and his third at 92 which Jefferson got a piece of to stay alive.

Jefferson, who had five hits in Aspendale's first three games, stepped out of the batter's box and looked over his left shoulder to his third base coach, who merely shrugged his shoulders.

Jefferson swung and missed at Kennedy's next pitch for the first out of the inning. He tossed his batting helmet away in disgust and took a seat in the dugout. "Good luck fellas. I've never faced anyone who throws that hard," the 23-year-old leftfielder said.

Aspendale's second hitter bounced out to second base to bring Jenkins to the plate. For a kid of 17, he strode to the plate like Willie Fucking Mays. He had more confidence than Carlisle had cigarettes.

This is going to be interesting, Carlisle thought.

Jenkins tapped his cleats with his bat to remove any excess dirt and grass and planted his feet firmly in the batter's box. Kennedy adjusted his cap, put his right foot on the pitching rubber and looked in at Harding, who was crouched behind the plate 60 feet, six inches away. Harding signalled for an inside fastball. It caught the inside corner for strike one. Kennedy's next delivery was waist high, and Jennings lined it into short centerfield. But the ball stayed up long enough for Willy centerfielder Craig Abrams to make a pretty shoestring catch for the third out of the inning.

When Jenkins next came to the plate in the home fourth, Kennedy had allowed just an infield hit, walked one and struck out four. He was also up 2-0 thanks to a two-run home run off the bat of third baseman Dewey Beckett in the top of the third.

With a man on first and none out, Jenkins was given the bunt sign to move Gus Andrews into scoring position for clean-up hitter Dom Brecianno. Jenkins squared to bunt and laid down a beauty down the first base line. With Willy expecting Jenkins to swing away, Jenkins was safely across the first-base bag before Willy's first baseman fielded the ball.

Better than average speed, knows how to handle the bat, Carlisle later wrote in his notes.

With runners at first and second and none down, and the Aspendale crowd cheering as the burly Brecianno walked to the plate, Harding called time and walked to the mound for a chat with his pitcher.

"A hell of a bunt, nothing we could have done about it," Harding told Kennedy. "Let's keep the ball down and see if we can turn a double play here. My mother is quicker than Brecianno."

Kennedy smiled and nodded. Harding took his position behind the plate, pulled his mask down and called for a curveball. The umpire behind the plate yelled out strike one as it crossed the plate knee-high.

Carlisle looked at his radar gun. It read eighty-four mph.

A curve at 84? Fuck me, Carlisle thought.

Brecianno was intent on seeing every pitch in Kennedy's repertoire and worked the count to 2-2. He fouled the next three pitches off and then lifted a fastball to medium leftfield which stayed up long enough to gather a few raindrops before it settled into leftfielder Rick Blair's glove. Neither runner was able to tag up.

Kennedy retired the next hitter on a pop-up which first baseman Jack McGovern snared and got out of the inning unscathed on a ground ball to shortstop.

On a pitch count due to his ongoing rehab, Kennedy was limited to 70 pitches on the afternoon. Willy's scorer told Harding he had already thrown 56 pitches. The next inning would be his last. He gave up a two-out, run-scoring double to Tucker Jefferson and then struck out Bob Romano to end his afternoon. Jenkins was on deck and would not get another chance to face Kennedy, who was given a warm round of applause by his teammates as he came back to the dugout.

"You were sharp mate," Harding told Kennedy as he took his gear off. "As long as you don't show any ill-effects from today's outing, we'll move you up to eighty pitches next Saturday and 90 in the game after that."

Kennedy nodded and took a seat in the dugout. "That scout you talked to before the game, who's he with?"

"The Stars. I reckon he came here to have a look at Jenkins, but your name will be scribbled in his notebook. You hit ninety-four on the gun."

"Really? Ninety-four?"

"Yup, but let's not get carried away, okay? It's just your first start of the season. Let's see how your arm and knee feel in the next few days," Harding said. He grabbed a bat and walked to the on-deck circle to start the top of the sixth. Harding gave Willy a 3-1 lead with a home run over the left field fence. The lead would hold until the home eighth when Billy Jenkins came to the plate with runners on the corners and one man out.

Batting against Williamstown right-handed reliever Steve McNally, Jenkins got a hold of a mid-eighties fastball and belted it to the gap in left-centre field. Both runners scored and Jenkins slid into third with a triple. He scored on a wild pitch to give the Aces a 4-3 lead.

Aspendale reliever Bud Belanger allowed a walk and base hit in the top of the ninth, but the Aces got out of the jam and walked off winners.

As the Aspendale and Willy players shook hands, Carlisle filled another page in his small notebook.

Next to Jenkins' name he wrote 'hits with power and has above average speed'.

There are five tools that scouts look for in a player: speed, power, arm strength, hitting for average and fielding. After just the one game, Carlisle was convinced Jenkins was the real deal. He'd wait until after Wednesday night's game with Sandringham and the following Sunday's game at Blackburn before deciding on the overall grade he would give Jenkins. Most organisations graded prospects on a scale of 20-80, with 20-30 being well below average and 70-80 being well above average. As a rule, anyone with a grade of 65 or better is one who could develop into a major leaguer.

As for Kennedy, Carlisle wanted to see him again and due to a quirk in the schedule which had Williamstown hosting Essendon on Saturday, he'd be able to watch both players the following weekend.

Pitchers are evaluated on velocity, command, mechanics and pitch arsenal along with attitude, knowledge, focus, confidence, preparation and judgement. With a smooth operator like Harding nurturing and monitoring him, Carlisle had a good feeling about the left-hander.

"If he pulls up okay and his knee and arm are sound, based on what I saw today, I'm going to recommend the Stars sign him," Carlisle said to himself as he packed his gear. "He'd jump at a hundred grand signing bonus."

As Carlisle walked to his car with his chair and bag, he was approached by middle-aged fellow wearing a Williamstown hat.

"What do you think of my boy?" Bruce Kennedy asked.

Carlisle didn't need to know the name of the player he was asking about.

"He's certainly got a lot of potential."

Kennedy stuck out his hand. "Bruce Kennedy. I'm Paddy's dad."

"Duke Carlisle."

"A couple of the boys said you're not with Atlanta anymore. Is that true?"

"It is mate. I joined the Stars a couple of weeks ago."

"New York, wouldn't that be something?"

"It would, but don't get carried away. I've seen hundreds of pitchers like your boy over the journey, and the majority never even get signed. Let's see how he pulls up and how he goes in his next couple of starts."

The elder Kennedy nodded. "Good to meet you Mr. Carlisle. Hope to see you again."

"You will."

CARLISLE WAS one of the first to leave the parking lot. It was just after 6pm. "Nine innings wrapped up in less than two and half hours, that's the way it ought to be, not like those damn four-hour marathons which is now the norm for a major league game," he said as he moved onto Edithvale Rd and then Nepean Hwy.

In need of a decent meal, Carlisle had earlier used *Google* to find a restaurant in the area and headed to the suburb of Highett, which was on the way back to the city, to a joint called the Buckingham International, a handsome red brick building which in addition to having a slew of hotel rooms featured a restaurant and bar. Carlisle found a spot in the crowded parking lot and walked into the bar/restaurant which had received numerous favourable reviews online.

A wedding reception was being held in front of the large room and Carlisle was lucky to be seated at one of the few available tables near the door. He ordered a scotch and soda before even looking at the menu. While he was waiting for the beverage of his choice to arrive, he glanced over at the young bride and groom, who were seated in the middle of a long table. Their table overlooked about 20 others and since it was mealtime the noise level in the room was comparable to a meaningless late September night game at any major league ballpark. Carlisle instantly thought of how much the new bride looked like his first wife, one Tammy Sue Bodine of Jackson City, Tennessee.

Tammy Sue had a mane of blond curly hair, big brown eyes which could see through to your soul and a pole dancer's body which once caused a driver of a Greyhound bus bound for Nashville to lose control of the vehicle and crash into a row of trees outside the local Dairy Queen.

None of the passengers were harmed nor was driver Earl Tatum. Several trees though ended up as firewood. In the days following the accident, DQ's business more than doubled. The establishment's owner, Duane "Banana Split" Jones, was able to catch up on his alimony and child support payments and buy a new deep fryer to continue hardening the arteries of his regular customers.

When their time was up, prematurely in most cases, their overweight and saturated fat-filled bodies went straight to The Dicky Jones Funeral Home and then on to the local cemetery which was owned and operated by Duane and Dicky's father, Homer "Dirt Nap" Jones. Homer was given his nickname 45 years earlier in high school when he tackled a pipsqueak of a running back from Jefferson Davis High School so hard, the kid stayed face down on the turf for over 15 minutes. "I was just taking a nap," Dewey Dickinson told his worried parents after the game. Dickinson never played another game of football – his choice – and went on to become one of Tennessee's top litigators. "I saw the light after that hit and decided to concentrate on the books. I owe my career to "Dirt Nap", he said at a party to mark his 50th birthday 10 years earlier. He even sent Jones an invitation to the bash, but Jones politely declined. "The gravediggers are threatening to go on strike and if there's one thing you don't want in the middle of summer, is bodies lyin' around waitin' to be buried," he said a brief phone call.

Tammy Sue was 21 and Carlisle 22 when they married at the local Catholic church one June afternoon a week before the start of the regular season. Carlisle had never been much of a religious man, although he had prayed to God every now and then when he came up to the plate. "C'mon Lord, give me something good to hit."

"Shit, Duke, the good Lord could serve up a fastball on a silver platter and you wouldn't be able to get it out of the infield," Kingsport catcher

Jock Adamson once told him after hearing him pray for a waist-high meatball.

Sure enough, Carlisle weakly bounced one back to the mound, turned right and took a seat back on the Spirit bench.

Tammy Sue's parents, Tommie and Beverley Bodine, went to church every Sunday, occasionally attended bible study classes and were members of the choir. They were adamant that the couple be married by a priest and so they were. The reception was held at the VFW (Veterans of Foreign Wars) Hall and nearly came to a premature end when the bride's two older brothers got into a fistfight after the last keg of beer ran dry.

"What the fuck Vern? You were supposed to be taking care of the beer," Bobby Joe Bodine yelled at his younger brother. "That was your gift to the newlyweds."

"Is it my fault Carlisle and his mob drink like fucking fish?" Vern asked. "Shit, I ain't made of money. Business has been slow. You know that."

"Slower than that sixth-grade brain of yours?"

Vern had always a bit sensitive about his lack of education, and despite having enough beer in him to piss out a three-alarm fire, he let go with a sweet right-hand which would have made Floyd Mayweather proud. It caught Bobby Joe flush on the jaw. He stood upright for a moment, wobbled and then went down like an imploded grain silo.

A full-out brawl ensued. It took twenty minutes and three squad cars of coppers to bring things under control.

"There's no need to make any arrests officer; just a simple family squabble. Take this here platter of ham and cheese sandwiches back to the station. Shit, you can even keep the platter. Cost us $5 at Walmart," father of the bride Tommie Bodine told Lieutenant Howard Dundee.

"Pay for the damages Bodine and we'll forget all about it," Dundee said. He motioned to the other officers to leave and go back to their cars.

"Who's the moron marrying into this family of yours Tommie?" Dundee asked.

"Why that would be Duke Carlisle of the Jackson City Spirit," Tommie Bodine proudly said.

"The outfielder who couldn't hit a curveball?"

"Yup. That's him standing right over there with my lovely daughter."

Dundee slowly walked over to the head table where Carlisle was standing. He was half bathed in beer and other assorted other alcoholic beverages.

"Son, I've got one word to say to you," he said into Carlisle's ear. "Annulment."

"Congratulations mam," Dundee said, tipping his cap to Tammy Sue.

After order was restored, the wedding cake was brought out of the kitchen. Tammy Sue was about to cut into the chocolate cake and feed the first slice to her new husband when she noticed the cake's white icing; it read *Happy Bar Mitzvah Ira.*

"Ira? Who the hell is Ira and what the fuck is a bar mitzvah?" Tammy Sue yelled out.

"I'm going to kill that fucking dim-witted son of mine," Tommie Bodine said. He grabbed Vern by the collar of his new suit jacket ($24.99 at Walmart) and pulled him over to the cake.

"Read that to me you halfwit."

"Happy Bar Mitzvah Ira." He paused. "Shit. I forgot to change it."

"Why the fuck did you buy it in the first place?"

"It was half price."

"It took the starting infield of the Jackson City Spirit to remove the hands of Tommie Bodine from his son's neck.

Unbeknownst to Duke Carlisle, who was in his second year as Jackson City's third base coach, Tammy Sue had a temper much like her brothers and father.

He found out one evening with less than a week to go in the three-month season when he arrived home late.

"The game went into extra innings, weren't you listening?" Duke asked.

"Is baseball all you ever think about Duke?"

"It's my job hun."

"Your job is to be here for me, especially when I'm ovulatin."

Duke Carlisle found himself in a predicament of sorts. There was no finer lay in all of Jackson City and Pioneer County, Kentucky than Tammy Sue Bodine.

He loved every inch of her luscious body and just thinking about her, especially when they were apart, gave him a hard-on he could have taken to the plate and batted with. But at the age of 22, fatherhood was the last thing on his mind. And after getting to know Tammy Sue's family a bit more in the weeks after their wedding, he had begun to put more thought into that annulment Lieutenant Howard Dundee had told him about.

"Listen hun, about this here ovulating business, I've been thinking that maybe we should wait awhile until we have children."

"Wait? What the fuck for? Everyone one of my friends from high school is already a mom. I want a baby Duke, and I want one now."

"You can have your baby Tammy Sue but it ain't gonna be with me."

"What do you mean it ain't gonna be with you?"

"I love you and all hun, but we want different things. I think it'd be a good idea to get an annulment."

"An annulment? What the fuck is that?"

"It means we end our marriage. I spoke to the priest who married us, and he thinks it would be the best thing for us being that we're more in lust with each other than love."

"You want to divorce me? Me? I'll fuckin kill you first."

And with that, Tammy Sue Bodine picked up every dish, glass and bowl in their one-bedroom apartment and started hurling them at her husband. Several found their mark, but the pain was nothing worse than being hit by one of them weak sliders Greeneville's Grover "Freight Train" Alexander served up.

Once Tammy Sue reached for the steak knives, Duke Carlisle raced into the bedroom, closed the door and slid a chest of drawers up against it.

"You open that door now Duke Carlisle or I'll call my brothers. And if they get a hold of ya, you'll be giving signs from the third base coaching box by blinkin' your eyes. You understand me, Duke?"

Duke was a bit busy cramming everything he owned into two duffle bags to hear every word, but the thought of giving signals to the Jackson City Spirit players without the use of his arms and legs was not one that appealed to him.

Nevertheless, he went out the window, threw the suitcase into the backseat of his Plymouth and raced back to the stadium where he decided to spend the night.

Tammy Sue rang Vern and then Bobby Joe but neither answered. She left a tearful message on each of their machines. "Duke dun left me. Said he'd be annulling me."

"Where the hell can they be at this time of night? It's a Tuesday damn it," she asked herself.

It was just after 11:30pm when the phone in the office of Vern and Bobby Joe's garage and towing service rang. Vern had just towed in a Cadillac owned by some Yankee which had broken down on the interstate just outside of town. The cop who came to the aid of the vehicle's occupants, rang their garage asking for it to be towed and dropped the Keatons of suburban New York City at a motel in town. "I'll get to work on it first thing in the morning," Vern told Bruce and Susan Keaton and their twin 10-year-old boys, Philip and Charles, as he hauled the four-year-old vehicle away. The Caddy had a three-year warranty which was bad news for the Keatons. Vern and Bobby Joe might not have been the smartest fellas in Jackson City, but they were smart enough to realise they had pulled in a live one.

"What ya think is wrong with it?" Bobby Joe asked as his brother unhooked the caddy from the tow truck.

"Probably needs a new set of plugs and a distributor cap."

"That all? Not even $100 worth of work," Bobby Joe said. "Put her up on the lift little brother and see if you can find something else wrong with it. I'll get the phone. Might be another breakdown for us to go to."

"Calm down sis, I can't barely make out what you is saying."

Bobby Joe listened closely as his younger sister poured her heart out.

"That son of a bitch. He can't do that to you. Vern and I will straighten that fuckin' weasel out. Don't you worry."

Just as Bobby Joe was about to hang up, he heard a loud crash come from the garage. He ran to the garage and found the Caddy laying on top of his brother. A mixture of blood, oil and anti-freeze oozed from the bottom of the vehicle which had fallen from the lift and crushed Vern Bodine.

Vern had put the safety locks in place when the car was loaded onto the garage's sole lift, but neither he nor Bobby Joe failed to figure in the excess weight of the massive four-door Cadillac, which was several hundred pounds over the lift's capacity. Vern was checking the Caddy's exhaust system when the lift gave way. The Caddy fell seven feet and landed right on top of Vern.

Bobby Joe managed to jack up the Cadillac and free his brother but there was nothing he could do to save him. He rang his parents, sister and the cops in that order. Two hours later Vern's body was taken to Dicky Jones's Funeral Home.

Overcome by grief at the loss of his younger brother, Bobby Joe forgot all about Tammy Sue and her marital problems.

Tommy Bodine and his wife Beverley grieved for months and when they were finally brought up to speed on their daughter's annulment, Duke Carlisle was safely back home in Pioneer County, Kentucky working at Calumet Farm mucking out the stalls of stallions during the day and trying to get into the panties of his old high school girlfriend Lori McAndrew at night.

"Not until we're married Duke," she repeatedly said.

He thought for a moment, "Can I meet your family again?" he asked.

By the time Carlisle returned to Jackson City in late spring to resume his duties with the Spirit, Tammy Sue Bodine was six months pregnant and had a rock on her ring finger that caused temporary blindness to anyone who looked at it if the sun hit it at just the right angle.

Tammy Sue had fallen head over heels with Steven Lucas, the owner of the local movie house. However, the bookish 32-year-old was beginning to wonder if she was more in love with the films she went to for free or him. It took just one roll in the hay with Tammy Sue to convince him that a night with her was far better than sitting alone in the projection booth whacking off to images of Sharon Stone and Sigourney Weaver.

Duke Carlisle stayed well clear of the movie theatre the next three years, and the Bodine family, and was the happiest person in town when a Blockbuster Video store opened just a few blocks from the stadium.

The day the Spirit offered Carlisle the job in their scouting department was the day he finally stopped looking over his shoulder for a member of the Bodine clan. In the three years since his annulment with Tammy Sue, he came face-to-face with a Bodine just once although they knew exactly where he was every time the Spirit had a home game. Carlisle was in the checkout line at Food City Supermarket one afternoon when Beverley Bodine appeared behind him. The two simply nodded.

Duke Carlisle thoroughly enjoyed his steak dinner at the Buckingham International. It came with all the trimmings and was washed down with a cold glass of Victoria Bitter, a decent enough replacement for the bottles of Coors he drank back in the states.

Meanwhile, the party for the newlyweds was just getting started. Several tables were moved to create room for dancing and a DJ started pumping out tunes Carlisle had never heard of. Before fists started flying at his reception nearly 30 years earlier, he and Tammy Sue had danced up a storm to “Love Shack” by the B-52s. It was an infinitely better song than what his ears were currently being assaulted by, so he got up, paid the bill and got back on the road.

Chapter 10

It was just starting to get dark. The night air was mild, so Carlisle drove with the windows of his rental car down which proved to be a mistake. At the next major intersection, somewhere near St Kilda, Carlisle was waiting for the light to turn green and fiddling with the car radio when he felt a pair of strong hands on his shoulder. "Get the fuck out of the car," some monster of a bloke started yelling.

Carlisle managed to put the Toyota in park and as he tried to fend off the would-be carjacker with his right hand, he reached for his thermos with his left. He got a firm grip on it and drove it straight into the thug's nose. Blood squirted from it like the fountain at Caesar's Palace. The thug let out a scream, crumpled onto the warm Nepean Highway pavement and started to crawl away. He didn't get very far. The driver of a petrol delivery tanker exiting a service station on a service road never saw the thug, who as instructed by an online site for wannabe crooks – www.howtorobamotherfucker.com.au – was dressed entirely in black. Carlisle turned his head as the tanker's back wheels turned the fellow into porridge. "That has to hurt," he said.

He picked up his thermos, examined it and was relieved to find that it hadn't been damaged. Carlisle got back in his car and rang 911. He heard a recorded message instead of an operator asking what his emergency was. "The number you have rang was incomplete. Please check the number and dial again."

He dialled 911 again and heard the same message.

"WHAT THE FUCK IS THE EMERGENCY NUMBER IN THIS FUCKING PLACE"? he screamed.

As he looked up, two patrol cars arrived on the scene. The two cars in front of him at the light were long gone as were the cars behind him. None of the cars travelling southbound towards Frankston had stopped. They were probably checking their phones while stopped at the light or with darkness falling had not seen anything.

"You see what happened here mate?" one of the coppers asked.

"I did," Carlisle reluctantly said. *There goes the rest of the night*, he thought.

"The Toyota yours?"

"Yes officer. It's a rental."

"You American?"

"Yup, here on business."

Carlisle thought the cop was about 50. The others with him were much younger. "Cassidy, set up some witches hats around the vehicle before we move it to the side road," captain Steve Chapman yelled to one of the constables.

"For your sake I hope we don't have to tow it," Chapman told Carlisle.

Carlisle told Chapman how he fought off the would-be carjacker, bashed him with his thermos and looked on as his attacker was run over by the back wheels of a petrol tanker.

"If it all checks out, you'll be free to leave Mr. Carlisle, although we may need to have you come down to the station for a more formal interview in the coming days. When are you going back home?"

"Not for another 10 days or so."

"We should have this wrapped up by then," Chapman said.

One of the constables on the scene covered the deceased's body with a dark green tarp while others directed traffic away from the service road.

Chapman lifted the sheet and had a look at the mangled body underneath. He looked like he was in his late teens. The senior constable reached into the fellow's back pocket and took out his wallet.

According to his driver's license, the deceased was 19 years old and from Dandenong; one of Melbourne's rougher and poorer neighbourhoods some 15 miles to the southeast.

According to information retrieved from the laptop in Chapman's car, John Deng had been arrested 15 times in the past four years for various infractions ranging from burglary to assault.

He should have been doing time instead of being on the street, Chapman thought.

"He was a violent, repeat offender," Chapman told Carlisle an hour later. "You're in the clear mate; you defended yourself. And since there's nothing else we need from the car, you can drive it back to wherever it is you're staying.

"We've got all your details and if one of our senior detectives needs to speak with you, he'll call you."

The driver of the petrol tanker, 52-year-old Ernie Vickers, hadn't felt a thing when he ran over Deng and kept travelling towards the city. He was pulling into Geelong when he was finally pulled over by cops, who tracked him down through the delivery he made at the Brighton service station. He was questioned and let go.

An ambulance took Deng's body to the morgue.

Thirty minutes later two officers knocked on the door of Deng's home and notified his parents of their son's death.

"At least he died doing what he loved," Deng's father told the senior constables. Douglas Deng wasn't joking. After being told of the death of his oldest son, he shrugged his shoulders, got back in his recliner and resumed watching a cooking show which was airing on a massive TV sitting on top of a huge entertainment unit. During the next commercial, while the senior constables were talking to his wife, Rhonda, Douglas Deng took a plateful of food from the fridge which his wife had put away for their son and finished it. "What are you going to do? Freeze it and save it?" he asked her.

Rhonda Deng cried on and off for the next week. "He was such a good boy. He never kilt no one. He just hurt them," she told relatives who stopped by their small mortgaged-up-to-the-eyeballs weatherboard house to pay their respects.

Duke Carlisle had been in Australia less than a week, been told by an emergency room nurse not to use his dick for anything more than urinating, had nearly been carjacked and watched a 19-year-old get run over and killed.

He smoked two cigarettes to calm his nerves, got back in his rental car and slowly drove back to the city.

Thankfully, Carlisle had left the scene before camera crews arrived. It was up to Lieutenant Chapman to brief the media. The identity of the attempted carjacking was not released although he was described as an American tourist.

"Jesus Christ. What does the good lord have in store for me tomorrow?" Carlisle asked himself as he pulled into his hotel's underground parking lot. "Maybe I should stay in and order room service. What's the worst thing that can happen? Food poisoning?"

Chapter 11

CARLISLE WENT outside just once the next day and that was to buy the two daily Melbourne newspapers. Since the death of the carjacker happened after both papers went to press, the incident was not reported. However, the story led both 6pm newscasts that evening. *If it bleeds it leads* is the gold standard used by TV news producers and editors of sensationalist tabloid newspapers, and there was plenty of John Deng's blood on Nepean Highway.

Carlisle spent Monday afternoon sending separate emails to Stars general manager Dan McLain and Stars field manager Darren Betts with his initial thoughts of Jenkins and told them about left-handed pitcher Paddy Kennedy.

I'll see Jenkins play on Wednesday night, watch Kennedy carefully on Saturday afternoon and Jenkins again the following day, he wrote.

Kennedy could be a real steal, but we'll have to move on him fast. I'd offer him somewhere between $100,000 and $200,000. He and his dad would jump at an offer like that and we could have him at Mosquito Lakes for spring training in February. Jenkins will demand north of over $2 million as a signing bonus and from what I've seen so far, he's worth it. He's a five-tool player and he's just 17. Nothing phases him. He just oozes confidence.

More coming in a few days,

Duke.

McLain and Betts quickly replied. McLain was happy to hear about Patrick Kennedy and the low signing bonus that could make him a Saint in time for spring training. The Stars farm system had a wealth of young right-handers but were thin on southpaws. "If he's half as good as Carlisle thinks, he could wind up playing A ball next season," McLain told assistant GM Ryan Maloney over lunch the next afternoon at their Snapple Stadium offices.

"Email Carlisle a Rookie League contract and ask him to get hold of Kennedy's medical records. We need to make sure his knee is sound. He's hitting 92, 93 on the gun so I'm guessing it is, but I want our people to have a look at those records before we make Kennedy and his old man an offer."

Maloney took down every word McLain said in a small notebook he carried everywhere. The young executive was as thorough as a Watergate prosecutor.

"Tell Carlisle to shoot some vision of him at his next start and email it over. I want to see how he looks on the mound. If he gets the thumbs up from me, you, Carlisle and Betts, we'll offer him a signing bonus.

"We'll start at \$130,000," McClain continued. "If they balk at it, we can go as high as \$200,000, even \$225,000. I want that kid at Mosquito Lakes in February."

Despite being just 32 years of age, Maloney, a former minor league infielder, who played AA ball in the Stars organisation, was very highly thought of by other clubs for his vision, business sense and confidence. He made deals others backed away from and preferred to go with his gut over those who were married to books of statistics and analytics.

Based on Carlisle's glowing assessment of Jenkins, Betts had the young Aussie pencilled in as his starting shortstop in as little as three years. Rookie League, a split season at A level and AA and then a year at AAA. His plan was to have current shortstop, 32-year-old Gold Glover Herbie "Scooter" Samuelson, work with Jenkins every day once he arrived in camp in south Florida.

"I want this kid, Duke," Betts said in an email. "Get some vision of him at the plate. I want to dissect his swing the way a high school kid cuts up a frog in biology class. If he's got a weakness, I'll find it and fix it. He's our guy."

After a couple of quiet days, meaning no visits to hospital or encounters with Melbourne's criminal element, Carlisle drove to the upscale bayside suburb of Sandringham and the Royals' home ground where the Royals were entertaining Jenkins and the Aspendale crew. The medium house price in Sandringham was over $850,000, which thanks to his new contract, was in his price range if he was so inclined to take up residence 15,000 miles from home. Once Carlisle got to New York he'd go house and apartment hunting or just take up residence in a hotel close to the ballpark in Flushing, Queens. Since he still hadn't heard from one Cindy Bartkowski of Atlanta, Georgia, a one-bedroom apartment was looking like the likely option.

The Royals had dropped three of their first four games – two of the losses coming by just one run – and in just a 27-game season, desperately needed a win to avoid tumbling to the bottom of the East Conference ladder.

They had used their ace pitcher three days earlier in a 3-2 last-inning loss to Waverley and would be depending on a trio of hurlers against Jenkins and the Aces. Their starter, Steve Whittaker, was 35 years of age, old enough to be Jenkins' dad.

The Aces countered with 17-year-old Brian Day, who had one thing in common with Jenkins; they had both played for Victoria since they were nine years old. From what Carlisle had gathered, Day was a fine player in his own right. But comparing him to Jenkins was like comparing tap water to champagne.

On a beautiful spring evening for baseball, Carlisle took his chair and backpack and set up camp about 20 metres past the first base bag.

Fifteen minutes before the first pitch he wandered over to the canteen behind the home plate fence to grab a bite to eat.

Who the hell puts ketchup on a hot dog? Carlisle wondered when he was asked if he wanted tomato sauce on the hot dog he had just purchased. "Don't you have any mustard here?" he asked the woman who served him. In Carlisle's time around the traps, it was the moms of high school ballplayers who volunteered to man the canteens. The dads raked the infield and pitcher's mound and marked the plate and foul lines. The one-percenters they were called. Without them, there'd be no baseball on the local level.

"Mustard? Who puts mustard on a hot dog?" she said.

"Three hundred million Americans, including this one."

"Here scouting Jenkins?" she asked.

"I am."

"I'll get you some mustard if you give me an honest assessment of my kid," she jokingly said.

"And he is?"

"David Merritt, he plays second for the Royals. I'm his mum, Wanda."

Wanda opened the fridge and handed Carlisle a container of mustard which he spread evenly on his dog.

"He thinks he is going to be a big leaguer but even I know he doesn't have a chance of being signed. He's hitting a buck ninety for goodness sake," Wanda said.

Carlisle bit into his dog and wiped a bit of mustard from around his mouth. "This isn't half bad. Can I get another one please? And ... you wouldn't have any sauerkraut back there, would you?"

"You're pushing it Slick. This isn't Coles, you know."

Carlisle laughed. "Throw in a bottle of water then if you don't mind. I'll write down a few notes on your boy and go over them with you after the game. Okay with you?"

"That's fine and kind of you too. Thank you."

Carlisle handed her a twenty, told her to forget about the change and walked back to his chair.

As it turned out the hot dogs were better than the game. The Royals were no match for Jenkins and Aspendale. The visitors scored early and often and won 11-4. Jenkins belted a long home run off Whittaker in the third inning and added a single and double off a pair of relievers for a three-for-five night at the plate. Delaney recorded all five of the at-bats on his iphone. Jenkins also sparkled in the field. After the last out was recorded and the warmth of the sun was replaced by an early evening chill, Carlisle introduced himself to Charlie and Cassie Jenkins.

"The New York Stars are very interested in your son," he told them. "I've come down from Sydney just to watch your boy," he lied. "The Stars organisation is prepared to make your family a substantial offer."

Carlisle jotted down his mobile number – he had picked up a new phone when he arrived in Melbourne – on one of his business cards and handed it to Charlie and Cassie Jenkins.

"I'll be in town until Monday."

"You're aware that Billy is intent on finishing Year 12?" Cassie Jenkins asked.

"I am. That's next November? Right?"

"It is. What kind of money are we talking about Mr Carlisle?" Charlie Jenkins asked.

"Seven figures."

"A million dollars?" Cassie asked?

"Yes mam."

Cassie's knees nearly buckled when she heard Carlisle's answer.

"Tell your people in New York that we have an agent and he'll be advising us," Charlie Jenkins said.

"That's standard procedure," Mr Jenkins. "I'm sure your agent is familiar with me and my time with the Atlanta Knights. Your son will be well looked after by the New York Stars. Our coaching staff is second to none. He won't be rushed to the major leagues, and let me tell you, he will love the facilities we have in Mosquito Lakes. You and your wife will receive business class tickets to Florida anytime you want to come down and visit, and we'll also put you up at a five-star hotel while you're down there."

The faces of Charlie and Cassie Jenkins lit up at the thought of business class plane tickets and a five-star hotel.

They've taken the bait, Carlisle thought. *Just reel them in.*

"I'll be at the game on Sunday and would be happy to meet with you both and Billy's agent either after the game or on Monday night over dinner. Give me a ring or let me know on Sunday."

Carlisle decided he would wait until Sunday's game at Blackburn before deciding on the overall grade he would give Jenkins.

Before leaving the ground, Carlisle stopped by the canteen to give Wanda Merritt his take on her son David. The second sacker went one-for-three and only had one ball hit his way. The lad was a bit small for his age, wasn't exactly quick and didn't have enough muscle on him to drive the ball. A bit of time in the gym could make him an adequate player at the level he was at, but his hope of being drafted was virtually nil.

"Mind you, one game is not enough to judge anyone, but I don't see David advancing any further," Carlisle told Wanda. "That's my professional opinion, I'm sorry."

Wanda nodded. "I guess I'll just have to find the right time to tell him."

Wanda Merritt was just one of the thousands of parents Carlisle had spoken with over the years at U.S. high school grounds, college stadiums and semi-pro ball parks throughout the northeast and south. He didn't enjoy telling them their kids weren't good enough but when asked he gave them his professional opinion. The majority took it well. But there were plenty of parents who told him to get stuffed – another expression he had picked up in the last week – or challenged his scouting credentials.

"What do you know sitting there with your binoculars and radar gun? I'm a better judge of talent than you."

"You wouldn't know a decent player if he jumped up and bit you on the bum."

"Take that radar gun of yours and stuff it up your ass."

Those were just a few of the comments he had heard over the years. One very chilly spring afternoon in Jacksonville, Florida about 10 years ago, one parent was so incensed with Carlisle's assessment of his son that he followed Carlisle back to his motel. Sometime during the night all four tires on his Ford pick-up truck were slashed to bits. Eight hundred plus dollars later he was back on the road. The Knights organisation reimbursed him for the new tires and hefty towing fee.

Parents just didn't seem to understand that signing bonuses and contracts were as rare as a Republican senator voting to raise the country's minimum wage. The kids lucky enough to be signed were still Prince of Penzance-like odds to ever make it to the big leagues.

Jenkins was the exception, and he thought Williamstown's Patrick Kennedy could be another.

Chapter 12

LIGHT RAIN was falling as Carlisle left his downtown Melbourne hotel for his first trip over the West Gate Bridge, which linked Melbourne's CBD and the western suburbs. He plotted his route that morning, and safely navigated his way through heavy traffic and got to Williamstown in just 30 minutes.

Carlisle had a walk around the quaint suburb, had a late lunch at a Chinese restaurant and arrived at the ground about 45 minutes before the 3:30pm start time of the seniors' game.

The showers had ended just before the reserves game began. The infield and pitcher's mound had been covered overnight. The outfield was a bit wet but playable.

Carlisle had a look at both the Essendon and Williamstown Facebook pages before leaving and saw that defending Victorian Division 1 champion Essendon had their ace scheduled to meet the home side. Riley Barrett had been signed to a minor league contract by the Boston Bean Eaters four years earlier but never advanced past A ball and was released. All that was left of the 24-year-old's $175,000 signing bonus was his truck, a top-end Toyota HiLux, which took the carpenter to and from building sites during the week.

Barrett was nearly unhittable for Essendon but in Rookie League and A ball he took a lot of early showers. At the end of his time with the Boston organisation the right-hander was a relief pitcher and was used only when his team was either way out in front or way behind.

He looked good warming up, but his fastball had little movement, and his curveball hung in the air like ripe fruit. But he was good enough at this level to be one of the league's top pitchers.

On the home side of the field Willy playing manager Terry Harding was warming up Patrick Kennedy. The ball made the same sweet sound landing in Harding's catcher's mitt as it did six days earlier at Edithvale. The plan today was for Kennedy to throw 80 pitches and continue to build up his arm strength.

With the ground a bit damp, Harding told Kennedy not to chase anything hit on the ground and take it easy on the basepaths when he came to the plate and batted.

Kennedy struck out two of the three Essendon hitters in the first inning and gave up just two base hits in six innings of work: both to Riley Barrett. He walked one, struck out seven and watched the last three innings of the game from the dugout.

Kennedy hit 94 miles an hour several times on Carlisle's radar gun and got another tick of approval from the New York scout. *His pitches have plenty of movement. He's the real deal, no doubt about it*, Carlisle thought

Riley pitched eight solid innings and left the game with the score tied 3-3.

"Shit, the last thing I need is an extra-inning game," Carlisle said to himself from his seat behind first base. "I've got to drive over that damn bridge, if I can find it."

The game did go into extra time, ending in the 12th inning on a passed ball which gave Williamstown a 4-3 win. The passed ball should have been scored a wild pitch. Johnny Bench would have had trouble stopping the pitch, which bounced in the dirt and skidded towards the screen behind home plate. The runner on third could have stopped for a coffee and still made it to the plate in time.

Carlisle approached Kennedy after the game and introduced himself to the left-hander.

"Any other scouts been around Paddy?"

"You're the only one – so far. It seems everyone wrote me off after I did my knee. But as you can see, it's not giving me a bit of trouble."

The kid was right. He wouldn't be able to throw 95mph with a dodgy knee, Carlisle thought. *He also knew that in just a matter of weeks or even days, scouts from other major league clubs would be getting in contact with him.*

"I reckon you've got a future Paddy and I'd like it to be with the New York Stars. I'm prepared to offer you a signing bonus of $200,000 – that's US dollars – if you put pen to paper in the next week. I've got a contract in my bag. Talk it over with your folks and Terry Harding and let me know. Here's my card. I fly back to New York on Thursday, so you have plenty of time to decide."

While Carlisle gathered his things and took off in his rental car, Harding and Kennedy talked things over in the clubhouse over a couple of cold beers.

"Carlisle had to impressed with what he saw today and last week. Did he offer you a deal?" Harding asked.

"He did and I was ready to sign there and then. He's talking a $200,000 signing bonus. Two hundred fucking thousand dollars Terry, US. Guaranteed."

"Shit. I thought maybe $150 large. But two hundred. That's a lot of coin mate. Talk it over with your folks, see what they say."

"What do you think?" Kennedy asked.

"If it was me, I'd sign right away. With that knee of yours ... you never know. One bad step and it could all be over."

He's right, Kennedy thought.

"I'll talk it over with mum and dad tonight. Carlisle said I would be at spring training at Mosquito Lakes with the Stars before being sent to a Rookie League team."

"The coaching you'd get over there would be invaluable Paddy. And you'd have the best physios and surgeons looking after that knee of yours."

The next afternoon Carlisle travelled to the suburb of Blackburn east of Melbourne to have another look at Billy Jenkins. The home side had one solid pitcher but had used him in an important mid-week game, which it won, and sent a 19-year-old with just mediocre stuff to the mound to face Aspendale. Jenkins and the Aces teed off on the kid while Blackburn did the same to a trio of Aspendale pitchers. Blackburn won the slugfest 12-10. Jenkins did most of the damage for the visitors. He doubled twice with the bases loaded, singled and hit a long sacrifice fly to the fence late in the game for his sixth RBI of the afternoon. The 17-year-old again played errorless ball in the field and displayed a strong throwing arm.

I'm sold, Carlisle thought after Jenkins' sixth and final plate appearance of the afternoon. *I've never been this sure about anyone as I've been about this kid. Admittedly, he wasn't facing much out there today, but he does it effortlessly. We've got to sign him, and fast.*

Carlisle relayed his thoughts back to New York in separate emails to McLain and Betts. "He can't miss," Carlisle wrote. "He's a once in a generation player. And we better get on to him quick. Every club is going to be after him. Some of them don't have deep pockets like ours, but that club in The Bronx does. Give me the go-ahead and I'll hand over a signed contract next weekend. Let's knock the family on its collective ass. Give me the go-ahead to make him an offer of $2.25 million. It will be the best money the NY Stars have ever spent."

McLain met with the organisation's bean counters later that day. "Due to the money we're saving by not re-signing Batista and his mate Stubby Hendricks, we can go as high as four million for both the pitcher and Jenkins," head bean counter Don Yates said. "I'd advise against signing any big free agents this season. Maybe in a couple of years when Kennedy and Jenkins are ready."

McLain agreed. He and Betts would build the club primarily through their farm system and look at a couple of middle-of-the-road free agents in the $4-$5 million price range to get the club competitive again.

Betts had his thoughts on who he wanted to see wearing blue, white and orange next season and what he wanted he usually got.

After receiving an email from McLain overnight with the words SIGN THEM in big bold letters, Carlisle was back in Williamstown late Monday afternoon for a meeting with Bruce and Carole Kennedy at their Williamstown home. They were a pleasant couple and after coffee and biscuits, it didn't take long for Bruce Kennedy to get down to business. He motioned to his son, who was sitting at the dining room table with them. "Paddy told me you offered him $200,000."

"I did Bruce."

"If you bump it up to $235,000 – guaranteed – we're prepared to sign."

That's all they want? Just an extra $35,000? Carlisle thought.

"The NY Stars would be willing to do that Mr. and Mrs. Kennedy."

"I just happen to have a contract with me," Carlisle said with a smile. He opened his briefcase, pulled out a standard free-agent contract and filled in the amount of $235,000 and handed the contract to Paddy's parents. Paddy left his seat and peered over his dad's shoulder. *My name on a major league contract. I can't believe it,* Paddy thought. *This is the greatest day of my life.*

"What do you say Paddy? Are you ready to become a New York Star? We've had a lot of great pitchers over the years; Stanton, Bergman, Reynolds, Goodman, Duncan."

He handed Paddy a pen and a Stars cap, which Paddy proudly put on.

Paddy's younger sister Anne Marie came in from the living room and took several photos of her big brother signing his major league contract.

"Congratulations Paddy. We'll see you at Mosquito Lakes in February," Carlisle said as he shook hands with his latest signing.

"Just one thing Carlisle," Bruce Kennedy said.

Uh oh. Don't throw a spanner into the works. It's a done deal, Carlisle thought.

"Can we have another signing down at the clubrooms tomorrow? We'll have the local media there and invite the TV networks too It would really help the club."

"Done," Carlisle said. "Shall we say 4pm?"

The Kennedys looked at each other and nodded.

"Four it is," Bruce Kennedy said.

"Make the arrangements," Carlisle told the Kennedys.

Kennedy was in constant contract with coaches from the Stars as he finished out the season with Williamstown, especially pitching coach Timothy Clyde Stuckey, who put him on a strict pitch count. "I don't want you reporting here with a tired arm son," Stuckey told him.

A strength coach outlined a weight and fitness program for him to follow and a nutritionist laid out a green and fruit-based diet which replaced the burgers, chips and sugar-coated junk he ate at the ballpark.

Kennedy bought himself a new car and put $50,000 towards the mortgage of his parents' home when the signing bonus landed in his bank account. "It's the least I can do," he told his teary-eyed mum and dad. "I wouldn't be where I am without your support."

Kennedy also gave the Williamstown Baseball Club a gift of $5000 which went to refurbish the clubrooms and the kitchen.

"Don't tell the local paper, okay? I don't want to make a big deal out of it," he told Terry Harding.

With the favourable exchange rate factored in, Paddy Kennedy had a tad over $200,000 left from his signing bonus.

He was loaded down with a couple of bags and eight added kilos of muscle on the day he departed for Florida.

On a warm early February night before he left, Paddy Kennedy handed the keys to his four-month-old sky-blue Mazda to his 18-year-old sister.

"This will make it a lot easier getting to and from uni," Paddy told her. "It's got a full tank of petrol, and the rego and insurance are paid. Just be careful with it."

"I'll take good care of it," Anne Marie Kennedy said, throwing her arms around her big brother. "I promise."

The next evening Paddy Kennedy boarded a Qantas flight at Tullamarine bound for Los Angeles. He had a business class ticket courtesy of the NY Stars. After a three-hour layover at LAX, he boarded an American Airlines flight bound for Miami.

Chapter 13

A CAR and driver sent by the Stars picked Kennedy up and drove him to the club's spring training home in Mosquito Lakes, two hours away. Despite its inhospitable name, Mosquito Lakes was no worse than any other city in the southern US when it came to insects – for 10 months of the year that is. The torrential rains of July and August and the odd hurricane were perfect breeding conditions for mozzies and they bred like a Kardashian – often and anywhere. During those two months citizens and visitors were urged to wear light coloured clothing and bathe themselves in mosquito repellent before venturing out after dusk. Some Stars fans even brought mosquito nets to the ballpark on nights when the mozzies were particularly bad.

Kennedy's knees were shaking when he stepped out of the car and looked at the sprawling complex. Pitching coach Stuckey, a former Major League pitcher who played his last game with the Chicago Cheeseburgers in 1998, pulled up in a golf cart and greeted Kennedy. He tossed Kennedy's bags in the back of the cart and showed him around. First stop was the hotel where he would be staying. They dropped his bags at the front desk. "Patrick Kennedy," Stuckey told the lad manning the front desk. "We'll be back in a few."

The late winter sun was beginning to set as Stuckey put the cart in gear.

"You'll be staying at the hotel the club owns until we figure out what we do with ya. Breakfast is at seven. Practice is at eight," he said in a southern accent which reminded Kennedy of Sheriff Buford T Justice of the *Smokey and the Bandit* movies.

Over the past few months, the two had only communicated via email.

"If I was you, I'd make sure I'm on time."

"I will be."

Stuckey drove them to the complex's main stadium which had seating for over 10,000 fans. Just enough lights were on for Kennedy to have a good look at the immaculate infield and outfield. They had a brief walk around.

This is fucking amazing, Kennedy thought.

"You'll be out on the back fields this spring. Depending on how you progress, you could be pitching right here for our Rookie League team in a few months," Stuckey said. "You've filled out a bit over the past few months. That's good to see. How's the knee?"

"It's the best it's been since I injured it."

"And your wing?"

"It's not where I want it to be yet, but I'm getting there."

"Let's get you back to the hotel so you can grab a late meal."

Stuckey threw his cigarette butt on the pavement and rubbed it out with his boot.

"You don't smoke do you?"

"Nope."

Stuckey pulled a pack of cigarettes from his jacket pocket, jabbed a fag in his mouth and lit it.

"Good. These fucking things will kill you," he said motioning for Kennedy to get back in the cart.

Billy Jenkins signed with the Stars the same week Kennedy did, but with a bit more fanfare. His "agent" turned out to be a local lawyer. It took him three full days to go over the standard contract and pronounce it "acceptable".

All three commercial TV networks turned up for the press conference at Southbank's Crown Hotel/Casino where it was announced that Jenkins had signed with the NY Stars for $2.5 million. A large novelty cheque, like the ones given to winners of pro golf tournaments, was given to Jenkins. He was surrounded by his beaming parents, sisters Susie and Vicky, both sets of grandparents, several of his Aspendale teammates and the president of the Aspendale Baseball Club, Bert Tonelli, who told anyone within earshot that Jenkins was the eighth Aces player to be drafted by a big-league club in the past 20 years. However, only one, a left-handed pitcher by the name of Bob Grove, had reached the show. None of the other nine had been personally scouted and signed by Duke Carlisle so Tonelli had a good feeling that Jenkins would make it.

For a 17-year-old, Jenkins handled himself quite well in front of the Melbourne media pack which included reporters and photographers from Melbourne's two daily newspapers, the *AAP* and Chris Bachman of the *Cheltenham Post*. Bachman had been writing about Jenkins' on and off-field exploits for the last 10 years and was still on the same salary, although earlier in the year he was given a laptop which he was supposed to file stories on when he was out of the office. The laptop remained in its box under his desk. "When I get a fucking raise, I'll file a story from the road. Until then, it's 9-5 Monday through Friday with a 45-minute lunch break," he said to anyone within earshot.

Since Bachman was the lone senior journalist at The Post and the only one capable of a writing a hard-hitting news story, he was given a wide berth by his editor, "Slippery" Pete Pilkington. He attended monthly council meetings and was well-respected by councillors and the young 23-year-old mayor, Ralph Whitby. Bachman got anything he wanted from Whitby in exchange for not writing about how his excellency cheated on his VCE exams.

Nobody made a stink about the laptop sitting under Bachman's desk. The box it came in however did serve as a functional footstool so at least it got some use.

Jenkins had been asked to be in a photo or sign an autograph every now and then, but since he was now more well-known in the state than

Victoria's premier, at least for this week, he was constantly being recognised and asked to pose for selfies. "What are you gonna do with all that money Billy? Don't spend it all in one place mate. Can you lend me a million mate?"

He really did have a million bucks to spare since his $2.5 million (US) signing bonus was north of $3 million Australian. It was wisely invested and each month he got a nice stipend. He didn't have to work at Coles or Woolies like some of his mates and spent the next year concentrating on baseball and his Year 12 studies. He was named MVP of Baseball Victoria's Summer League competition even though the Aces lost their end-of-the-season semi-final in three games. They didn't have enough pitching to make it through to the grand final series. Kennedy and Williamstown made it to the final but were defeated by perennial powerhouse Essendon in three games.

Jenkins did well on his VCE exams the following November and to no one's surprise had another strong season for Aspendale. The Aces were on top of the ladder when it came time for Jenkins to travel to Florida for spring training. In an emotional scene at Tullamarine, which all three networks got vision of, Jenkins said goodbye to his family on a rainy early February night and boarded a *Qantas* flight for Los Angeles. Charlie Jenkins wanted to accompany his son to Florida and help him settle into his new surroundings but had to travel to Far North Queensland for an important meeting with area banana growers who had been battered by a cyclone just a few weeks earlier. "Even with the time difference (16 hours this time of the year), we'll try and Skype every day. Just enjoy yourself. You're doing something you've wanted to do since you were a lad," Charlie Jenkins told his son who was nearly a head taller and 10 kilos heavier than he was.

Billy Jenkins had his mitt and a baseball in his carry-on bag and every so often during the 14½-hour flight took them out and tossed the ball into his mitt to settle his nerves. "What am I worrying about? I can do this," he said to himself. "The Stars gave me two and half million dollars and a business class seat for goodness sake."

But Billy Jenkins was not going to be playing against Australians and a sprinkling of older Americans anymore. The best young athletes back home gravitated to cricket and footy. He was going to be facing the best young baseball talent the United States had to offer. Duke Carlisle had the confidence Jenkins could make it. Jenkins, who had never once doubted his own ability, needed a confidence boost before he took the field in a NY Stars uniform.

Chapter 14

THREE DAYS later, Billy Jenkins was in the clubrooms at Bank of Florida Field. Gene Short, manager of the Class A advanced Mosquito Lakes Saints of the Gulf Coast League, welcomed him to the NY Stars organisation and introduced him to several other free agent signees and coaches. Jenkins was one of about 40 players. Each was assigned a locker which matched their uniform number. "Get dressed fellas. We'll meet up on one of the back fields. Coach Joe Keneally will march you out there. If you have any questions, he's the one to speak too."

Jenkins found his locker, got undressed and pulled on his NY Stars uniform – white pants, white cleats, blue top and a blue cap with an orange NY insignia. The cap was a little stiff, so he bent it back and forth a few times until it fit better. The number 56 was on his back. It could have been higher. The draft picks and free agents who have little chance of making it usually get stuck with numbers in the high 70s or even 80s. Jenkins grabbed his mitt and followed the others onto the field.

Since Paddy Kennedy was a pitcher and Billy Jenkins an infielder, their paths rarely crossed during the day. They hung around with different crowds at night too. Being over the legal US drinking age of 21, Kennedy, occasionally went out for a beer with his new teammates. They swapped baseball stories, showed each other photos on their phones of the girls they dated back home and wondered where they would be headed once management handed out assignments. The lucky ones would get to stay in Mosquito Lakes and play for the organisation's Gulf Coast League side, which kicked off the first week of April. Other locales included Kingspoint, Tennessee, home of the Stars' Rookie League team and the New York Penn League's Class A Poughkeepsie (New York) Bandits.

The Kingspoint and Poughkeepsie sides didn't begin their season until Mid-June which is where those who had finished their college baseball careers got sent. The cream of the crop wound up in Columbia, South Carolina of the Class A South Atlantic League or were assigned to the Class A advanced team based in Mosquito Lakes.

Mosquito Lakes College sophomores Sophie Hall and Erica Cosgrove showed up at Bank of Florida Field just after 10am. They became friends on the very first day of volleyball practice in their freshman year. Hall hailed from Tallahassee in the northern part of Florida while Cosgrove grew up a few hundred miles northwest of there in Macon, Georgia. Both were given athletic scholarships after earning All-State honours in volleyball and softball in their junior and senior years of high school.

Each had a tight grip on a Starbucks coffee cup. Sophie had a small pair of binoculars hanging around her neck. Stars ballcaps kept the warm late-winter sun off their faces as they walked to one of the back diamonds. Blonde hair spilled out of the back of their caps.

Their phones were tucked into the back pockets of their shorts, which were tighter than a camel's arse in a sandstorm. Those lucky enough to be walking behind them often wondered if Apple's iPhone logo had been permanently etched onto their shapely arses. Sophie and Erica had a couple of hours to kill until their next class – advanced basket weaving – and were eager to check out the new talent which had arrived in town over the past few days.

Sophie, all five feet ten inches of her, and Erica, who was two inches shorter and two bra sizes larger, played volleyball during the autumn and softball in the spring and had earned all-conference honours for the

Flyswatters – what else would the school nickname be? – in both sports. They were vital components to the school's athletic success and were given courses softer than a down-filled pillow; baseball/softball theory, American geography – the final was a toughie – to locate Hawaii and Alaska on a map, film appreciation – in which they each had to direct a 10-minute video – and another on the music of Taylor Swift and its effect on young women. "It takes money out of our pockets and puts it in hers," Sophie wrote in one essay. She was not wrong.

Sophie and Erica rated young ballplayers too, but not the way Duke Carlisle did. They put ballplayers in three categories; unfuckable, fuckable, and depends on how drunk we are. Those with money were deemed potential boyfriends. However, if any player with money was on the dorkish side – think Sheldon of the *Big Bang Theory* – they were immediately written off.

"They have to be Instagram or Facebook material," Sophie was fond of saying. Erica agreed.

Initially they seemed pleased as they checked out this year's new crop of players, who were taking infield and batting practice. The pitchers were off in a group of their own down the left field line. Sophie put her binoculars up to her green eyes and started scanning the field. Erica took her phone from her pocket. She'd be taking notes. In the batting cage was a tall, muscular lad with the number 56 on his back. "I think we got us a keeper," Sophie said. "Number 56. Put a star next to that one."

She continued. "Cross off number 47. He looks like he just stepped off the set of *Hillbilly Catfishing.* He's probably got a month's worth of Macca's stuck in that dopey beard of his."

Number 47 belonged to outfielder Eugene Donaldson of Natchitoches, Louisiana. He was patiently standing by the batting cage, waiting to take his cuts. Next to him was Elrod Stokes of Rattlesnake Valley, Texas. "Woo wee," Sophie cried when Stokes came into her line of vision. "This number 68 is fine."

"Let me have a look," Erica Cosgrove said, taking the binocular from Sophie's hands.

"Definitely fuckable," Erica noted. "Although I don't know what my daddy would say if he found out I was screwing a black ballplayer. But we don't discriminate, do we Sophie?"

"Not when they look like that."

Stokes was a switch-hitting outfielder who batted over .400 in his junior year at Rattlesnake Valley HS. But a run in with a four-foot rattler while he was doing some work on his father's small ranch left him hospitalised for nearly a month and caused him to miss his senior year of ball. He graduated with his class last May and now, nine months later, after a vigorous conditioning program, was finally 100 percent fit and ready to prove to the Stars that they hadn't throw away $65,000 signing him.

By the time Sophie and Erica finished their scouting work and headed back to campus, a half-dozen players – highlighted by Jenkins and Stokes – were on their "definitely fuckable" list, another 10 were listed as "fuckable". The others had the "depends on how drunk we are" tag attached to them.

Donaldson topped the unfuckable list of seven.

All Sophie and Erica needed to do was put names to the numbers they had jotted down and introduce themselves to the newcomers. "They might have girls back home, but I'm pretty sure we've got them covered," Sophie Hall correctly noted.

After weeks and weeks of endless drills and intra-squad games, the Stars managers, coaches and front office staff started handing out assignments. Paddy Kennedy was one of the lucky ones. Stuckey, New York's pitching coach, had taken a keen interest in the Aussie recruit. He talked Kennedy up to New York manager Darren Betts every time they went over the organisation's list of pitchers. "Physically he's fine Darren. That knee of his won't give him any trouble and since he's a few years older than the others I'd like to start him out at Columbia," he said one morning in Betts' small, crowded office. "If he holds his own there, I'd like to move him up to Kingspoint in July and see how he goes against them college fellas.

"You think that much of him?" Betts asked.

"I do," Stuckey said. "He's hitting 94, 95 on the gun and still improving. He's going to make it to the show."

"I hope you're right. Them lefties we have in AA and AAA ain't worth their weight in horse shit," Betts said.

Six days later, Kennedy and about 20 others flew from Fort Lauderdale into Columbia, South Carolina, a good-sized city of over 125,000 located right smack in the middle of the Republican-leaning state. They were met by a bus which took them to the ballpark they'd be spending most of their days and nights for the next couple of months. Hollings Park had seating for nearly 8000 and was a lot better than some of the other ballparks they'd be visiting as they started their pro careers. Columbia was in the Southern Division of the 14-team league. A pool was started by bench coach "Digger" Murtaugh on where the team bus would hit the 300,000-mile mark. Would it be on the highway to North Carolina (Asheville) or Georgia (Augusta and Rome), or South Carolina (Charleston and Greenville) or Kentucky (Lexington)? It was five bucks to join. Kennedy chose Augusta since it had the best nickname in the league, the GreenJackets. Plus, it was the only city Kennedy knew since every year it hosted The Masters. To him the other cities were just places on a map. Kennedy was off by 2100 miles. Catcher Ernesto Armosa of the Dominican Republic, who knew even less about US geography and only a dozen or so words of English, took out the pot of $145 with his guess of Del Marva in Maryland.

Del Marva was part of the Northern Division of the "Sally" League, as the South Atlantic League was often called, and it had some of Columbia's longest bus trips. "Why Del Marva?" Armosa was asked. "Yes, Del Marva. I win," he replied. The team travelled as far north as New Jersey (Lakewood) and played in Maryland (Del Marva and Hagerstown), North Carolina (Kannapolis, Hickory and Greensboro) and West Virginia (Charleston).

Although Kennedy could afford his own place thanks to his handsome signing bonus, he stayed with a host family as did the rest of his new teammates. When the season started in early April, in just two weeks, Columbia's players would start drawing their salaries. It wasn't much. Kennedy's first cheque for two weeks work was $420, about $30 a game.

Once taxes, clubhouse dues and insurance were taken out, Kennedy was left with less than $300.

During spring training, players are each given $120 per week in meal money. Once the season starts players receive $25 per day meal money when they're on the road. When the team was in Columbia players paid for their own food and drinks.

All the players stayed with host families in Columbia and Kennedy was assigned to one of the better ones. Sarah Dowling and her husband, Tom, had two youngsters, aged 10 and 12, who loved baseball. Ty and Christopher peppered Kennedy with questions about Australia and baseball day and night. But the only time Kennedy got to sit down and have dinner with the Dowlings was after selected day games. On game nights, Kennedy had to be at the ballpark two hours before the 7pm start time so he missed out on Sarah Dowling's cooking.

Sarah and her husband made sure their boarder was well-fed. They often left a plate for him in the fridge which he ate after night games or had for lunch the next afternoon.

Clubhouse managers took charge of the pre- and post-game spreads but never served up much. If you didn't like peanut butter and jam sandwiches, you were out of luck. On a good day the "clubbies" got some cheap deli meat like ham or bologna and maybe a tub or two of potato salad and bags of plain potato chips. Players washed the grub down with tasteless supermarket brand names of cola since they were cheaper than Coke and Pepsi. On some nights, if they were lucky, Kennedy and his teammates ate leftovers from the concession stand. Nutritionally, cold hot dogs and soggy nachos offered little. But since they were free, they were gobbled up. Fellow pitcher Willy "Catfish" McGee of Gainesville, Florida was the only one on the 10-man pitching staff who knew how to cook and introduced them to grilled catfish which he bought fresh from a local fish shop and fried up on the barbecue of the home where he was staying. In return, Kennedy supplied fresh fruit and salads to McGee and his fellow hurlers.

"Word is you signed for some big bucks Mr. Australia. That true?" Catfish asked Kennedy a few days before the start of the season.

"Don't believe everything you hear mate."

"I read that."

"Don't believe everything you read either."

The Stars won four of their six games. Kennedy started the side's third game against the Asheville Tourists on Thursday afternoon April 4 and allowed two runs on four hits before he left the game for a pinch hitter in the bottom of the sixth. The Stars snapped a 3-3 in the home eighth on a sacrifice fly and won 4-3. The win went to reliever Humberto Colon. Kennedy struck out eight and walked two and was pleased with how he threw in his first professional appearance.

"I was a bit nervous to tell you the truth," he told reporter Allison Symonds of the *Columbia Herald*, the city's daily paper. "It took me a few innings to settle down. Once I found my rhythm, I felt pretty comfortable out there."

Symonds was also a rookie but lived just 15 minutes away from the ballpark. Every member of the South Atlantic League Saints was at least 500 miles from home. The 23-year-old brown-haired starlet graduated from the University of South Carolina in Columbia the previous May and had impressed Don Mackey, the paper's long-time sports editor with her willingness to cover anything; including the annual lawnmowing races just outside of town. Nobody in the sports department of five wanted the assignment which always drew a big crowd. Her colleagues were more interested in the University of South Carolina's spring football (gridiron) game which in the past had drawn crowds of up to 15,000.

Symonds put her hand up to cover the lawnmowing races. Her smart yarn and the accompanying photos were well received by the locals. As a reward she was named the Stars beat writer for the entire 2025 season. After every home game she filed a yarn from either the rickety press box or her desk if the game was over within three hours. The *Herald* couldn't afford to send her on the road, so she listened to the away games on radio or watched them – if they were being live-streamed – and rang team manager Dusty Dyer 30 minutes after the game for a comment.

Dyer wasn't a fan of reporters since his marital difficulties were disclosed in the pages of the *Herald* the year before. But he was told by Stars management that he was contractually obligated to speak to all members of the local media no later than 30 minutes after the last out of every ballgame.

Dyer didn't particularly like having a woman poking her head in the clubhouse but relented once he started reading Symonds' stories. She knew her baseball and his players let their guard down and were more honest with her than they might have been with a male reporter. Only one player, Johnny Roman, of some hick town in west Texas, tried to come on to her and when she said no, he flicked his wet towel at her. Symonds responded with a well-placed knee to his groin which put the back-up outfielder on the disabled list for 14 days.

Roman missed the Stars' first road trip of the year, 10 games, which started in Charleston, West Virginia. The club left on their 500-plus kilometre long journey at 8am the following morning. As they boarded the team bus, a Stars official handed each player an envelope with $250 cash, a dozen twenty-dollar notes and a tenner. It was their meal money for the next 10 days. After a stop for lunch, they hoped to get to the Coalminers home field by 3pm. Spending six hours on a bus was not the best way to prepare for a game but if the Stars organisation was able to save money on motel rooms for a night it did. Every other Class A side did the same thing.

For the Stars first road trip of the year, fruit and assorted drinks – all bought by the players – were placed in several coolers and topped up with ice. Occasionally after a game, a few six-packs of beer were stashed among the cans of Coke. Kennedy was the only player on the 25-man roster over the legal drinking age of 21 but Dyer never made a fuss. "They'd be having a beer or two at home. No harm in having one on the bus after a game. They ain't driving," he told first base coach Ricky Estacion. "Shit, they're so tired they'll be asleep before we get to the motel.

"You make sure you stay awake Bussy," Dyer called out to bus driver Randy Murray as the team travelled to its three-star accommodation following a 5-4 loss. In his early 60s, Murray was in his third year of driving the team bus. When the club was at home, Murray drove buses for the City of Columbia's Mass Transit system.

"I had a good nap before the game," Murray said in return. "I'll have us at that motel before you can say Jackie Robinson."

"Hell of a ballplayer that Robinson," Dyer said. "Hell of a ballplayer."

Rather than being sent to a city he had never heard of, Billy Jenkins, as expected, was assigned to New York's Gulf Coast League side in Mosquito Lakes along with a bunch of other recent high school graduates and free agents. Despite a bit of good-natured ribbing from his new teammates about his multi-million-dollar signing bonus, the now 18-year-old was enjoying life as a professional ballplayer and felt at home in Mosquito Lakes despite being there just six weeks. He was thankful he'd be staying put.

"There haven't really been any surprises," he told his dad on one of their twice weekly skype calls from the hotel room he would be vacating in the next week. Once the regular season began, he would either share an apartment with a couple of his teammates or be billeted with a host family. The Stars organisation didn't frown on players getting their own apartments, since several of them had gotten decent-sized bonuses. But it preferred having its players stay with a local family so they would be better looked after, better fed and less likely to get into trouble.

It had been nearly two months since Billy had left home and Charlie Jenkins was surprised at how much muscle he had put on.

"The strength and conditioning coach has our group in the gym three and four times a week and we've even had a nutritionist working with us," Billy told his dad.

"How are your coaches, Bill? Easy to work with? Teaching you lots?"

"They're amazing dad. They're top-class, patient and Scooter has been fantastic."

"Scooter? You've told me about him, haven't you?"

"Yeah. Scooter Samuelson, the New York shortstop. He has taught me so much. No wonder he wins all those Gold Glove awards. He's like a vacuum cleaner. He picks up everything, and with such ease too. He's taught me a lot about footwork and how to read hitters, where to position myself."

"What's Mosquito Lakes like? Enough to do?"

"It's a good place to live dad. It's just starting to warm up. I've played golf a few times and been out fishing with a couple of the guys. But playing ball eight hours a day leaves us pretty spent at night."

"Anyone giving you a hard time about your signing bonus."

"Nah. It's all in fun. And some of the other guys signed for a couple of hundred thousand dollars, so I'm not the only one with a bit of money."

"Just be careful son. Once the locals know how much you signed for, they're going to be hitting you up for loans, asking you to help get a business off the ground."

"I've heard a few interesting proposals, but I just tell them that all my money is tied up in a fund that I won't be able to access for another three years, and they move on."

"And the girls?"

"There's a few of them at practice and our intra-squad games. They've got their eyes on this lad from Texas, Elrod Stokes. He's a ripper bloke."

Billy didn't tell his dad about Erica Cosgrove, the college sophomore he'd been making small talk with, and her friend Sophie Hall, who had been keeping Stokes company.

"All she wants to do is fuck Billy. Two and three times a night; in the morning, in the shower," Stokes told Jenkins over dinner one night. "If she keeps going at this rate my pecker's gonna wind up on the DL."

Jenkins laughed.

"You should hook up with her friend Erica. Sophie told me she's keen on you. And if she's anything like Sophie, you won't be getting much sleep at night."

"I might have a word with her. We'll see."

"We'll see? Bill. This is a slam dunk. It'll be the best fuck you've ever had."

Billy wouldn't know if Erica would be a good lay or not. She'd be his first. He couldn't tell Elrod that, and if Erica found out there was a fair chance she might blab it all over town.

He could see the headlines. *Virgin bonus baby finally scores, Jenkins doesn't measure up says local girl, Billy through wankin'.*

The night before the Mozzies got on the bus for their Gulf Coast League season opener in Daytona, Jenkins scored his first run of the season in the Mosquito Lakes College dorm room of Erica Cosgrove.

"I'm your first, aren't I Billy?" she asked when they were lying flat on their backs just five minutes after they started.

"Technically, yes."

"What's that supposed to mean? Technically?"

"I've gotten, you know, blow jobs before ... but this was my first time."

"Well, you could have fooled me. You're a natural."

Jenkins didn't know how to answer so he just shrugged his shoulders and said, "Well, it's easier than turning a 6-4-3 double play."

Erica laughed. "You ready to step up to the plate again slugger?"

"Let's play two," he said, quoting Chicago Cubs hall of famer Ernie Banks.

By the time Erica Cosgrove had finished with him, Billy Jenkins felt like he had played a week's worth of games in one night. "Why didn't you tell me you rode horses. I'm going to need a day off," he kidded.

Jenkins took an Uber back to the upscale home of June and Bryan Harper where he was staying. In the end, being billeted with a local family held more appeal than living by himself or with one of his teammates in a rented apartment for the next five months.

The Harpers had a boy and a girl, both under the age of 10, and were extremely easy to talk too. He felt like he was staying with his favourite Aunt and Uncle. And since Bryan had played a little bit of college ball himself, Billy picked his brain on how to stay focused during the long season and how to deal with all the travel.

The next afternoon Billy Jenkins started at shortstop and went 1-for-4 in his professional debut. "You all right son?" manager Gene Short asked him in the clubroom after the Mozzies' 6-4 loss. "You looked a little sore out there."

"Just nerves skip. Was good to get that first one out of the way. I'll be better tomorrow."

After some stretching back in the motel room he shared with Stokes, and a leisurely swim, Jenkins felt like himself.

"What do you say Stokesy? Let's go out and spend that meal money of ours."

Game time the next day was 7pm which meant that everyone had a full day to kill until the bus took them to the ballpark about 3:30. Most of the guys hung around the pool. Others played computer games or watched TV shows on their laptops and phones. A group of six played cards; dropping nickels, dimes and quarters onto the centre of the table. To keep anyone's nose from getting out of joint, raises were kept to $1.

Jenkins took a stroll by himself around noon and had lunch at a nearby Denny's Restaurant. He bought a copy of the local paper from a vending machine out front to see if anything had been written about the previous day's game. Forgoing the usual burger, fries and Coke, Jenkins ordered a Caesar salad, fruit cup and an iced tea.

After the middle-aged waitress took his order and left, Jenkins turned to the back of the paper and the sports pages. Since it was opening day there were two full pages on the game and several good photos. His name appeared twice. There was bit about tonight's game with some information on the starting pitchers. Daytona was sending Rick Yeager to the hill while the Mozzies were giving the ball to "Slim" Tim Robertson. "Slim" was over six feet tall and didn't weigh more than 160 pounds. He was all arms and legs on the mound and hid the ball so well hitters had no idea when and how the ball left his hand. By the time they found the ball, it often had whizzed past them. It took Jenkins a few at bats in the club's intra-squad games to get a read on him. Even then he was hard to hit since he had so much movement on the ball. You had to wait him out, go deep in the count and wait for your pitch. Jenkins liked Mosquito Lakes' chances to even the series.

Jenkins left $5 of his daily meal money on the table as a tip and paid the $13.50 tab at the cash register. Jenkins was luckier than most minor leaguers. He had $1900 flowing into his bank account from his signing bonus on the first of each month along with his $812 monthly salary – minus taxes – which was deposited into his Florida bank account every two weeks.

With Stokes by the pool and the motel room to himself, Jenkins took Scooter Samuelson's advice and took a nap in the afternoon.

"It takes your mind off the game, even if it is just for an hour. You need to be relaxed come game time. I'm not saying it will work for you, but it has for me."

A little over an hour after he closed his eyes, Billy was woken by the buzz of his phone. He looked at the screen and saw a text message from Erica.

Missing me, Billy? Good luck tonight. I'll be listening. Can't wait till you get back. xoxox.

Billy felt a bit bad since he had given little thought to his bedroom partner and hadn't even sent her a text.

Instead, he had been looking for some information on Daytona's Rick Yeager, who he would be facing in Game 2. All manager Short and coach Keneally knew about Yeager was that he was drafted in the sixth round by Cincinnati and had led his side to the state high school championship game in central California 11 months earlier. Jenkins found some stories on him as a high schooler courtesy of Google and was able to learn that the left-hander had an outstanding curveball which was his out pitch.

As for Erica, curiosity got the better of him, so he punched her name into his phone. A couple of volleyball and softball yarns popped up along with her Facebook page. There wasn't much to see there except for a shit load of photos with her and Sophie and the arms of blokes all over them. *Is she just being playful or sleeping with half of the guys on her campus?* Billy wondered. *Damn, why did I have to look? I've got a game to worry about.*

Stokes returned to their motel room half an hour before the bus was due to leave for the ballpark. He stretched out on his bed, turned on the TV and started flicking around looking for something to watch. "Can you believe this shit Bill? No cable. We can't even watch *Sportscenter* for fuck's sake. Dr Fucking Phil? Really? I can't watch this shit."

He threw the remote down and stared at the ceiling.

"Take my laptop mate. Everything is on YouTube, the highlights of every major league game from last night."

"Thanks Bill." He fiddled around and settled on a 15-minute package on New York's game with Florida, a 10-3 loss for the Stars. "Shit, they look bad. At this rate the big club will be calling us up in September."

Jenkins laughed. "September 2027 is my guess."

"You think we'll ever make the highlights Bill?"

“Why not. I like to think we have as good a shot as anyone else playing A ball.”

“You’re right man. I sure hope I do better tonight. A sacrifice fly? That’s all I could get off their pitchers last night. I was shit.”

“At least you knocked in a run Stokesy. Hey, listen up. I’ve been reading some stuff about Daytona’s pitcher tonight. Rick Yeager is his name and he’s supposed to have a mean, mean curveball. If he throws a fastball in the zone go for it.”

“I sure will. I really need to get off to a good start. In my junior year at high school, I was hitting around .200 halfway through the season. I was about to get benched and replaced by a freshman, a fucking freshman Billy. Next game, boom: two doubles, legged out an infield hit and made a running catch in the outfield to save a couple of runs. I need some of that magic tonight or in the next couple of games.”

“You’ll make it happen mate. Just be patient. Don’t try too hard.”

“You ever go through a slump? One of them 2-for-25 slumps when you can’t hit shit?”

“Never that bad. I’ve been lucky. But I did the hard yards; took extra batting practice, extra ground balls. My dad always told me the more work you put in the more you get back.”

Stokes nodded. “You were playing ball, and I was dodging rattlesnakes; all but one anyways.”

“How bad was it? We’ve got some of the most dangerous snakes in the world back home, but I’ve never even seen one.”

“I’ll tell you Bill. I don’t wish that sort of pain on anyone. The fucker got me just below the knee. I didn’t think I’d make it at first. Thank God my dad heard me yelling for help. He took me straight to hospital.”

“Geez”.

“Took me a good month before I felt like myself. Missed my whole senior year, the whole year. I thought I’d never be drafted. Bud Hartnett, he was my high school coach, he went to bat for me. He called everyone he knew and talked me up. Told them I had recovered and was worth being drafted or signed. I wasn't drafted, but when the Stars offered me $60,000, I tell you, it was the happiest day of my life. I'd have signed for a dollar mate. One US greenback."

Jenkins smiled. "I'm sure glad you're my roommate."

"Ditto," Stokes said.

"Hey, Stokesy," Jenkins said as he sat up. "What do you know about that filly you're hanging around with and her mate Erica?"

"Probably as much as you do. Sophie just likes to screw, and she's obviously got a taste for dark meat. They play volleyball and softball for the college, take some ridiculously easy courses to stay eligible, that's about it."

"What about their pasts?"

"Not sure Bill. I'm only thinking about today and tomorrow."

"I slept with Erica for the first time the night before we left, at her dorm."

"No shit?"

"Fair dinkum mate."

"Details. Do I get any details?"

"She can get pretty wild. But ..."

"But? What's wrong with pretty wild?"

"I checked her Facebook page, and in every photo, she's got blokes hanging all over her."

"It's all for show Bill. They talk a good game and like to show off their bodies."

"So, you don't think ..."

"That they're fucking half the school? No way. In all seriousness Bill, I'm not going to throw away what's been given to me by hooking up with someone like that."

"They've probably slept with five, six guys between them. One or two in high school. Another one or two college guys and a ballplayer or two."

"I hope you're right. I like her, and I hope she likes me too and not my signing bonus."

"They're not after money Bill. They know we might not be here for long. Especially you. You'll be playing Class A short season or Class A advanced ball in two months. You've got all the tools. I wish I had your talent."

"Thanks mate. I sure hope we get to the show together."

"Let's start by hitting the shit out of the ball tonight against that Daytona pitcher. What'd you say his name is?"

"Rick Yeager."

"I'm predicting he'll be having an early shower."

Just as Jenkins was about to reply there was a loud knock on their motel room door.

"Bus leaves in five minutes fellas. Five," coach Keneally yelled.

"We better get a wriggle on," Jenkins said.

"A what?"

"A wriggle on. Time to haul ass."

"Now that, I understand."

Thirty minutes later, the Mosquito Lakes Saints got changed in what passed for a clubhouse.

"I've got a shed in my backyard nicer than this," first baseman Donaldson the Unfuckable said to a chorus of laughs.

"Settle down boys, settle down," Short said.

There was a good-sized crowd on a balmy night for Game 2 of the three-game series and they gave it to Jenkins when he emerged from the dugout and walked to the on-deck circle in the top of the first inning.

"Hey Billy. Lend me a couple of million, will ya?"

A group of fans chanted "Overpaid, overpaid."

One young girl held a sign with the words 'Marry Me Billy' in big block red letters.

Jenkins heard the comments but didn't turn around. He was focused on Daytona pitcher Yeager as he pitched to centrefielder Craig McCallum, a 19-year-old from Finger Lakes High School in upstate New York who had the build of a fire hydrant. McCallum got ahead in the count and was looking for a curveball. Yeager served one up and McCallum lined it into left field for a base hit.

The voice of the home side's public address announcer, Dale Sterling, the host of Daytona's top-rated morning radio show, filled the air as Jenkins walked to the plate.

"Now batting for Mosquito Lakes, number 12, shortstop Billy Jenkins."

Jenkins heard a few boos as he stepped in the box. He looked to the third base coach box where Keneally relayed the signs. Since the Mozzies knew little about Daytona's catcher and McCallum wasn't all that fast, Keneally instructed Jenkins to swing away. Jenkins had seen a lot of major league curveballs during the last two months but nothing like the one Yeager had. His first pitch dropped about a foot and a half as it crossed the plate for a strike. Jenkins took a few pitches and then fouled off two curveballs to even the count at 2-2. Most hitters would be looking for another curveball at this point, but not Jenkins. He figured Yeager would throw his heater and he did. Jenkins drove the ball into the left-field corner for the first extra-base hit of his pro career. Keneally held McCallum at third and just like that the Mozzies had two runners in scoring position with one man out.

Stokes was next to bat and sent a long fly ball to centre field which was caught. It allowed McCallum and Jenkins to tag up. McCallum scored and Jenkins advanced to third. "Good piece of hitting there Bill," Keneally said. "Two out, so take off at the crack of the bat."

Jenkins was stranded at third when Yeager fanned third baseman Bernie Harris on a wicked curveball to end the inning.

"Another fucking sacrifice fly," Stokes told Jennings as they grabbed their gloves in the dugout and took their positions in the field.

"And another RBI," Jennings said. "You nailed it. Another 20 feet and it would have gone over the fence."

Jennings and Stokes each went hitless the rest of the night against Yeager. First baseman Donaldson was the star with two hits. His two-out, two-run single in the top of the seventh snapped a 1-1 tie and put the Mozzies on top 3-1.

"Slim" Robertson gave up two hits and a run in the bottom of the seventh and left the game with the visitors on top 3-2. Reliever Todd Mann came on to get the last out of the inning and pitched a scoreless eighth and a scoreless ninth to give the Mozzies a 3-2 win. Stokes made a routine catch in shallow left field for the final out of the game.

In the small clubhouse the Mozzies celebrated their first win of the season like they had won a pennant.

"Shall I tell them to put a lid on it?" Keneally asked Short

"Nah, let 'em enjoy it. It's their first win as pro ballplayers."

Their second win came the next night in a slugfest. The Mozzies jumped out to a big early lead, but Daytona rallied to tie the game 7-7 in the home seventh. Stokes broke the deadlock with a two-run homer in the top of the eighth. Jenkins, who had led off the inning with a single, greeted Stokes at the plate. "Two more ribbies. At this rate you're going to lead the league," Jenkins joked as they jogged back to the visiting dugout.

The Mozzies squeezed out another run in the top of the ninth and they needed it as Daytona rallied off closer Mann in the bottom of the ninth to close to 10-9. With the tying run on first and one out, Daytona's Kurt Sather smacked a hard ground ball towards second base. Jack Halloran fielded the ball cleanly and flipped it to Jenkins, who stepped on second for the force and threw to first to complete the inning and game-ending double play.

The Mozzies were a happy bunch as they showered and changed. It was after 11 pm when they boarded the team bus which was filled with all their gear. Ten minutes later it pulled into McDonald's. It either that or

Denny's. When Keneally had asked the players where they wanted to go, Donaldson the Unfuckable started the chant of "Maccas, Maccas."

"It's 11:30 at night and we're eating quarter fucking pounders," Stokes told Jenkins, who sat across from him. He shook his head. "If I see one more peanut butter and jam sandwich or one more Big Mac, I'm gonna lose it."

Jenkins laughed.

"Have a look at Donaldson. He's actually enjoying himself."

Jenkins turned around. Donaldson had fries stuck in his nose and ketchup was hanging off his beard.

"I'm gonna make it to the show just for the food," Stokes quipped.

The team bus arrived back at the Daytona Motel after midnight.

"Be at the bus by 9:45 in the morning fellas," Keneally shouted as the players filed out and went to their rooms. "The bus leaves for Clearwater at 10 whether you're on it or not. "We'll be in Clearwater by lunchtime, but I'd have myself some breakfast if I was in your shoes."

Situated on the west coast of Florida, Clearwater, the home of the Sharks, an affiliate of the LA Legends, was a three-hour drive away.

The only Mosquito Lakes player to miss the team bus last season was starting first baseman Tommy Palmer.

The Little Rock, Arkansas teenager was fined $1000, or two and-a-half week's pay, and was also suspended for three games. Had the Mosquito Lakes coaching staff or management found out about his dalliance with Mary-Anne Sidebottom – the wife of Bradenton Marauders manager Salty Sidebottom – following the last game of a three-game series in early May, his suspension might have lasted until the fourth of July.

A third-round draft pick who could have been drafted by an NFL team as a linebacker, Palmer was taking off his uniform in the visitors' clubhouse and waiting his turn to shower after a tense 2-1 win when he was handed a note by the clubhouse boy. At first, he thought the lad wanted an autograph. "You have a pen?" he asked.

"I was told to give you this," the lad said before scampering off.

Palmer flipped open the piece of paper and read a brief handwritten message which was so neat it looked like it had been typed.

Meet me at Bernie's after 9. You won't regret it. I was wearing the green halter top today. I'll be in green tonight. MA.

A tall brunette, with breasts the size of in-season rockmelons, Mary-Anne Sidebottom sat in the first row behind the Bradenton dugout at nearly every home game. Everyone in the ballpark that afternoon – the paid attendance was 2,612 –noticed her, even the umpires.

Palmer snuck out of the team motel after his roommate, Hank Logan, fell asleep. He hailed a cab and arrived at the massive country music venue at 9.15. At six foot four and a solid 225 pounds with scattered facial hair, Palmer, just 18, wasn't even carded when he walked up to one of the nightclub's bars and asked for a beer.

He downed it in three gulps, asked for another and started walking around looking for Mary-Anne Sidebottom. Since it wasn't a Friday or Saturday night there were only 300-400 people on the premises which resembled an airplane hangar. The difference was that an airplane hangar smelled better.

A bearded and bald-headed DJ cranked out country tunes. On weekends, MC Propecia was replaced by live acts who mainly performed covers.

"The crowd don't want to hear your shit. They want to hear some Garth Brooks," proprietor Bernie "Hacksaw" Jackson told the Meth Heads during their first and nearly last gig two weeks earlier. "You boys either play some Garth or some shit by Tim McGraw or you get the fuck off my stage," Jackson yelled after their first set.

The Meth Heads opened their second set with 'Friends in Low Places'. Jackson nodded his approval from the VIP seats where he was entertaining several young lovelies.

Mary-Anne Sidebottom attracted a fair share of attention on the dance floor in her tight green top, painted on jeans and boots.

"If she's 46 I'm Babe Fucking Ruth," Palmer said as he looked her over. Mary-Anne easily spotted Palmer in the crowd. He was a head taller than most. She gave him a wave and walked over to him when some shit song he had never heard before mercifully ended.

"I was wondering if you were gonna show," she said. "Let's grab a table. My damn feet are killing me. While you're up, get me a drink hun. Gin and tonic please."

Palmer got himself another beer at the bar, handed Mary-Anne her drink and sat down across from her.

"So, tell me Tommy, any other pretty ladies been sending you notes at the ballpark?"

"A few," Tommy lied. The only offers Tommy had gotten in the eight weeks he had been in the sunshine state had been from girls young enough to be Marry-Anne's daughters. Tommy Palmer was itching to get laid but wisely decided against hooking up with anyone under the age of 18.

"You know who I am?" Mary-Anne asked.

"Well, judging from where you were sitting today, I'd say you either work for the Sharks or know someone at the club. You can't just walk up on game day and get the best seat in the house, can you?"

"Well," Mary-Anne said. "I know someone."

"Who would that be if you don't mind me asking?"

"Salty Sidebottom."

"Sidebottom? The manager of the Sharks?"

"That's the one. I'm his wife."

Tommy Palmer leaned back in his seat and took a long sip of his beer. "You're fucking kidding me, aren't you?"

Mary-Anne poked at the ice in her glass with a plastic straw and said just one word. "Nope."

"And you want to sleep with me?"

"I don't figure on doing much sleeping hun, do you?"

Palmer felt himself blushing and scrambled for a suitable answer. "I'll sleep on the bus tomorrow," he said.

Mary-Anne smiled and rubbed Palmer's crotch with her left foot.

"What if he finds out?" Palmer worriedly asked.

"He won't find out. He's on a bus tonight. The Sharks play in Jupiter tomorrow afternoon. He doesn't like travelling on game day. Says it tires his players out."

"You sure he won't find out?"

"You want to get laid hun or should I walk over to that long line of arseholes over there who want to get in my pants?"

Palmer's head was saying no. His 18-year-old Louisville slugger won the argument. Mary-Anne Sidebottom and Tommy Palmer finished their drinks, walked outside and hopped in a waiting taxi.

"The Hampton Inn downtown," Mary-Anne told the driver.

"Tommy was here when I turned in," Hank Logan told Mozzies coach Joe Keneally the next morning while the team bus idled in the motel parking lot. "His bag in the room?" Keneally asked.

Logan walked back to the motel room he shared with Harper and came out carrying Harper's bag.

"Toss it on the bus," Keneally said. "They'll get reacquainted in Clearwater, if he ever shows the fuck up."

Palmer arrived at the ballpark in Clearwater an hour before game time.

"Don't bother getting dressed son," manager Gene Short told Palmer when he saw him enter the visitor's clubhouse. "Come to my office."

"I don't want to hear any excuses son," Short said. He was seated in an office chair behind an old desk that wobbled as he filled out the night's line-up card.

"You're suspended for three games – without pay," Short told his first baseman. "If you want to fuck up your career before it even gets started, that's your business, understand?"

"Yes sir."

"You've let your teammates down, your coaches down and me. We need your bat in the line-up. Reynolds is taking your place for this series, and you better hope you don't turn out to be another Wally Pipp."

"Who?" Palmer asked.

"You're a pro ballplayer and you don't know who Wally Pipp is? Google him for cryin' out loud. Now get the fuck out of this rathole they have the nerve to call an office. You'll be sitting with the locals tonight. I want you keeping track of Hennessy's pitches, every single one. Keneally will give you a scorecard."

Palmer slowly walked out of Short's office, found Keneally and got a scorecard from him. "If you miss another bus Palmer, miss curfew, or fuck up in any way, you'll be on a bus back to Little Rock," Keneally told him.

Palmer took a seat in the stands and as asked, kept track of Walt Hennessy's pitches. Hennessy threw a cracker of a game, striking out 12 and walking just two, but was on the losing end of a 3-2 score. Ben Reynolds went 1-for-4 with an RBI as Palmer's fill-in.

Palmer got reacquainted with his teammates on the bus after the game. He took a seat next to roomie Logan. "What the hell happened last night?" Hank Logan asked. "Where were you man?"

"I went out, had way too much to drink. I didn't want the coaches to see me hung over, so I took a Greyhound bus over here."

"Jesus Tommy."

"I know. I fucked up big time. It won't happen again. I'm not going back to Little Rock to work at a fucking Walmart."

"Coach told us you're suspended for three games without pay."

"That's right. He let me off easy."

"Hey Hank. You know who Wally Pipp is?"

"Played for the Yankees way back, didn't he?"

"He did. He didn't feel good one day and sat a game out. Lou Gehrig replaced him and went on to play over 2100 straight games. That was the end of Pipp's career. I'm not going to be this league's Wally Pipp, that's for fucking sure."

Palmer was lucky. Reynolds had just two hits in 12 at-bats filling in for him. In his first game back from suspension, Palmer singled, homered, drove in three runs and never looked back. He made the league All-Star team and got promoted at the end of the season.

Reynolds got released and wound up taking a coaching job at a middle school in Wichita Falls in northern Texas. Denny Rousseau, his former high school coach in Plano, just outside of Dallas, pulled a few strings to get him the gig. "I owe him," Raines told his wife Shirley over dinner one night. "If it wasn't for Ben, I wouldn't be a two-time state championship coach."

Reynolds was happy to get into coaching, but nearly blew a gasket when Wichita Falls Middle School principal and athletic director Bernie Fleming told he'd have to enrol at the local community college and get a teaching certificate. Reynolds did just enough schoolwork to get by and 18 months later received his certificate and officially became the lowest paid member of the Wichita Falls Middle School athletic department. Luckily, he hadn't tossed away the signing bonus the Stars gave him less than a month after he graduated high school. He rented a one-bedroom flat a few miles from the middle school, furnished it, paid for his tuition and books, and bought a 10-year-old Ford pickup truck to get around town with the $18,000 left in his bank account.

Denny Rousseau had neglected to tell Reynolds that Wichita Falls was smack dab in the middle of tornado alley. Three times in his first season as coach, games had to be abandoned when the city's tornado sirens sounded. Players, coaches, umpires and parents ran for cover as fast as their legs could carry them. They hunkered down in the school gymnasium for more than an hour on each occasion until they were given the all clear.

"My old teammates are sitting poolside somewhere in Florida while I'm riding out a fucking tornado in a gym that smells like a wrestling room. Shit, I should have taken extra batting practice, listened to the coaches, gotten better," Reynolds said to himself.

Chapter 15

A FULL contingent of Mozzies filed out of the team bus when it arrived at their motel in Clearwater, another three-star job with hot and cold running cockroaches. Players and coaches checked in, unpacked and then got back on the bus for the short ride to the ballpark where peanut butter and jam sandwiches greeted them in the visitors' clubhouse.

"Are they fucking kidding? More peanut butter and jam sandwiches? Is that the state sandwich of Florida?" a fired-up Stokes said loud enough for all to hear.

Donaldson the Unfuckable didn't seem to mind. He jammed several into his gob. "They're free," he said. "You guys don't want them? More for me."

"Easy Stokesy," Jenkins said putting an arm around his roomie's shoulder. "I'll order us some pizzas. Enough for everyone," Jenkins said. "And I'll treat you to a good meal after the game."

"Thanks mate," Stokes said. "Let's wrap this game up in two hours twenty so we can find someplace decent that's still open."

The Mozzies headed to their ancient lockers and got dressed for batting and infield practice which was scheduled for 4pm. Stokes, Jenkins and the others sat in uncomfortable wooden chairs that were older than their parents.

The subject of new chairs and lockers was brought up at a Clearwater Sharks board meeting in the off-season.

"As long as the chairs have four fucking legs and the lockers can hold a jockstrap, they're staying," thrifty Clearwater owner Roger Moody told

Tony Floyd, the Clearwater general manager who brought the subject up. "I'm just relaying what I heard from the other GMs during the season," Floyd said in his defence.

"Fuck the other GMs and while we're at it, how about coming up with some ideas to bring some fans to the fucking games. You're the damn marketing manager. Put some asses in the seats, paying asses, and then we'll talk about upgrades. Anybody got anything else they want to bring up?" Moody asked.

The six other men and one woman around the table in the boardroom shook their heads no.

"Nothing? Then the meeting's adjourned," Moody barked. He checked his watch. "And just in time too. I'm having lunch with the Trump 2024 Florida campaign chairman."

"Why doesn't that surprise me?" Floyd said after everyone had left the room.

"Who is going to be keeping an eye on our stuff when we're out on the field?" Stokes loudly asked. "Anyone know?"

His teammates shrugged their shoulders.

Coach Keneally walked to the centre of the locker room.

"That'll be Dizzy Hoskens," Keneally said. "He's been looking after visiting clubs for nearly 30 years now. Nothing has ever been stolen on his watch."

Keneally yelled across the room. "Hey Dizz. Come on over and meet a couple of the boys."

"Good to see you again Dizz. You're looking well," Keneally told the septuagenarian. He hugged the clubhouse man and motioned for Stokes and Jenkins to stand up. "This is Elrod and this is Billy. They're our two stars. They asked if their gear will be safe."

Hoskens laughed. "You boys serious?" he asked in a slow drawl punctuated with a few healthy coughs. "Nothin' has ever been taken on my watch. Nothin'. And if anyone ever tries anything, they'll get a slug in their bum."

He pulled the left side of his windcheater open. A large handgun was strapped in a holster. Stokes and Jenkins each took a step back. Keneally laughed.

The ballpark's gates had not yet opened so the Mozzies went about their pre-game drills in near silence. Baseballs occasionally bounced off empty seats down the right and left field lines and landed in the gloves of outfielders shagging flies. Stokes warmed up his strong arm with near-perfect throws to third base and then to the plate.

The club's pitchers ran laps in the outfield under the watchful eyes of pitching coach Herb Templeton. "Why do they make us do so much damn running," right-handed reliever Chuck "Beer Nuts" Klein asked fellow reliever Sonny Raines during a brief water break. Klein was dripping with sweat in the 27° heat and 90 per cent humidity. "You can't throw 95 mile per hour heaters without the drive your legs give you. Didn't your coaches have you run laps in high school? Raines asked.

"Nope. We took batting practice and that was it."

"How in hell did you get drafted Klein?"

"I pitched a two-hit, complete game shutout in the state semi-finals in front of a shitload of scouts, that's how."

"That doesn't mean shit anymore," Raines told him. "If I was you, I'd run and run and then run some more. And get on those stationary bikes we have back home too. At the rate you're going you'll be released before we get to July."

"Bullshit," Klein said.

"What's your ERA?"

Klein didn't answer. It was over 6.

"And your walks and hits per inning?"

Again, Klein didn't answer. It was 1.45.

Klein was the last pitcher to return to the clubhouse and nearly passed out when he got to his locker. His T-shirt, hat and shorts were drenched in sweat. Once he had something to drink and cooled down, he walked over to Raines's locker.

"Thanks for the advice, Sonny."

Raines looked up and nodded. They exchanged fist pumps. Klein went back to his locker and then straight to the showers to cool off before he got dressed for the night's game.

"I hope Kirky – starting pitcher Alan Kirk – is on tonight. I'm so fucking exhausted I don't think I could walk from the bullpen to the mound if they called on me," he said as cold water from an old shower head trickled down on him.

By July 1 Klein had whittled his ERA down to 4.75 and gotten his WHIP down to 1.26. He had also put five miles an hour on his fastball, dropped five kilos and was fitter than he'd ever been.

After batting practice Keneally hit ground balls to Jenkins and the rest of the infielders while manager Gene Short looked on from the dugout. A smile appeared on his face as Jenkins and second baseman Mitch Larkin effortlessly turned double plays.

To end the drill, Keneally hit sharp ground balls to each infielder starting with third baseman Chuck Perry. Perry fielded a two-hopper cleanly, fired a throw to first baseman Donaldson the Unfuckable, who threw the ball to catcher Tom Stockdale at the plate while Perry ran off the field. Stockdale flipped the ball to Keneally, who sent Jenkins scrambling to his left to field a grounder. Jenkins caught the ball in the webbing of his glove, turned and fired a rocket to Donaldson, and without breaking stride, jogged off the field. Larkin gobbled up the ball hit in his direction, made a looping throw to Donaldson and followed his double play partner into the dugout. Keneally then laid down a bunt which Stockdale pounced on and threw to Donaldson. The drill ended with Donaldson spearing a ball hit right over the bag.

"This infield of ours is one of the best we've ever had," Short told Keneally. "I like the way Jenkins and Larkin click. Seems like they've been working together for years. It's been a month."

Short took off his cap and ran a hand through his thick grey hair. "Jenkins is a fucking gun Joe. I don't think the step-up next season is going to affect him one bit. He'll be in New York sooner than you can say Joe DiMaggio."

"You're not wrong Gene. I've never seen a kid that young with so much natural ability. Betts in New York asking about him?"

"Every week Joe, every week."

"What do you tell him?

"That New York is a long way from Mosquito Lakes."

The two coaches shared a laugh and went back into the clubhouse. Short filled out the night's line-up card. It was the same as the previous night except for the number nine spot. Pedro Hermosa was pencilled in to make his first start. The just turned 19-year-old from the Dominican Republic was so nervous he threw up twice before he even put on his uniform.

"Try and relax kid," Templeton told him. "Make believe it's an intra-squad game. Block everything else out and you'll do fine."

When the last Mosquito Lakes player left the field and was in the clubhouse, the Clearwater mob took the field for their batting and fielding practice. The few hundred fans in the stands – the game didn't begin for another two hours, at 7pm – cheered as the Sharks emerged from their dugout. Kids of all ages, many carrying their gloves, ran to the fences down the left and right field lines with the hope of snaring a foul ball or an autograph. Most got one or the other. Players were constantly told to sign autographs and even pose for selfies at home games to create a bond with fans. "We've got to get them to come back," Tony Floyd said.

Since the Mosquito Lakes players and coaches had never set eyes on Clearwater's players – they were just names in newspaper season previews and numbers on a scorecard – several watched the Sharks go about their pre-game drills.

Jenkins, Stokes and Donaldson the Unfuckable ran the ruler over Clearwater starting pitcher Richard Rasmussen as he did several stretching exercises in the outfield. "He's not all that big for someone who's supposed to throw hard," Stokes said.

About 30 minutes before game time, Rasmussen and Hermosa went to their respective bullpens down the right and left field lines and began warming up. Hermosa was more of a finesse pitcher. He nibbled away at corners and had a variety of off-speed pitches while Rasmussen relied on his heater.

"He's going to be tough, but I'll get a hit or two off him," Stokes promised. The Texan didn't get a hit or two against Rasmussen, he got three to lead the Mozzies to a 6-3 win over the Sharks.

Chapter 16

BACK IN New York, three days remained until the Stars' 2025 season-opener on April 2 against the visiting Pittsburgh Miners. General manager Dan McLain and field manager Darren Betts were seated at a table in McLain's luxurious office on the first level of Stars Field putting the final touches on their 25-man roster.

Betts had flown in from Orlando earlier in the morning where the night before the Stars had wrapped up their Grapefruit League campaign with a 10-5 win over the Kansas City Chargers, who were picked by most pundits to contend for the AL Central Division title.

The Stars had won 16 of their 30 spring games, better than many had expected, but McLain and Betts were expecting the club to play no better than .500 ball once the regular 162-game season began.

After jettisoning their high-priced free agent busts, the club had one of the lowest payrolls in either league. After deciding to keep second-year outfielder Danny Gatt and jettison veteran outfielder Rod Garvey, McLain and Betts had one last decision to make; who would be the 10th man on the pitching staff? Ricardo Castro had pitched brilliantly during the spring but had never thrown a ball in a regular-season Major League game. Jeff Cash had just one good outing during the spring, and after a mediocre season in 2024, Betts and McLain decided the club was better with the untested Castro and put 26-year-old Cash on waivers. It was the one part of the job that McLain and Betts each hated. "I'll tell him, Betts said.

If no other club put in a bid for Cash's services and his $800,000 a year contract – modest for anyone in 2025 – Cash would be kept as an insurance policy and be reassigned to the Stars AAA affiliate in Roanoke, Virginia.

When the Stars arrived in New York, Cash was told by one of the Stars coaches that Betts wanted to see him. Cash read the papers, was active on Twitter and knew what was coming. He was just hoping the Stars would not release him outright. Then he'd be out of a job.

"I'm just 26, surely someone will take a chance on me," he told himself.

Cash's agent of eight years, Cliff Peterson, frantically worked the phones once his client was put on waivers. Only the Seattle Coffee Grinders showed an interest.

"Seattle? Three thousand miles away? Shit Cliff. I can't just uproot my family and move out there, especially without a guaranteed Major League contract. I'd rather go to Roanoke – there's no new blood there – put up some good numbers and hope for a mid-season call-up."

"Leave it with me Jeff. I'll get in contact with the Seattle people and McLain."

Duke Carlisle also had a decision to make. He could either find himself an apartment in New York for the next six months or stay at a local hotel. He still had his place in Atlanta but when Cindy Bartkowski texted him with news that she had found her own place and was seeing one of her fellow realtors, he decided to put the two-bedroom apartment on the market. It was in a nice complex in a well-to-do, quiet suburb and was paid for. He'd miss sitting on the balcony overlooking the pool in the morning and kibitzing with several of his neighbours, but that was about it. He thought of hanging on to the apartment as an investment and renting it out, but decided he didn't need the aggravation of dealing with tenants – who no matter how well they were vetted – turned into Keith Moon every weekend.

Six weeks after the apartment was listed, it was sold to a couple from Macon who were downsizing. Carlisle was asking $290,000 and got $302,000 after a mini bidding war broke out between several interested parties. He took a couple of days off and flew down to Atlanta to clear out the apartment. He packed all his clothes and personal belongings in several large boxes which a United Parcel Service (UPS) truck collected. Carlisle had the boxes shipped to a storage unit he had recently rented about a five-minute drive from the Stars ballpark in Queens. He donated everything else to goodwill. A truck from the Salvos came by on the morning he flew back to New York. Two older fellows in much better shape than Carlisle was, easily carried his couch, fridge, washing machine and dryer, kitchen table, two beds, end table and dressers down a flight of stairs, hoisted everything into their truck and were gone in 30 minutes.

Carlisle jumped in his rental car, stopped at his realtor's office – not the one where Cindy worked – handed over his keys, signed and initialled several documents and was told that $272,612 would be transferred and deposited into his account within twenty-four hours. The rest of the money, approximately $10,000, went to Carlisle's lawyer, realtor, Uncle Sam and the condominium board. He was back in his hotel in New York before dark.

Like many players and front office personnel settling into New York for the first time, Carlisle decided to stay at a hotel near the ballpark. His suite set him back $5000 a month but he was on good coin, and free maid and laundry service were part of the deal. Plus, there were no landlords, utility companies or removalists to deal with and no need to buy furniture. Carlisle wouldn't be spending that much time in New York anyway – he'd be off looking for the next Billy Jenkins – but at least he had a place to call home.

His car in Atlanta, a light blue Ford Explorer, not even two years old, was driven to New York by a college kid named Dusty Nelson, who scored the ride through an online vehicle relocation company Carlisle rang and registered with.

Nelson had to put up a $1000 bond with youcandrivemycar.com and was given six days to drive from Atlanta to New York. He was charged $10 a day and had to pay for petrol and road tolls. There were no other charges to pay unless he took more than the allotted six days to get to New York or the vehicle was damaged.

Nelson recruited mate Jonas Wagner for the road trip. Two weeks earlier they drove down from New York – where they were sophomores at New York University in lower Manhattan – in fellow student Randy Feldman's Buick so they could spend the Easter holiday back home. With three people taking turns behind the wheel, the trip from New York to suburban Atlanta was covered in just 22 hours. They stopped only to eat, shit, pee and fill the car's petrol tank. Its back seat was big enough for one person to spread out and be somewhat comfortable. The other napped in the front passenger seat while the third drove. Feldman got them from New York to Virginia – the most congested part of the journey – and then turned the driving duties over to Nelson and Wagner. Also, a sophomore, Feldman was having trouble adjusting to life in the city that never sleeps and was heading home to continue his studies at the University of Georgia. The large boot of his car was filled with several suitcases and boxes. Nelson and Wagner had to shove their sports bags behind the driver and passenger seats.

Covering the same route on their way back, but driving at a much more leisurely pace, Nelson and Wagner left Atlanta on Easter Monday in the much larger Explorer. They connected to I-95 for the run north through the Carolinas, Virginia, Washington DC, Maryland, Delaware, New Jersey and finally New York.

Nelson did all the driving. The two 20-year-olds stopped every evening about 6pm, got a motel room, had dinner at one of the many fast-food restaurants that dotted I-95, grabbed a few beers, split of bag of chips, watched a ballgame on TV and turned in. Nelson and Wagner agreed beforehand they would spend a day sightseeing in Washington. It was a crisp, sunny spring day when they pulled into the nation's capital. They somehow managed to snare a parking spot near the mall although Nelson blundered his first try attempting to parallel park. Horns blared behind him and then applause rang out as he safely steered the Explorer into the smallish spot. Several trees along the mall were just beginning to bloom. There was barely a ripple on the water in front of The Lincoln Memorial Reflecting Pool. Nelson and Wagner were walking to the Smithsonian Air and Space Museum when three guys in their mid-20s stopped them.

"Where are your caps?" the bigger of the three said pointing at his red 'Make America Great Again' baseball cap, which was made in China.

"Back at the car," Wagner said. "I like to feel the sun on my face."

"You're disrespecting the president, the greatest president this country has had; ain't that right boys?"

The two other blokes nodded in unison. One pointed to his large belly which his Trump 2024 T-shirt laboured to cover.

Wagner and Nelson looked at each other but didn't panic. The mall was teaming with tourists. *They're not going to do anything stupid,* Wagner thought.

He was wrong.

The bigger of the three, who had a face like former Attorney General William Barr, punched Nelson in the gut while the other two pushed Wagner down and kicked him several times in the ribs.

"If we see you two faggots again, you better be wearing your Trump hats and T-shirts. Understand?" Barr said.

Nelson and Wagner were sprawled on the footpath but not one person stopped to help. "I got this," Nelson said to Wagner.

"Don't Dusty. Let it go."

Nelson was not a particularly strong bloke. He didn't play any competitive sports, and didn't lift weights, unless pieces on a chess board counted.

But he was seething. He slowly got up, told the three Trump backers to go fuck themselves and kicked Barr right in the balls. Barr went down faster than the president's poll numbers and started screaming like Ivanka Trump.

By this time Wagner had gotten to his feet. "Get the fuck out of here," he told the other two.

They looked at Barr writhing in pain and sprinted off. Nelson removed the Make America Great Again cap from Barr's unevenly shaped head and took a few steps to his right where a dog had recently done his business. Using a stick, Nelson pushed the pile of dog shit into the hat and then plopped it back on Barr's head, making sure it fit snuggly.

To make sure Barr stayed down for at least another few minutes, Nelson gave Barr another swift kick in the nuts.

"Why'd you do that?" Wagner asked.

"We can't have someone like him reproducing, can we?" Nelson said.

"No, we can't."

Nelson and Wagner walked off and seamlessly blended into the crowd.

They arrived in New York in the early afternoon of April 3. Nelson dropped their belongings at New York University in lower Manhattan and then after an hour's drive somehow found the players and management parking lot at Stars Field where he and Wagner were greeted by Carlisle. Nelson gave Carlisle his keys and Carlisle made a quick inspection of his car. "No hiccups on the drive? She handle alright?" Carlisle asked.

"The hardest part of the trip was finding this parking lot," Nelson joked.

Carlisle nodded and handed the NYU sophomore a hundred-dollar bill as a tip and a pair of tickets right behind the plate to that night's game against the Miners.

"It's only 3pm," Carlisle said looking at his watch. "The gates don't open until 5, but I can give you blokes a tour of the clubhouse and stadium if you're keen."

"That would be fantastic," Nelson said.

"Braves fans?" Carlisle asked.

"Through and through," Nelson answered.

"Do me a favour and cheer for the Stars tonight."

"We will," Nelson and Wagner said.

"It's going to be a cold one tonight. Is that all you guys have with you?' Carlisle asked pointing to their T-shirts.

They nodded.

"You'll freeze. I'll get you a couple of sweatshirts from the clubhouse man. Fifty bucks each."

Nelson turned to Wagner. "Fifty bucks?" he whispered.

Relax boys. I was just having a little fun with you. No charge.

The day before, in beautiful spring sunshine, the Stars won their season opener 6-5. Game two of the three-game series was going to be played on an 8° night thanks to the power of television. The networks shelling out several billion dollars over five years for the television rights, decided what time games began. Fuck the 14,000 fans who braved the cold and showed up at the ballpark. The number of eyeballs tuning in at home at night far outnumbered those able to watch the game on TV in the afternoon.

Carlisle, McLain and the rest of the front office staff watched the Miners take game two from their heated suite behind home plate. Nelson and Wagner stayed warm by downing coffees and hot chocolates. They spent half the game running to the toilets.

Thanks to Carlisle's generous tip, Nelson and Wagner were able to take a cab back into Manhattan instead of the number 7 train which was not the safest place to be at 10pm.

Carlisle stayed in New York for two weeks before he jumped into his Explorer and hit the road to scout college and high school players. He spent what was left of April, all of May and the first few days of June travelling through upstate New York, New Jersey, Massachusetts and Pennsylvania.

Out of those 50 days, Carlisle spent just 10 of them in his hotel suite. He drove through snow in Syracuse, New York in late April, the picturesque Berkshire Mountains in Massachusetts in the middle of May and Amish country in Pennsylvania in early June.

Dick Doncaster, the athletic director of Monmouth College on the Jersey shore, had told Delaney several weeks earlier about three solid prospects who were attending the four-year university.

Doncaster knew his baseball, so Carlisle headed to the campus on his way back from western Pennsylvania to watch a couple of ballgames. The light breeze from the nearby Atlantic Ocean and the sweet smell of the ocean air made for a couple of enjoyable afternoons. Carlisle took a seat in the near-empty bleachers lining the third base line and took out the tools of his trade from his well-worn bag; binoculars, radar gun, thermos and cigarettes. The light wind blew his cigarette smoke away from the few spectators.

He did his paperwork that night on the table of his Best Western hotel room. Even though it was after 8pm, rays of sunshine filled the room. Monmouth College third baseman Hank "The Tank" McClintock was the best of the three. He was only 5 feet 10 inches tall but was as strong as an ox and an outstanding fielder with a strong and accurate arm. He hit for average and power. Carlisle pencilled him in as a mid-to-late round draft pick. Since the Major League draft consisted of 40 rounds, Carlisle figured McClintock could go as high as Round 20-25.

Outfielder Bryant Webb was a speedy sort with a good arm but lacked power. "Maybe a very late round pick if he bulks up," Carlisle wrote.

Right-handed pitcher Armando Delgado was an interesting proposition. Tall and lean with an above average fastball and a curveball which danced around the plate like Travolta in *Saturday Night Fever*, he never seemed to get any offensive support. Delgado's record of 8-12 turned many scouts off. But he had a very good ERA of 4.22, a good WHIP of 1.29 and plenty of upside.

"A real sleeper," Carlisle wrote. "A mid-rounder. Put him on our board."

Carlisle emailed all the information to McLain in New York. He'd meet with the rest of the scouting department on his return to New York and put together a full report for McLain and Betts in time for the draft which was held June 6-9 in New York.

The odds of picking a winner at nearby Monmouth Park Racetrack were infinitely better than the odds a college player had of playing professional baseball – just 10 per cent.

A high school player's chances of being drafted by a Maor League club was less than one percent.

However, college players personally selected by Carlisle had a one in four chance of making it to the big leagues while a high school player on Carlisle's draft list almost always played some level of minor league baseball.

Chapter 17

WITH HIP hop music blaring through several large speakers, Major League Baseball Commissioner Herb Lincoln – resplendent in a $3000 beige suit and a US flag pin on the lapel, which if anyone had looked was made in China, $125 silk tie, and $600 shoes – strode to the podium in the Jackie Robinson room of the Jacob Javitz Convention Centre in New York exactly at 12 noon on Monday, June 3. The noise stopped as Lincoln approached the mic. He made a few brief opening remarks, picked up a card handed to him by one of his assistants and slowly said ..." With the first pick in the 2025 Major League Baseball Draft, the New York Stars select outfielder Christopher Cole of Scottsdale High School in Arizona.

Polite applause from fans, many of them wearing Stars and NY Bombers apparel who paid $20 a head to watch the draft in person, greeted the selection of Cole.

Most draft experts expected Cole to be a top-three pick and with the Stars having so many good young pitchers in the minor leagues, the selection of Cole made sense.

Wearing a brand-new sky-blue suit which flattered his six-foot three-inch muscled-up frame, 18-year-old Cole hugged his mom and dad and slowly strode to the stage. He was handed a New York Stars cap, shook hands with Lincoln and smiled for the many cameramen on stage. "Get used to it kid. New York is not Scottsdale," Lincoln told him.

Cole was interviewed live on ESPN by its baseball expert Clyde Sanderson, who six weeks later was inducted into baseball's Hall of Fame.

"Will you'll be able to handle the pressure of being the number one pick and playing in New York?" Sanderson asked.

"I am going to love playing in New York. The bigger the stage the better I perform," he said.

"How many years in the minors do you feel you'll need before you're ready?"

"Two at the most."

"Two? Most need three or four."

"I'm not like them. Two tops."

Sanderson looked straight into ESPN's camera. "There you have it folks. Expect to see Cole in a NY Stars uniform in two years."

The New York media couldn't get enough of the confident Cole. He was the lead story on that night's newscasts and was on the front page of the *NY Post* and the *NY Daily News* the next morning.

While Cole was being interviewed backstage as the draft continued, Carlisle, his staff and McClain crossed players off their board while Lincoln called out the first-round picks of the other 29 teams.

The Stars chose outfielder Logan Kenworthy of Blue River High School in Northern California with their second-round pick, the 31st overall. "That's two-thirds of their future outfield right there," ESPN's Sanderson said. "I'm really surprised Kenworthy was still available. Rumours of off-field issues caused his stock to tumble and have cost him a few million dollars."

Sanderson didn't get into Kenworthy's off-field "issues" – which included an alleged rape and the theft and torching of a motor vehicle. Neither offence ever became public but rumours regarding Kenworthy's character continued to swirl as the draft approached.

Once touted as a top 10 pick, ever major league team passed on selecting the switch-hitting 18-year-old in the opening round even though some scouts had ridiculously compared him to Hall-of-Famer Mickey Mantle.

Blue River High School homecoming queen Donna Atherton was the victim of the sexual assault and was shattered that Logan Kenworthy, someone she valued as a friend, had forced himself on her at a house party despite her repeated cries for him to stop. She was too ashamed to report the rape to police but told her mother, Sarah, who in turn told her husband, Thomas.

Full of rage, Thomas Atherton drove to the Kenworthy home in his Ford pickup truck and banged on the large front door of their two-storey Tudor style home with his fist.

Randolph and Stacey Kenworthy were sipping margaritas in their pool in the backyard when they heard the racket coming from the front of their half-million-dollar home. Randolph Kenworthy, the mayor of Acacia Springs, put on a pair of thongs, draped a towel around his big shoulders, walked to the front door and opened it. He was met with a roundhouse right from Thomas Atherton which missed his head by inches.

Atherton was quickly put into a headlock by Kenworthy – a former heavyweight wrestler in his high school and college days – and wrestled to the ground.

"You'd be better off going to the council offices with any grievance you have instead of coming to the home of the mayor and attempting to assault him," Kenworthy told Atherton, who was pinned to the foyer floor.

"Two nights ago, your son, Logan, raped my daughter," Atherton said as he tried to regain his breath and wriggle out of Kenworthy's hold.

"He did what?"

"He raped my daughter Donna."

"My son?"

"Your son, the Blue River High baseball player."

Kenworthy let Atherton go and sat on the foyer floor.

"Is she sure it was Logan?"

"Of course, she's sure. What do you think, she's sleeping with everybody on the damn team?"

"No, no. I didn't mean to infer that. I just never thought Logan could do something like that."

"He did it alright. My daughter hasn't stopped crying since the attack. She trusted him and he's going to pay. When the cops toss his ass in jail, he'll be playing ball in a prison yard."

"Have you gone to the police?" Kenworthy calmly asked.

"Not yet. I just found out about it."

Kenworthy ran his fingers through his greying hair and motioned for Atherton to join him in the kitchen. He grabbed two beers from the fridge and hopped on a chair at the breakfast bar. Atherton did the same just as Stacey Kenworthy entered the kitchen.

"What's going on Randy. Who is this?"

"This is Thomas Atherton. He's claiming that Logan raped his daughter at a party two nights ago."

"He did what?"

"Raped my daughter Mrs Kenworthy. And he's going to pay for what he's done to her."

Stacey Kenworthy sat down next to her husband. "Surely there must be a mistake," she said. "Logan would never do that to anyone."

"He did it alright and Donna is prepared to say so in court."

"Court?"

"Yes, court. I'm going to the cops as soon as I leave here."

Kenworthy motioned to his wife to relax.

"Let's see if we can keep the cops out of this Thomas."

"Worried about your job Mr Mayor."

"More worried about your daughter testifying in court. Do you really want all her dirty laundry aired in public?"

"What dirty laundry are you talking about? Donna is a top student, the Blue River High School Homecoming Queen."

"Let's just say I've heard a few rumours."

"Rumours? I ought to knock your fucking head off for even saying that."

"Easy now Thomas. She's a high school senior and we all know what high school kids get up to these days; the sexting, the promiscuousness."

"We'll let a jury decide how promiscuous she is. Who do you think they'll believe, eh? A teary young woman or a rich, spoiled athlete and the son of the city's mayor?"

Fuck, Kenworthy thought to himself. After a few moments of silence, he asked Atherton if he'd be open to a deal.

"A deal? What kind of a deal?"

"A nice cash payout?"

"You think you can buy me and my family?"

"I'm just thinking of the kids," Kenworthy said. "Why ruin both of their lives?"

"Donna could go to whatever college she wanted; get any psychological help she may need and be set for life."

"And your son just walks away scot free?"

"No. I'm going to disown the prick."

Atherton reportedly accepted a cash payout of $300,000 from an untraceable company in the Cayman Islands in exchange for not bringing charges against Logan. The motor vehicle theft never went to trial thanks to Lance McNamee, the Kenworthy's family attorney. A judge dismissed the case for "lack of evidence" and spent the warmer than average summer at a "newly acquired" beach house on Lake Tahoe.

"You have cost me well over half a million fucking dollars," Randolph Kenworthy told his son several nights later over dinner. "And you're going to pay it back with interest. Understand?"

"Interest?" Logan said.

"That's right, interest you bloody halfwit. You make Jonah Ryan look like a Rhodes Fucking Scholar."

"Must you use that sort of language dear?" Stacey Kenworthy asked her husband.

Randolph Kenworthy turned to his wife of 24 years and loudly uttered one word – "YES".

"As the mayor of this city, do you have any idea what would happen if the press got hold of this and it was plastered all over TV, radio and the papers? I could kiss that run at the Senate goodbye for starters. Rape for fuck's sake? Rape? What the fuck were you thinking? If it was up to me, I'd be seeing you once a month at San Quentin," Randolph yelled.

"I believe it's been closed down dear," Stacey Kenworthy quietly said.

"Then I'll pay the fucking state to re-open that shithole."

Randolph Kenworthy moved his chair closer to his son. He was still taller and bigger than Logan but not as much as he was a year ago when Logan shot up four inches in three months. "I wouldn't lose a night's sleep if you did time. Do you understand son?" he asked.

Logan looked at his mother, who nodded.

"I do."

"Good. Now go upstairs and do your damn homework so you stay eligible to play ball. The day you graduate, get picked in the draft and get the fuck out of here can't come soon enough."

The words were harsh, but Logan knew he was lucky he had a high-profile father with money who was able to pull some strings. He told only one person, his closest mate Barry Walsh, the truth about what had happened with Donna Atherton. The two had a few drinks at a house party and went to one of the home's many bedrooms. Daisy went to the bedroom willingly but protested when he wanted more than a blow job. No one heard her screaming over the loud music as Logan forced himself inside her.

He tried to apologise to Donna at school the following Monday, but Donna ignored him. The theft of the motor vehicle which took place on the night of the party, was also kept quiet. Logan Kenworthy set a late-model Mercedes coupe on fire after joyriding around the city for a couple of hours. The offence was kept out of the city's arrest reports after his father intervened.

Randolph Kenworthy paid the owner of the vehicle $65,000 and arranged a substantial discount on a new car at the city's Mercedes dealership in return for his silence.

Logan Kenworthy never against set foot in the family home after he was drafted by the Stars. "I wish he had been drafted by Uncle Sam and sent to fucking Afghanistan," Randolph Kenworthy told his wife by phone on the day of the draft. "That's what he deserved. Not a million-dollar contract and the fame that comes with it."

Stacey Kenworthy accompanied her son to New York for the draft and smiled for the cameras like every other proud parent that afternoon.

Three days after being drafted, Logan Kenworthy arrived in Mosquito Lakes, Florida and was assigned to New York's side in the Rookie League along with Chris Cole. Logan received a $700,000 signing bonus which he told the Stars to deposit directly into his father's account. As predicted, Cole made it to the big leagues in just two years. It took Kenworthy four years to reach the show. Two years after that, he had paid his father back in full.

Carlisle signed off on both Cole and Kenworthy, and New York's 35 other draft picks, spent two nights at his hotel and flew to Omaha, Nebraska for the College World Series to have a closer look at the half dozen college players the Stars had drafted and the juniors who would be eligible to be drafted in a year's time.

He did not walk away disappointed. Many were playing in front of TV cameras and large crowds for the first time but excelled over the 12-day tournament. Carlisle arrived early each day to try and find an out-of-the-way seat in the crowded ballpark which would allow him to smoke his cancer sticks but couldn't. However, he was told of a small area off the main concourse which was reserved for smokers and every few innings ducked out for a couple of ciggies. He grabbed a coffee from a concession stand on the way back to his seat where he took out a fresh notebook and his binoculars from his bag and went to work.

By the end of the 12-day tournament Carlisle had filled three notebooks, went through 18 packs of cigarettes and two lighters, and had a stack of empty coffee cups taller than six-foot-10 University of Texas left-hander Freddie "Major" Burns.

"I need a vacation," Carlisle told himself on the flight back to New York's LaGuardia Airport. "I've seen so many fucking games in the last three months I'm seeing bats and balls in my sleep instead of blondes and brunettes."

Good friend and fellow scout Pete Giacomin, and agents Subway Stemkowksi and Saul Bernstein, who were just acquaintances of Carlisle, had rented a house on the shore of Lake Saratoga, just a few miles south of the city of Saratoga Springs in upstate New York for a couple of weeks after the July 4th holiday. A small country town for 45 weeks a year, Saratoga Springs quadrupled in size when the seven-week thoroughbred racing season started the second week of July.

When asked how to get to Saratoga Race Course, which opened in 1863, making it the oldest track in the US, legendary *New York Times* sportswriter and *Pulitzer Prize* winner Red Smith once said ... "you drive north from Manhattan for about 175 miles, turn left on Union Avenue and go back 100 years." The characters of that era, long before the tote came into operation and bookmakers ruled, were long gone, but plenty of conmen and tricksters still descended on Saratoga every summer.

"Come on up mate. The house has four bedrooms, four bathrooms and the fish start biting just after the last race of the day," Giacomin told Carlisle in a late-night phone call soon after the July 4th fireworks show. "The fourth bedroom is yours for 10 days if you want it and for just $1000. What do you say? Are you in?"

"Who cancelled Pete?" Carlisle asked, figuring he was not the group's first choice to fill the last bedroom.

"Kevin McEvoy of the *News*. He's having some plumbing work done."

"And for that he has to stay home?"

"He's having his own plumbing done Rick, downstairs plumbing."

"Prostate troubles?"

"The poor bastard is up four times a night to pee."

"Shit. He's a good bloke. I'll send him a note."

"He'd appreciate that, Rick. Macca's wife told him that if his pecker is out of commission he'll be sleeping alone. He might have to wear adult diapers after his op. Can you believe that? A 56-year-old man in diapers. Fuck me."

The thought of Macca in diapers touched a nerve with Carlisle. Twenty years earlier his old man was diagnosed with prostate cancer and had to have the damn gland removed. He kept extra pairs of underwear and pants in his office and car in case he peed himself due to the incontinence – one of the side effects from surgery. Incontinence and impotence, how's that for a quinella?

To prevent any leakage, Sid Carlisle took a pee, or tried to, every hour on the hour, and kept his fluid intake to a minimum when he was working. Despite the precautions, Sid Carlisle wet himself several times in the months following his surgery. He was so embarrassed by the first incident that he snuck out of the building of the engineering firm he worked for, covered the stain on his tan-coloured trousers with his overcoat, dashed to his car and drove straight to the nearest service station where he changed.

"Fuck", he screamed while he took off his wet pants and underwear for the third time in as many months. "I'm going to have to start wearing fucking diapers. Diapers."

He rinsed his wet underwear and pants in the warm water of the bathroom's sink, stuffed them in a plastic bag, put on a fresh pair of undies and pants and drove home. The soiled clothes went straight into the washing machine.

Sid Carlisle had many good years after his surgery. His pecker worked on occasion, which he and his girlfriend at the time, were thankful for. He died 22 years later, in his sleep, aged 82.

McEvoy was luckier than Sid Carlisle. In the quarter century since Carlisle had been operated on, treatment and surgical techniques had greatly improved. Two weeks after McEvoy was operated on, he was back at his desk in midtown churning out stories. He wet his pants just once, at an afternoon training session of the New York football Giants in East Rutherford, New Jersey. McEvoy was given a pair of sweatpants by a sympathetic assistant coach, who it turned out had the same operation in the off-season. McEvoy tossed his wet undies and pants in a trash bin, tapped out two stories at the team's press centre, emailed them to his editor, sprinted to the parking lot and drove home.

McEvoy made it up to Saratoga Springs for the final week of the summer racing season. It was a quiet week, coming after the running of the Travers Stakes which was known as the midsummer Derby, but it was still nearly impossible to find accommodation in town. He and his wife Lois stayed at an overpriced motel 10 miles away from the track for five nights, and while it was good to get out of the stinking heat and humidity of a New York City summer, he didn't have nearly as much fun as Carlisle, Giacomin, Stemkowksi and Bernstein had earlier in the summer. The four left town thousands of dollars poorer, 27 pounds heavier and with a suitcase full of stories.

Giacomin, "Subway" and Bernstein had a three-day head start on Carlisle and were glad to see their mate arrive since he was the best handicapper of the bunch. Known as the graveyard of favourites, the mighty Secretariat was even beaten there, Giacomin, "Subway" and Bernstein could not find a winner on the track or off. The fish weren't even cooperating. They were half-expecting the pier where they were dangling their rods from to crumble beneath them.

Carlisle hadn't been to Saratoga for at least six or seven years and as he pulled into town just after lunchtime on a Tuesday afternoon, he was pleased to see that not much had changed. His favourite restaurants: The Olde Bryan Inn, Harvey's Restaurant and Bar, The Country Corner Café, were still standing and packed more tightly than the cigarette butts in his car's ashtray.

The town was still clean and welcoming and right on Union Avenue was that gorgeous racetrack where on most days general admission tickets were $7 and clubhouse tickets just $10. The magnificent grandstand glistened in the mid-day sunshine. However, on a handful of days over summer, afternoon thunderstorms were known to rip through the Saratoga area which often caused three or four races to be transferred from the turf track onto the muddy main track. Fields of 13 or 14 were reduced to six or seven, but punters didn't seem to mind since there were still races to bet on.

Racing was now conducted five days a week instead of the previous six – Mondays and Tuesdays were dark – which gave punters and horsemen alike a chance to freshen up. The previous summer – in 2024 – Saratoga set a record for money bet over the 40-day meeting, a staggering $US146.6 million on course. Wagering from all sources, including simulcasts, totalled $US705.3 million. For the fifth straight year over a million fans paid their way in. The sport of kings was being propped up by casinos in many states, but in Saratoga, racing didn't need any outside help to thrive.

If 10 races weren't enough for punters, the Saratoga Harness Racing Track, which now incorporated a casino, had meetings four days a week during the summer months. They mostly started at 7pm and it wasn't uncommon to see hundreds of punters march to the harness track after the last thoroughbred race of the day. Had they been carrying placards, they would have read *new track, new opportunities.* It was a mystery to many where the punters got the money to go to two meets in a day especially if they had crapped out in the afternoon. But they came, and they wagered and ate and drank until the last race of the night. Some even wound up in the casino, putting their hard earned on the blackjack and roulette tables if the trotters failed them.

Carlisle pulled over near the main entrance to the racecourse and bought a copy of Wednesday's *Daily Racing Form* from an old-timer seated behind a large wooden table in the shade of an even older tree.

It couldn't be, could it? Carlisle thought. He looked at the fellow more closely. His face had a few more lines than it had the last time he had been in town. But his blue eyes gave him away. When it came to blue eyes there was Newman, Sinatra and James Longfellow. Every regular Saratoga racegoer over the last sixty years or so knew James. He couldn't remember all their names, so he called everyone champ.

Longfellow had exercised horses in the mornings for several prominent trainers in his younger days, was a barrier attendant in the afternoons and then sold tip sheets at the main gates on Union Avenue for decades. James was on course for the Travers Stakes in 1962 when Jaipur and Ridan locked horns for the last quarter mile. Longfellow tipped Jaipur and he prevailed by a nose. He was there in 1973 when Triple Crown winner Secretariat was beaten by 100-1 outsider Onion in the Whitney Stakes. Red Smith even wrote a yarn about him one August. And here he was in the summer of 2019, still skinny as a rail and still working at the racecourse.

Bundles of the Daily Racing Form were stacked on and under the table Longfellow sat behind. Despite its $10 cover price, they'd all be gone by post time of the first race on Wednesday. The paper's speed figures, Beyer numbers, race comments, latest workouts and news stories made it a must for the serious punter. The cost was about a third for those who went online and printed out the past performances, but Carlisle preferred the full printed edition as did thousands of others. Racetracks around the country had started to put together their own form guides, and while some were surprisingly good, Carlisle thought they were a clear second when compared to the *Daily Racing Form.*

"Got any winners for me James?" Carlisle asked.

Longfellow cupped his ear. "What was that champ?"

"Got any winners for me James?" Carlisle again asked.

"They're in there," Longfellow said pointing to a copy of the form.

Carlisle laughed, scooped a copy of the paper off the table, and handed Longfellow a tenner. Longfellow stuffed the $10 bill in a money belt, took a few sips from a water bottle sitting on the end of the table and watched Carlisle walk back to his car. He waved as Carlisle drove off to the house Giacomin, Stemkowksi and Bernstein had rented.

He recognised Giacomin's black late-model Lexus in the driveway and pulled up alongside it, leaving plenty of room so either car would be able to back out. He took a suitcase, a small carry-on bag and the *Racing Form* from his car and knocked on the front door. When no one answered he turned the doorknob and let himself in. He put his bags down in the large living room and looking through a sliding glass door found the trio seated around a round white table by the pool. Remnants of breakfast littered the table. A large umbrella shielded the three from the strong mid-day sun. White towels were draped on the back on an empty chair. Subway was reading the *New York Times.* Giacomin and Bernstein had their faces buried in the form.

Carlisle opened the screen door and quietly walked to the table. He tossed an envelope with $1000 in it in front of Giacomin. "Nice digs Pete," he said. "Here's my share."

The three jumped to their feet and warmly greeted Carlisle with handshakes and slaps on the back.

"How the hell did you find this place Pete?"

"I know a guy who knows the owner and the owner is very particular to whom he rents the place to. He goes to Europe every summer. Go figure. Why go overseas when the best action is right here in Saratoga?"

"Action day and night fellas?"

Giacomin laughed. "Just during the daylight hours. Maybe you'll change our luck. You always could pull the ladies."

"I'm not 25 anymore, or even 35," Carlisle said. "Those were the days."

"Word is you had a bit of trouble with your pecker down in Australia. That true?"

"How the fuck do you guys know about that?"

"There was something on Facebook."

"Facebook?"

"Yup."

"What did it say?"

"Something along the lines of 'which high-profile scout nearly lost his boomerang on a trip down under'"?

Subway and Bernstein laughed as if they were hearing the story for the first time.

"Let's just say the item is still with me and in good working order. Now let's find some winners tomorrow," he said tossing his form guide on the table in a bid to change the subject.

"Or are you boys going to the trots tonight?"

"We have a dinner reservation at Harvey's at 7," Bernstein said.

Delaney looked over at Subway, who was fiddling with a bandage on his right hand.

"What happened to you mate?" he asked.

"Ahh, not even worth talking about."

"I can smell a story a mile away. Details guys, details."

Giacomin glanced over at Subway. "Go on, tell him."

Giacomin began to tell Delaney all about Subway's run-in with a gardener/handyman earlier that day.

"Subway was up before we were. He made some coffee, went outside to collect the papers and brought the *Times* and his coffee to this same table.

"He wasn't out here for more than 10 minutes before his quiet morning was ruined by a loud noise which sounded like a jet engine. Subway went to investigate. He opened the front door and saw some middle-aged fellow wearing a pair of headphones and a backpack connected to a contraption which he was using to blow a few scattered leaves from one end of the driveway to the other. A pickup truck full of gardening gear was at the end of the driveway

"Subway looked at his watch. It was 7:45."

"I'll take over from here if you don't mind," Subway told Giacomin, who sat back down and gave Subway the floor.

"I yelled out to him, but he couldn't hear me from the noise of that fucking leaf blower. I walked up to him, got in his line of vision and ran my hand across my throat telling him to shut the fucking thing down which he did.

"What the fuck are you doing chief? It's 7:45 in the morning. I'm on fucking vacation here.

"The fellow took off his headphones. 'I come by twice a week,' he said with some sort of Spanish accent. 'Mr Costa likes to keep his property neat.'

"He does? Well, Pedro, I am paying Mr Costa a shitload of coin to stay here this week, so if you don't mind, get that plastic rake from that piece of shit you call a truck, rake up the three leaves I see, put it in a garbage back and get the fuck out of here."

Giacomin and Bernstein broke into laughter even though they had heard the story before. Delaney was amused not only by the content but by Subway's story telling abilities.

Subway continued. "Pedro, or whatever the fuck the guy's name is, put his headphones back on and turned on the leaf blower. So, I took the leaf blower from his hand, turned it off and took the backpack off him. There was a bit of a struggle and then I threw it onto the driveway, stomped on that fucking thing and broke it into a few pieces. He's lucky I didn't take one and shove it up his ass. But I cut my hand bad enough that it required a trip to the local hospital. Three stitches, a few lacerations and now I have an over mitt made up of bandages. And a damn tetanus shot. Best $500 I ever spent."

The boys spent the rest of the afternoon shooting the breeze, having a few beers, chips, pretzels and ice cream before driving to Harvey's for dinner. They drove towards the sun which was still an hour away from slipping beneath the horizon.

The four gorged themselves on Harvey's steaks, baked potatoes, onion rings and pints of Guinness until their stomachs and bladders nearly burst.

Despite their best efforts to reel in a tableful of adorables seated next to them, who were picking at their salads and downing pitchers of Margaritas, strictly a no-no at an Irish establishment, Carlisle and his mates struck out swinging on three straight pitches.

Wishing the gals a pleasant good evening on their way out, Bernstein took the keys to Giacomin's Lexus from the scout's hands, and since he was the most sober of the quartet, steered then to the parking lot.

"Wait here a second fellas," he said scrambling back inside the restaurant.

"What in the wide, wide, wide of sports is he up to?" Carlisle asked.

Bernstein had taken a liking to one of the two blondes seated at the table next to them – 'she looks just like my first wife,' he later explained. The sports agent was not the best-looking rooster in Saratoga, but far from the worst, and with the courage of three pints of Guinness under his belt, approached the four women.

"Excuse me ladies," Bernstein said interrupting their desserts. "I want to apologise for some of the crude things my friends may have said over the course of the last few hours. They're on holiday and had a few too many," he said looking directly at Laura Yokum.

The natural blonde, and the wife of leading horse trainer S.B. Yokum, looked Bernstein over as he spoke, trying to figure out where she had seen him before.

Unbeknownst to Bernstein, Laura Yokum, Naomi Treloar, Paula Sheets and Lorraine Mahr were all married to successful horse trainers who journeyed to Saratoga each summer with some of the finest horseflesh in the country seeking their share of the tens of millions of dollars in prizemoney on offer.

Laura Yokum was the youngest of the four adorables, and about two decades younger than Bernstein. Due to his 4am starts, SB Yokum was fast asleep by 9pm nearly every night. Every morning except Sunday, the 45-year-old personally checked the health of all 37 of horses under his care in Saratoga. He had another 150 or so in work in Kentucky, Florida and California. Wealthy owners paid the bills for their horses to be floated or flown to Saratoga where they were kept at the track's immaculately kept stables.

Yokum mixed their feed, consulted with the stable's vet and supervised their workouts and gallops. If he was lucky, he was able to take a nap around 11. He then changed into a suit, walked to the track's clubhouse and had lunch with an owner or two. By 12:30 he was at the tie-up stalls putting a saddle on his runner in Race 1. He saddled up five or six horses each afternoon, gave instructions to jockeys and watched the races from the grandstand with his binoculars and Laura at his side. With every race being televised across the nation and overseas, producers of the broadcasts made sure they had a camera on Yokum and the vivacious and often braless Laura when he sent off a favourite. Laura had a habit of jumping up and down during the last furlong as she cheered on her husband's horse and sealed every victory by giving her husband a long tonsillectomy.

"Shit, I wish SB won every damn race on the card," broadcast producer Ron Sinclair said after Yokum collected another winner. "The only time my wife jumps up and down and kisses me like that is when the network sends me overseas."

With their husbands asleep before the sun even set on glorious Saratoga, Laura, Naomi, Paula and Lorraine gathered at one of their rented homes several nights a week for drinks. But being that it was Naomi's 40th birthday, they had decided to go to Harvey's and celebrate.

"I know who you are," Laura shouted at Bernstein after his long-winded and unnecessary apology. "You're the agent for Wylie Sinclair, the Texas Longhorns quarterback, ain't you," she asked.

"I am."

"I saw you on the TV when he was drafted in the first round by the Cowboys. We like to keep our studs at home, not have them go off to Green Bay or some ass-backward town. You got him over $50 million. Ain't that right?"

Bernstein blushed a bit as he answered. "Somewhere in that neighbourhood."

"Well, that is one neighbourhood I would not mind living in. How 'bout you girls?" she asked, looking around the table.

Naomi, Paula and Lorraine all nodded.

"And you get about 10 per cent of that $50 million, is that right Mr Agent?"

"Not that much," Bernstein said.

"Pretty close though. And I bet you don't wake your wife up at 4am for a quickie and smell like manure half the time," Laura added.

"I'm not married."

"No girlfriend Mr Agent?"

"No."

"Pull up a chair then Mr Agent. I have something to discuss with you."

Laura moved her chair close to Bernstein, so close he could smell her perfume and the shampoo she had washed her blonde locks with several hours ago.

"You get me a football autographed by Wylie Sinclair for SB's birthday next month and in return I'll give you a night you will never forget. But it has got to say Happy Birthday SB on it with Wylie Sinclair's John Hancock. Got it?"

"Got it," Bernstein stammered.

Back in the parking lot, Giacomin, Carlisle and Subway stood alongside Giacomin's Lexus.

"What the heck is Bernstein up to?" Subway wondered. "If he thinks he's a chance with one of those women he is out of his mind."

"What's your name Mr Agent?" Daisy asked.

"Saul, Saul Bernstein."

"Like the guy in Better Call Saul?"

"Yup."

"What do you think girls," should we call us an Uber to take us home or should we call Saul here?"

"Let's give Saul a shot, see if he's a better lay than your pool boy," Lorraine said to a tableful of giggles.

Just as Carlisle was about to turn and go back into Harvey's, the restaurant's front door open. Bernstein walked out with a blonde on each arm. Two brunettes walked behind them.

"Do you see what I see Subway or am I hallucinating?" Carlisle asked. "Those are the women who were seated next to us. How the fuck?"

"Our man Saul must be one hell of a negotiator," Carlisle said.

"Looks that way," Giacomin added.

As Bernstein and his quartet of adorables got close to Giacomin's Lexus, Bernstein did the introductions.

"Hey fellas. This here," he said, nodding to the girl on his left, "is Laura. This is Lorraine," he said nodding to the blonde on his right. "And these lovely ladies are Naomi and Paula."

Carlisle, Subway and Giacomin tied to speak but nothing came out of their mouths.

"Saul says you have a pool back at your place," Laura said.

"We do," Carlisle replied. "And a lake."

"Then what the heck are we doing wasting our time here? Let's get going."

Bernstein opened the Lexus. He got in the driver's seat. Laura squeezed in next to him and Lorraine followed.

The back seat was barely big enough for Carlisle, Subway and his foot long, Giacomin, Naomi and Paula. They were packed in tighter than passengers on a TigerAir flight.

Bernstein safely guided Giacomin's Lexus through Saratoga's wide, quiet streets and had them all safely back at the rented home in less than fifteen minutes.

"Nice spread. This your place Saul"? Laura asked as she had a look around.

"No, we're just renting it. We're here for the week. We come up every year for the races."

"Oh yeah? Well if you don't back Strait off the Boat in The Hopeful tomorrow, you're all hopeless."

"He's in with a chance," Carlisle answered.

"A chance? He'll win by a fucking furlong," a fired-up Laura Yokum said.

"What makes you think that?"

"Cause my husband trains him and he's been busting every single stopwatch since he has been here."

The ears of Bernstein, Carlisle, Subway and Giacomin simultaneously perked up like a Kelpie's ears.

"Your husband is SB Yokum?" Carlisle asked incredulously.

"Yup. But don't worry. It's not like Saul here will be the first guy I've fucked since I've been married. Where do you fellas keep the booze?"

"There's some beer and wine in the fridge outside by the pool," Bernstein said.

"You have a fridge by the pool? Shit. Even we don't have that, and we live in a $3 million spread in the best neighbourhood in Fort Worth."

Lorraine, Naomi and Paula followed Laura to the pool. They took a seat around the main table as Laura opened a bottle of chardonnay.

"Hey Saul. How 'bout a few glasses here for me and the girls?" Laura yelled out.

Bernstein grabbed half a dozen wine glasses from inside and brought them to the pool area.

"Thanks lover. Whatcha boys having? Wine or beers?" Laura asked as she bent over to look inside the fridge.

Bernstein looked at his mates who just shrugged their shoulders.

"Beers please Laura."

Mrs Yokum placed four cold bottles of beer on the table while Bernstein scrambled to find some snacks for his unexpected guests. He returned with a couple of bags of chips and two containers of dip. He dumped the contents of the bags into a large bowl. "Help yourselves," he said taking the seat nearest to Mrs Yokum.

Laura Yokum broke the uncomfortable silence.

"Are you fellas agents here like Saul?"

Carlisle spoke up for his mates.

"Subway is, Pete and I are baseball scouts."

"No shit," Lorraine Mahr shouted. "My husband is a part owner of the Dallas Tornadoes."

"I scout for the Stars here in New York and Pete scouts for Philadelphia."

"The Stars? You've got as much chance of winning a pennant as I do of riding a Derby winner."

Carlisle laughed, looked at the slim 39-year-old, five-foot-two brunette and asked if she rode for any stable in particular.

"I just ride trackwork now lover, but I had my share of winners when I was in my prime. Didn't I girls?"

Naomi Treloar, Paula Sheets and Laura Yokum nodded enthusiastically.

"And we cashed plenty of tickets too," Paula said, high fiving her girlfriends.

"Nobody but my husband really gave her a ride in the bigger races," Laura said. "Said she wasn't strong enough. She's still strong enough to kick any of their arses from Santa Anita to Gulfstream Park."

Subway, who knows a little something about backing a winner – think of Mine That Bird in the 2009 Kentucky Derby which he backed at 50-1 and pocketed in excess of 50 large – piped up and said that he would put Lorraine on any horse he owned over the objection of any trainer.

Lorraine promptly sat on Subway's lap as a way of saying thank you and in less time that it took Secretariat to run the length of the Churchill Downs stretch, had a good idea of why Mr Stemkowski was called Subway.

"This one here is no gelding girls. He's got all his equipment and then some."

With Lorraine and Subway paired off and Laura and Saul eying each other like a couple of teenagers, the conversation around the table came to a sudden halt. Carlisle broke the silence by saying he was going for a swim.

"The pool is heated? isn't it Pete?"

"Hotter than a Hooters waitress."

Carlisle scooted off to his room to pull a pair of trunks from his suitcase and on his way back to the pool was nearly bowled over by a stumbling Naomi Treloar, who needed a bathroom, quickly.

Carlisle pointed down the hallway. "It's the second door on the right," he said. Instead of continuing out to the pool, Carlisle waited to see if Naomi was okay. Five minutes passed, then six. He debated whether to go knock on the bathroom door.

I certainly wouldn't want anyone to see me barfing up my dinner, he thought.

Carlisle knocked on the door. "Everything alright in there," he asked. "Naomi?"

When there was no answer, he slowly opened the door and found the 45-year-old sprawled on the bathroom floor. She hadn't even flushed the toilet and had passed out. Carlisle flushed the toilet, grabbed a hand towel, wet it and wiped the gunk off her face. He winced as he did.

She'll have to drink half a bottle of Listerine to get rid of the stench.

Slowly, the married mother of two came around. She spoke but made no sense. Carlisle helped her to her feet and then half carried Naomi to his bedroom. He laid her down, pulled the covers over her and made sure she was sleeping on her side just in case there was anything left in her stomach.

He closed the door to what was supposed to be his bedroom. It was nearly 11pm.

"Well, a fine night this turned out to be," Carlisle said.

Deciding to forgo his swim, Carlisle had a look outside. Paula Sheets and Pete Giacomin were nowhere in sight. He had a good idea of where they were though.

This is just great. Pete, Subway and Bernstein are getting laid, and I'll be sleeping on one of the couches.

Carlisle found a blanket and an extra pillow in a linen closet and made himself comfortable on a long, beige-coloured couch It faced a TV screen which took up most of a large wall. He turned on racing station TVG for a few moments, got bored and with visions of a day at Saratoga Racecourse in his head, drifted off to sleep.

The next morning, a loud bang on the front door woke Carlisle. He glanced at his watch. It was not even 8am. *Who the fuck is at the door at this hour? If it's the fucking newspaper being thrown against the door, the son of a bitch is two hours late and needs to learn the first rule of newspaper delivery; never throw a paper which wakes up the home's occupants.*

Carlisle got up, walked to a window at the front of the house and slowly pulled back a curtain to the left of the front door. Banging on the door was none other than SB Yokum.

Holy shit, holy shit. if he finds his wife here, we are all fucked. Think Duke, think.

Carlisle's few functioning brain cells – the rest were soused in Guinness – sprang into action. He walked away from the door and yelled. "Hold on mate. I just got up. I need to take a piss. Keep the food warm."

"I ain't no goddamn delivery boy," the country's leading thoroughbred trainer said. "Open this damn door now."

Carlisle raced down the hallway, burst into the four bedrooms, and quickly woke everyone up.

"SB Yokum is at the front door," he told his housemates and their overnight guests.

"Holy shit," Bernstein said.

"I've already said that. Get the girls out of here, now. There has got to be a back door out of this fucking place. I'll go and stall him as long as I can."

Carlisle saw a robe hanging on the back of Subway's bedroom door, tossed it on and slowly walked back to the front door.

Rubbing his eyes, he gingerly opened the front door. "Glad you are here; I can really use a coffee."

Yokum barged past Carlisle and stormed into the house.

"Where the fuck is my wife?" hollered.

"Your who?"

"You heard me."

"Are you sure you have the right house? Me and my mates are renting this place."

"This is the right fucking house MATE. It's Jim Costa's place. He rents it out every summer to city suckers like you. Some of my boys saw my wife with you last night at Harvey's."

Yokum backed Carlisle up against a wall. "If you fucked her, I'll will brand your ass just as I do my longhorns."

Carlisle had nothing to defend himself with except his wit.

"What did you say your name was? I didn't get it."

"You know who I am. Everyone in town knows who I am."

"Listen, Mr Yokum, may I call you SB?"

"No, you may not," Yokum said. He punched Carlisle once in the stomach and when Carlisle bent over to catch his breath, followed up with a stiff upper cut which grazed Carlisle's jaw. The Stars' top scout sank to his knees, more from the punch to his breadbasket, which left him gasping for air.

"What the fuck is going on out here?" Subway yelled as he and Giacomin entered the living area. "And who the fuck are you?" Subway asked getting right in SB Yokum's face.

"You know who I am."

"Actually, I don't. You have two choices understand? You either get the fuck out of this house now, or I call the cops, and have you arrested for assault," he said pointing to Carlisle who was getting to his feet.

"This ain't over," SB Yokum said. "Not by a long shot."

Yokum turned and started for the front door.

"Oh SB," Carlisle called out.

As Yokum turned, Carlisle landed a haymaker which landed flush on the trainer's jaw. Yokum's legs wobbled and down he went. Giacomin cradled the trainer's head, so it did not smack the floorboards.

"That's very sporting of you Pete," Carlisle said.

"Let's get him out of here," Subway yelled. "I've got an idea."

The three carried a barely conscious Yokum to his late model Mercedes and dropped him into the front passenger seat. "Now to finish the job," Subway said.

Subway went to the pool area, grabbed some of the empty beer bottles from the previous evening and tossed them on the floor in front of Yokum. He opened another bottle, poured some beer over Yokum and left the rest of the bottle on his lap.

"What a waste of perfectly good beer," Carlisle said.

"I'll drive his car, you guys follow me with mine, okay?"

"Where we headed?" Carlisle asked.

"To the backstretch of the racecourse. We'll leave him and his car there. A simple DUI."

"That's devious mate, but I like it."

"And hopefully when he wakes up from that beauty of a right hand of yours, he won't remember a thing."

"You think he will?"

"Shit Duke, if somebody slugged me the way you nailed him, I wouldn't remember the last six months."

"Hey, where the heck is Bernstein?" Giacomin asked.

"Probably hiding under a bed," Subway said.

Chapter 18

BY THE time Billy Jenkins and Elrod Stokes got to the player appearance sign-up sheets pinned to the wall in the Mozzies' clubhouse, there was no room left for another signature.

All 12 spots were taken within minutes of the sheets being posted. Those who put their names on the sheets for the meet and greets, signings and speaking engagements at local schools, shopping centres and car dealerships weren't doing it to push the Mozzies' brand in Mosquito Lakes, they were doing it to supplement their meagre incomes. In A ball or below, most appearances netted the ballplayers $50 or $100 and for many the extra cash was desperately needed. Some would not have been able to pay their bills or have a decent meal without the fill-ups.

It came with a cost though. The appearances were scheduled either on a rare off day or when players returned from overnight bus trips when they should have been inspecting the inside of their eyelids.

Jenkins and Stokes didn't need the money but were always curious to see what sort of appearances their teammates signed up for.

One Tuesday afternoon, nearly halfway through the season, and several hours before a home game, Jenkins and Stokes were asked by Mozzies manager Gene Short to see him in his office.

"Sorry fellas, I haven't asked you in to tell you you've been promoted to A ball, although that conversation is not too far off. I need a favour."

Jenkins and Stokes looked at each other and shrugged their shoulders.

"Sure coach," Stokes said. Jenkins nodded. "What's up."

"A good friend of mine, Hank Whitlock, runs the local Ford dealership and is in a bit of strife. His young son has been ill and he has more medical bills than you guys have hits and RBIs. To put it simply, he's got to move some cars – quick – or he could lose the dealership."

"If you fellas can go over there on Saturday, let's say from 11-2 and schmooze with the customers, sign a few autographs, pose for a few photos, he and I would appreciate it.

"There's no money in it. But someone will pick you up and shout you lunch. That is the saying, isn't it, Billy? Shout you lunch?"

"It is coach."

Short smiled. "Can I tell Hank you guys will do it?"

"You can," Stokes said.

"Outstanding," Short said. "Outstanding."

Ordinarily, Short would not have asked his two stars to make a personal appearance on the day of a game, but since the Mozzies were playing last-placed Fort Myers, he was willing to risk it. *Shit, I reckon I could pencil my name and Keneally's on the line-up card to replace them and we could still beat Fort Myers, Short thought.*

He was right. The Mozzies flogged the Fort Myers outfit in all three games. Jenkins and Stokes had a quiet night on Saturday – three hits and three RBIs between them

"Hank moved 30 vehicles thanks to you guys, some high-priced items too, so it looks like he'll be okay," Short told Jenkins and Stokes before batting practice on Sunday morning.

"It's going to be a scorcher today so I'm giving you guys the day off. We need to keep you fresh for the series with Dunedin. You okay with that?"

Any other time, Jenkins and Stokes would have said no. But they were buggered after playing Friday and Saturday night and needed a break.

"As long as we're back in the line-up on Tuesday night," Stokes said.

Short laughed. "You will be. I want everyone at their best for Dunedin. They are a damn good club."

After the Mozzies squeaked past Fort Myers 4-3 to sweep the three-game series, Short told the playing group they had the next day off. "Back here at 3.30 on Tuesday. And boys, don't do anything stupid, alright? Get some rest. We've got a pennant to win."

Everyone took Short's advice and behaved although Donaldson the Unfuckable came close to getting into a bit of strife on Monday afternoon when the burly first baseman was told by a young cashier at the local MacDonald's that it was temporarily out of Big Macs.

"How the hell could you be out of Big Macs? That's like us being out of baseballs," he yelled. "What the fuck am I supposed to have for lunch?"

Donaldson's tirade brought the fast-food outlet's manager to the front of the store.

"Sir, I am going to have to ask you to leave if you do not watch your language. We have young kids here," Roger Tidrow said pointing to several tables filled with youngsters gobbling down their happy meals.

"Do you have any Big Macs?" Donaldson yelled at Tidrow, who was half his size.

"Easy big fellow," slick-fielding third baseman Chuck Perry said trying to calm his teammate down. "We'll have something else, okay?"

Perry turned and faced Tidrow. "Everything is under control, go back to your office son."

Donaldson looked at the electronic menu boards facing him and in a much calmer voice asked the same cashier for two quarter-pounders, two large orders of fries and two large chocolate shakes.

"I'm sorry sir, but we are out of quarter-pounders."

"She's joking, isn't she?" Donaldson asked Perry. "Tell me she's joking. 'Cause there is no way I am having a fucking fish sandwich or a bloody salad. I need meat."

The cashier smiled at Perry.

"She's joking mate."

Perry and Donaldson took a seat outside and waited for their orders to be delivered. "You even get a waitress here," Donaldson said. "And you don't have to tip her."

Perry looked on in amazement as Donaldson scarfed down his lunch in less time it took to issue an intentional walk.

Living the dream, Perry told himself. *Living the dream.*

With the Mozzies rested and ready, Dunedin barely fired a shot in the three-game series which ended on Thursday afternoon. Dunedin, which came into the series in second place, four games behind the first-placed Mozzies, left Mosquito Lakes late Thursday afternoon seven games behind the frontrunners.

Dunedin sent its ace, Hermano Vasquez, to the mound in game 1 of the series and when he didn't make it through the fifth inning, Stokes knew the game and the series was over.

"Look at 'em Billy, heads down, they are toast," Stokes told Jenkins in the on-deck circle while they waited for Vasquez's replacement to jog in from the visiting bullpen. "Look at the junk this guy is throwing Billy. Holy shit. My grandmother throws harder than that."

Stokes's grandmother might have thrown harder, but she did not have the change-up or slow curve that Rodrigo Gomez had.

Stokes was the first Mozzie to face Gomez and went down swinging on a nasty curveball, while Jenkins popped up to end the inning. "It's a good thing we have a 5-1 lead," Jenkins told Stokes as they took their places in the field. "He's got some nasty shit," Stokes said. "I hope he stays in. I want another crack at him."

Stokes got his chance in the bottom of the seventh but again struck out, this time looking, on a slow curve ball that darted in, out and then down. "Jesus," Stokes said as he saw the home plate umpire's hand go up, signifying a called strike. "Even he can't help you son," the ump said as he adjusted his face mask and dusted off home plate.

"Make sure we throw Stokes a lot of off-speed stuff the next time we take BP," Short told Keneally in the dugout. "He's got to be able to handle this sort of shit."

Up the southeast coast in Columbia, South Carolina, Patrick Kennedy was putting up the kind of numbers Duke Carlisle expected from his Australian signee.

The hard-throwing left-hander had the best record in the Class A South Atlantic League and one of the lowest earned run averages. For every batter he walked, Kennedy struck out nearly six. He toyed with opposing hitters over the first 12 weeks of the season. Even when they saw him for the second time, hitters struggled.

One of the few hitters to have any success against Kennedy was Verne Boyne of Charleston.

The well-put together third baseman and native West Virginian was Washington's second round draft pick. Boyne was assigned to Charleston to make sure plenty of arses filled the stands of Coalminers Stadium. Boyne was able to live at home in his first season of professional ball while his teammates were billeted with families they had never laid eyes on until the day they were dropped off at area doorsteps and porches with their few belongings.

His momma's cooking and being able to sleep in his own bed were some of the reasons bandied about for Boyne's success.

The slugger was hitting well over .300 on the season and sent Kennedy for his only early shower of the season the first time the two clubs met earlier in the year in Columbia, when he belted a long three-run home run that was still climbing as it cleared the left-field fence. Boyne was looking forward to facing Kennedy again, this time on his home turf, while the Columbia left-hander had not forgotten the pitch that Boyne lifted into orbit. "He's not going to be seeing any fastballs," Kennedy told Allison Symonds of the *Columbia Herald* earlier in the week.

Kennedy pitched the second game of the three-game weekend series in Charleston smack dab in the middle of summer. The temperature was 31° and the humidity unbearable when the first pitch was thrown at 7:05pm. Thanks to an aggressive marketing campaign by the Charleston front office featuring Boyne and Kennedy, the sold-out sign went up thirty minutes before game time.

Both sides went down in order in the opening frame. Boyne led off the home second. "Now batting for your Coalminers, third baseman, number 12, Verney Boyne," public address announcer John Beasley said as Boyne walked from the on-deck circle to the plate.

Half of the crowd was on its feet. Boyne took his time getting comfortable at the plate. He knocked the dirt from each of his cleats with the tap of his bat, planted his feet, adjusted his batting helmet and was ready. Home plate umpire Doug Aulden lifted his right hand, signalling Kennedy to start the inning.

Kennedy went into his wind-up and delivered a curve ball which caught the outside of the plate. "Strike," Aulden said. The crowd booed. Kennedy's next delivery was a change-up which Boyne let go. Aulden lifted both index fingers to signal that the count was 1-1.

Two curve balls missed the mark which put Boyne ahead in the count at 3-1. *He's gonna bring the heater now, he's got to, Boyne* thought. He thought wrong. A change-up at the knees was a called strike to bring the count to 3-2.

Kennedy took his foot off the rubber, took off his cap and wiped the sweat from his forehead with the wristband on his right arm. He put his foot back on the rubber and peered in for the sign from catcher Tom Stockdale. He waved off the first sign and nodded at the second set of signs Stockdale gave.

If you're gonna get beat, get beat with your best, Kennedy said to himself. He took the ball from his glove, rolled it around in his hand and went into his wind-up.

Boyne fouled off the waist-high heater down the right-field line.

Boyne fouled off three more pitches, two curve balls and another fastball. Most of the crowd was on its feet as Kennedy again looked in for the signs.

He's gonna bring the heat, I just know it, Boyne thought. This time he thought right. Kennedy's fastball stayed up and Boyne got enough of it to smack into the right-centre-field alley. The ball rolled to the wall. Boyne cruised into second base with a stand-up double. Kennedy glanced at Boyne and nodded his head as if to say, *you got me this time but just wait.*

Boyne smiled at the league's top pitcher. *He's good, but I think I've got him figured out,* Boyne thought.

Kennedy struck out the next hitter, leaving Boyne stuck at second base.

Charleston leftfielder Julian Malone was up next and after falling behind in the count 0-2, was looking for a curveball. He got it and singled sharply up the middle. Boyne was held at third, putting runners at the corners with one down.

Stockdale went to the mound for a chat with Kennedy. "This number seven hitter isn't much. He won't be able to get around on your heater Paddy. Keep it low. If he puts the ball in play, we can turn two and get out of the inning."

Kennedy nodded.

Stockdale went back behind the plate, adjusted his mask and signalled for a fastball. Kennedy blew one past Tommy Melbourne and then another. He was ahead 0-2 in the count. Melbourne swung at the next pitch and popped it up behind home plate. Stockdale tossed his mask away, took a few steps to the screen behind home plate, snared the ball in his glove and ran back to the plate, keeping an eye on the Charleston runner at first, who had drifted a few feet from the safety of the bag. "You're not going anywhere," Donaldson the Unfuckable told the baserunner.

With two down, the Mozzie middle infielders took several steps back to their normal positions.

It was now up to Charleston's number eight hitter, Warrick Jones to get the Coalminers on the scoreboard.

Jones looked at two curve balls and with the count 1-1 was looking for a fastball. He got a curveball, swung hard and badly missed the pitch. The ball bounced once in the dirt and somehow got passed the sure-handed Stockdale. Ninety nine out of a hundred times Stockdale would have stopped the ball with his chest protector and kept it in front of him. But Kennedy's pitch had too much English on it and the ball rolled about twenty feet to his right. As soon as the ball got passed Stockdale, Boyne broke for the plate as did Kennedy. Stockdale picked up the ball and fed Kennedy, who turned and slapped a tag on the sliding Boyne. Home plate umpire Aulden signalled that Boyne was out which ended the inning. Boyne took the legs out from Kennedy with his perfectly legal slide and quickly bounced up, but Kennedy stayed down.

Kennedy rolled onto his back and grabbed his left knee. Stockdale rushed to his side. "It's my knee Tommy. I've done my knee."

Columbia team trainer Bud Grantham was at Kennedy's side in an instant. He gingerly examined Kennedy's knee. "It's my ACL Bud. The same one I did back home. I just know it."

"Maybe not. Let's hold off and see what the scans say Paddy."

Kennedy was carried off the field by Stockdale, Donaldson and Grantham and taken directly to the locker room. Grantham immediately taped an ice pack to Kennedy's knee to keep the swelling down. Not even 10 minutes later the Charleston trainer and team doctor brought a pair of crutches to the Columbia locker room.

Kennedy watched the rest of the game from the visitor's dugout on the third base side of the field. In the middle of the fourth inning, Boyne unexpectedly ran from his position in left field to the Columbia dugout to have a word with Kennedy.

"I'm sorry Paddy. It was an accident, a simple accident. I would never try and hurt anybody."

"I know mate. I'm not blaming you for what happened."

The two shook hands. Boyne walked back to Charleston's dugout on the first base side and was met by Charleston manager Bob Northland.

"Nice gesture son. Now get a bat in your hands. We got a game to win."

In New York, Carlisle and McLain were notified of Kennedy's injury within an hour and had a Zoom call. Carlisle was in Saratoga. McLain was in his office in Stars Field where the Stars trailed Chicago 3-1 after seven frames.

"On a play at the plate? Fucking hell," Carlisle said when he heard the news.

"We'll bring Paddy back here and have our doctors examine him. If the scans show a tear and surgery is needed, he'll have it here," McLain said.

Carlisle slumped down in a chair and put his head in his hands. "I feel awful for the kid, just awful. Shit. He actually had a chance of making it. He actually had a chance."

"It's not like you to show this much emotion Duke. You alright?"

"I'll be okay. I'm just thinking of Paddy. The calls he'll have to make to his parents, his mates. Let's fly his folks out here Dan so he'll have some support if he goes under the knife."

"Good idea."

Two mornings later McLain and team physio Bert Carney greeted Kennedy when his plane landed at LaGuardia airport.

Kennedy was wheeled into the terminal by a pretty flight attendant, raised himself from the wheelchair and steadied himself on his crutches. His injured left knee was supported by a cumbersome brace.

"How are you feeling Paddy?" McLain asked after he introduced Carney.

"Not too bad mate. It's pretty swollen."

"As soon as the swelling goes down our team orthopaedic surgeon will have a good look at your knee and order the proper scans," Carney told

Kennedy while McLain waited for Kennedy's bag. "Let's not assume the worst. Okay? It could be a partial tear."

Kennedy shook his head in agreement but knew his ACL was fucked. He had gone over the play at the plate in his head a hundred times. If he had stood a foot to the left or a foot to the right, if Stockdale had blocked the pitch, if Boyne hadn't taken his legs out from under him.

"Everything is being taken care of by the Stars," McLain told Kennedy as they waited outside for the limousine which brought him and Carney to the airport to return. "You've got a suite in the same hotel Duke Carlisle is in; all your meals will be brought to you and we'll take you to and from the doctor's office. It won't cost you a nickel Paddy."

"Thanks mate. Appreciate that."

"How'd your parents take the news?" McLain asked.

"They were upset, but I reckon it's because I am so far away. I told them I was getting the best care and would be seeing the best orthopaedic surgeon in New York. That calmed them down a bit."

"Next time you speak to your folks tell 'em we'll fly them over if they want to come and see you. We'll put them up in the same hotel and take care of everything. It won't cost them a cent," McLain said.

"Thanks. I'll call them later."

The limo finally pulled up to the curb. Carney held Paddy's crutches as he got into the car.

"Back to the team hotel Pete," McLain told the driver.

"Bert will have a look at your knee this afternoon Paddy. If the swelling has come down, the team orthopaedic will examine you tomorrow morning at his office in Manhattan and arrange the scans."

Chapter 19

IN MOSQUITO Lakes, Billy Jenkins was in a slump. He hadn't had a hit in his last 12 at-bats and was benched for the first time in his short career.

"Everyone goes through a slump Billy," manager Gene Short told him before he posted the line-up card. Billy's name was on the bottom of the card along with the other bench players. "Take a couple of days off, clear your head."

Jenkins had an idea why he was struggling. Teams were now seeing him for the second time and his strengths and weaknesses at the plate were getting around the league.

I'll talk to our hitting coach, take extra batting practice. This is the first and last time I'm going to sit on the bench.

His dad tried to cheer him up when they spoke after that night's game, a loss where Billy wasn't even used as a pinch-hitter, a pinch-runner or a defensive replacement.

"Everyone goes through a bad patch Billy. Mickey Mantle wanted to go back home to Oklahoma after his first slump. Willie Mays was sent down to the minor leagues. They are both in the Hall of Fame. When you get back out there in a couple of days, relax and have fun. The hits will come."

MORNING WORKOUTS were all but over when a lone security guard spotted SB Yokum's Mercedes near the barn area on the Saratoga backstretch at 8.47am.

Employed by Equine Security, Cal Ford, 36, was completing week three of his eight-week summer stint at Saratoga Racecourse. Everyone in Saratoga knew who SB Yokum was and most knew what he looked like. Not Ford, who got paid $10 an hour and shared a shack on the backstretch with five others. Abe Lincoln's cabin had more amenities, but Ford was happy to trade the suffocating humidity of a Queens summer, his nagging wife and their two young kids for eight weeks of relative peacefulness, even if it meant cooking his meals on a hotplate and storing his beers in an old fridge that couldn't freeze an ice cube.

Ford slowly approached the vehicle. Its headlights were barely visible in the early morning sunshine, but they were on. He crouched down and looked inside the car through the passenger side window. The engine was running, the handbrake was on, and the car was in park. Had Carlisle left the car on Union Avenue, it would have been a matter for the Saratoga Police Department, which did not like drunk drivers on its streets, especially in broad daylight.

Ford had been drilled since day one that if he saw anything suspicious near the stables and barns, he was to immediately contact the on-track stewards. Someone else might have called Yokum's backstretch stable office and asked whoever answered the phone to come collect their boss and bring some bugs bunny with them.

Unfortunately for Yokum, Ford rang the stewards. Their dark green Ford Explorer arrived on the scene within minutes. The stench of stale beer hit head steward Hank Swenson like a punch in the face as he opened the driver's side door and turned the car's engine off.

"Holy shit," Swenson said to fellow stewards Herm Wiley and Doug Adkins. "It's SB Yokum." While Swenson tried to rouse him and Wiley thanked Ford for ringing them, Adkins quickly snapped a couple of photos with his phone. *Those New York tabloids will pay through the nose for these,* he thought.

He was right. Later that morning he transferred the photos to a cheap phone he picked up at a local market, created a fake gmail account and emailed them to the *NY Herald* and the *NY Tribune.* He got 10 grand from the Tribune and another 12 grand from the Herald. The photos were on the front pages of both papers the next morning. Photo credit was given to a D Duck.

"Who the fuck took these photos?" Swenson angrily asked the next morning as he held up both papers in the steward's room.

"Someone must have gotten to the scene before the damn security guard," Wiley said.

"That fucker is toast, whoever it is" Swenson said.

"I wanted this handled internally. A full investigation by our integrity unit, hearings. Now, we'll have to suspend Yokum until we get to the bottom of this. I sure hope this turns out to be a simple driving under the influence and not some sort of payback by another trainer or a big gambler. This sport of ours has enough fucking problems."

Yokum came to soon after he was escorted back to his stable. His head assistant, Patrick James, told him he had to front the stewards before the following day's first race,

"What the fuck happened SB?"

"I'm not sure but my jaw feels like it was kicked by a fractious colt," he mumbled.

Yokum was driven to Saratoga General Hospital's emergency department where his swollen jaw was X-rayed. After an hour-long wait he was told by an overseas emergency room doctor he had suffered a broken jaw. The same doctor wired it shut. Just after 1pm he was released with a bagful of pills into the care of local attorney and frequent racecourse visitor RG Gaines, who had been called by James.

"Holy shit SB. You look like that Jaws guy from those James Bond movies."

Yokum glared at his attorney and motioned for Gaines to come closer.

"Get me the fuck home," he whispered.

"Stay put. I'll bring the car around.

"I've some good news," Gaines said after helping Yokum into the passenger side of his year-old BMW. "Your hearing has been postponed until the day after tomorrow. It will give you a chance to get some rest and give me some time to piece together what happened. Your assistant told me you don't remember anything. Is that true?"

Yokum nodded.

Patrick James saddled the stable's mounts for the next two days. It had two wins and a third from nine starters. Yokum was happy to hear the news at the rented house he and wife Laura shared on Lake Saratoga.

Even though it wasn't the first time she had cheated on her husband, Laura felt guilty over her one-nighter with Bernstein. She had no idea it was Bernstein's pal Carlisle who had broken her husband's jaw and set him up. SB was known to knock back a few on occasion, and since SB had no knowledge of what happened to him, Laura figured he had gotten into a late night or early morning scuffle and come off second best.

For the first time in ages, she looked after him. She made his meals, put them in a blender and watched on as he sucked the contents down with a straw.

"You're not going to like this hun," she said after breakfast. "But you need to see this."

Laura gently placed copies of that morning's *Herald* and *Tribune* on the kitchen table and took several steps back.

Yokum's eyeballs nearly popped out of their sockets when he saw the front page of each paper. He tried to yell but was only able to squeak out a few undecipherable sounds.

When I find the fucker who did this to me, I'll cut off his fucking nuts and stuff them down his throat, he said to himself.

RG Gaines accompanied Yokum to his hearing with the stewards. Laura Yokum did not, citing a hair appointment that could not be changed.

Impeccably dressed in a tan three-piece suit, Gaines asked the stewards to look at the big picture. Yokum had no history of drink driving, had an exemplary record as a trainer and his jaw was so badly swollen that he could have passed for former *Tonight Show* host Jay Leno.

"This is all a set-up Mr Swenson. Mr Yokum was obviously assaulted. Look at the medical report. His jaw is broken. The poor bastard will be drinking his meals for the next six-to-eight weeks."

Yokum slumped in his chair and winced as he put his hand to his jaw. He reached into his breast pocket and pulled out a handkerchief to wipe the drool from the corners of his mouth.

"Are the police investigating?" Swenson asked Gaines.

"Yes they are sir, but unfortunately my client has no memory of the attack or where he was that morning."

"Do you have anything to say Mr Yokum?"

The trainer pointed to his jaw and then to Gaines.

"I would like the opportunity to bring forward people who can vouch for Mr Yokum's character."

"Save it for the full hearing Mr Gaines. If you do not have anything further to add I shall consult with my colleagues Mr Wiley and Mr Adkins and deliver our decision within the hour."

After 45 minutes of deliberation, Swenson, Wiley and Adkins rendered their decision. Yokum was suspended for 30 days for being drunk on the premises of the racecourse and for bringing the sport of racing into disrepute. He was denied access to the racetrack, its stables and the training track.

Yokum mouthed the word fuck as he heard the decision.

"I am going to get the motherfuckers who did this to me," he mumbled into Gaines's ear. "They have fucked with the wrong guy. And tell my staff that they are not to talk to anyone from those two fucking newspapers. I don't care if Jimmy Breslin himself comes back from the dead. Nobody from those two rags gets an interview, ever."

"Don't worry SB. I'll get a court order this afternoon allowing you to continue training," Gaines told Yokum as they left the steward's room.

"You bet your Yankee ass you will, or you'll never spend a dollar from the retainer I gave you," Yokum mumbled. "Ten fucking thousand dollars. A fellow Texan wouldn't have charged me shit until it was all over with."

Gaines applied for the court order that afternoon but was turned down by Saratoga County Judge Elaine Kramer. She took all of two minutes to announce her decision. "This is a matter to be dealt with by the stewards of the New York Racing Association," Ms Kramer said. "Request denied."

"Don't you think you're being a little harsh your honour?" Gaines said as he stood in front of the defence table. "How is my client going to be able to make a living?" Gaines pleaded.

"He's got stables in every state Mr Gaines. I'm sure he'll survive until his hearing with the stewards."

"May I approach the bench your honour?" Gaines asked.

Judge Kramer rolled her eyes and motioned him to come forward.

"What is it Mr Gaines?"

"Your honour, my client would be extremely grateful if you would allow him to keep working. He was assaulted and set up. The only one hurt was my client and his reputation. You saw those NY papers this morning. It is shameful."

"And," Gaines continued in a voice barely above a whisper, "he would be very happy to make a donation to your re-election campaign."

Judge Kramer took off her reading glasses and gave Gaines a long, hard look. "Five large, in cash," she whispered.

"Step away from the bench Mr Gaines. I've heard enough out of you."

Gaines walked back to the defence table and remained upright.

"Motion granted." Judge Kramer announced.

She slammed her gavel down and called for the next case.

Gaines closed his briefcase, adjusted his tie, and walked out of the 100-year-old courtroom. *I just love dealing with judges who are up for re-election.*

He rang Yokum from outside the courthouse. SB was seated in a recliner in his summer rental watching the previous day's replays on TVG. He removed the icepack from his jaw, tossed two painkillers into his mouth and answered his phone.

"You've been cleared to keep training SB. I'll notify the stewards."

"How much did it cost me Gaines?"

"Five large."

"I can live with that. First place prize money in tomorrow's feature is a hundred and twenty grand. I own 50 per cent of the nag. I transferred your fee into your account. Come by the stables in the morning and I'll sort out the rest of it."

"He got a fucking court order?" a disbelieving Hank Swenson asked Herm Wiley and Doug Adkins later that afternoon.

"Yup," Adkins said.

"Who issued it?"

"Judge Elaine Kramer."

Swenson shook his head from side to side. "All those freebies we give the judiciary on race days, and they can't even back us up this one fucking time. What a joke."

"Yokum is saddling up the favourite in tomorrow's feature and you can bet your ass he'll have something to say if it gets up. We need a scandal somewhere – anywhere – to get racing off the front and back pages and those damn radio call-in shows."

Swenson got his wish.

JUST A few hours later in Mosquito Lakes, Florida, Republican presidential candidate and frontrunner Carl Tucker threw out the ceremonial first pitch prior to the Rookie League game between the Mozzies and the Clearwater Sharks.

The ball landed squarely in the glove of Mozzies catcher Stan Shearwater. He handed the ball back to Tucker, wished him well and shook the 52-year-old US senator's hand. Tucker doffed his Mozzies' cap to the polite applause of the capacity crowd.

"Is there a bar in this fucking place?" Tucker asked Mozzies' publicity director Will McNeil, who led him to his seat just behind the Mozzies dugout.

"I'll bring something to you. What would you like?"

"Scotch and soda. A double. On the rocks. Put it in a Coke cup and if they're edible, bring me a hot dog while you're at it."

Tucker, the two-term senior senator from the deep red state of Kansas, took a seat next to his advance man and trusted staffer Zach Nolen.

"How'd it look Zach?"

"It could not have gone any better Senator. You threw a strike and there was not a boo from the crowd. I am just about to post a video of the pitch on Twitter and Facebook."

"Good man. Hey, did those two hotties I talked too when we arrive get back to you?"

"They sure did."

"You get it all set up?"

"They'll meet you at the Marriot in town. Room 309. It's all been paid for – in cash."

"Outstanding. I'll stay a couple of innings and get over there. And if my wife calls tell her I'm at some damn fundraiser.

The two hotties Tucker was due to rendezvous with were none other than Mosquito Lakes College sophomores Sophie Hall and Erica Cosgrove, the girlfriends of Billy Jenkins and Elrod Stokes.

Jenkins and Stokes combined for four hits and drove in five runs in the Mozzies 7-4 win over the Sharks. The game took well over three hours due to numerous walks and pitching changes. By the time Jenkins, Stokes and their teammates had showered and changed it was nearly 11pm. There was hardly a soul waiting outside the clubhouse or the players' parking lot.

"Didn't the girls say they'd meet us here after the game?" Stokes asked Jenkins.

"They did. I saw them in the stands earlier."

Both checked their phones for any messages. There were none.

Jenkins rang Erica. His call went straight to her voice mail. Stokes rang Sophie. His call went straight to her voice mail.

"That's a bit odd, isn't it Stokesy? What do you think is going on?"

"Maybe they just got bored and went to the movies. They didn't say anything about an early class in the morning. I doubt they're asleep."

Sophie Hall and Erica Cosgrove were in bed, the same bed, a king-sized bed in room 309 of the local Marriott waiting on Senator Carl Tucker, who was showering before his tryst with the two lovelies. "Fucking mosquito repellent," he said while soaping himself up. "What a fucking town. But they'll remember me come primary day. Who the hell else is going to come down here and campaign?"

Dressed in shorts and a halter, Erica Cosgrove was having second thoughts about coming with Sophie to the hotel room.

"I feel a little guilty, you know, about cheating on Billy. He really is such a sweet kid," Erica told her roommate and bestie.

"Don't be. This is a big step up for us. Tucker is running for President Erica, President. I don't know about you, but two years in Mosquito Lakes is starting to wear a little thin. I'm crazy about Elrod, but who knows where he and Billy will be playing ball next year. We take care of Senator Tucker and he'll take care of us."

Erica leaned forward. "What do you mean he'll take care of us?"

"He'll give us jobs on his campaign. We'll fly all over the country, meet all the big wigs."

"And we'll have to fuck him. We'll be his personal whores."

"Not whores hun, staffers."

"What about his wife?" Erica asked.

"Every politician fucks around. Tucker is a decent looking bloke. He's got so much money coming into his campaign his people can't even count it. He's the frontrunner for the Republican nomination."

"How do you know all that? Aren't you majoring in basket weaving?"

"I Googled him during the game wise ass."

At that point, Senator Tucker emerged from the bathroom with just a towel wrapped around his 34-inch waist.

"Who is going to show the senator a little love?" Tucker asked.

Erica gave Sophie a poke in the ribs.

"I will Senator," Sophie said. She took off her top, hopped off the bed, threw her arms around Tucker, checked his tonsils and adenoids with her tongue and then sank to her knees.

"You're next honey," Tucker said, winking at Erica. "The least you can do is take your top off, so I have something nice to look at while your friend is polishing my knob."

Erica thought about it and nearly backed out. But seeing Sophie on her knees in front of Tucker turned her on a bit. She took off her top and when Tucker motioned for her to come closer she did.

They were locked in an embrace when *Mosquito Lakes Daily News* junior reporter Jimmy Kellogg slowly and quietly opened the door to room 309. Wearing a baseball cap and black-framed glasses which he did not need, Kellogg had earlier seen Tucker and his staffer chatting with Sophie Hall and Erica Cosgrove.

On a hunch he had followed the Senator from the ballpark to the Marriott, parked his beat-up Honda behind the four-storey hotel, grabbed a few essentials, stuffed them into a travel bag and walked into the hotel lobby.

Tucker grabbed his room key from the front desk and scurried to the elevator. He was nearly there and would have been on his way before Kellogg got there when he was recognised by an older couple from his home state who were on holiday.

"Just resting up after another day on the campaign trail," he told Doris and Reg Nathan. "Can we get a picture Senator?" Doris asked. "We both voted for you last time."

"Of course," Tucker said.

That extra minute gave Kellogg enough time to saunter over to the elevator and wait with Tucker and a few others for the next one. Tucker was nervously fingering his room card when the elevator stopped on the third floor.

Tucker got out and so did Kellogg. The 27-year-old general assignment reporter saw Tucker open the door to room 309 and then continued down the hallway. He took careful notice of where the security cameras were positioned.

Kellogg opened the door to the stairwell and waited. After thirty minutes passed, he stuffed his cap and eyeglasses into his travel bag, threw it over his shoulder and put thin gloves on both his hands. With a hoodie covering his face, a can of spray paint in one hand and burglary tools in the other, he emerged from the stairwell and quickly went to work. He spray-painted the camera lenses, pressed the elevator button, sent it to the fourth floor and quietly walked to room 309.

He glanced in both directions and went to work on the door with his burglary tools, a skill he learned from his older brother Lenny, who had a criminal record longer than a Louisville Slugger.

In 22 seconds, the lock was sprung. He slowly opened the door and put down a rubber stopper to keep it open.

With the two girls and Senator Tucker otherwise occupied, Kellogg started shooting video with his iphone. By the time he was spotted, he had shot about 10 seconds of video and gotten a dozen still photos. Erica let out a scream when she saw Kellogg, who took off. He scooped up the door stopper, jammed one of his tools into the lock and shut the door behind him. Sophie disengaged herself from Tucker's pecker and ran to the front door with Tucker. They tried opening the door, but it wouldn't budge.

By the time Tucker rang the front desk Kellogg was long gone. He had covered all his tracks, but his heart was racing. "Thanks Lenny. I couldn't have done it without you," he said as he drove off.

Kellogg slowly drove to the office of the *Mosquito Lakes Daily News*, an odd name for a newspaper which published just three times a week, wrote a short story and was about to upload the video of Tucker and his two playmates, and the story to the paper's website, its Twitter feed and its Facebook page when he stopped.

"Should I ring Frank and give him a heads-up?" he asked himself.

Frank being Frank Leishman, the paper's veteran editor, the man who hired him two years ago and was likely asleep even though it was barely 10pm.

Kellogg had an inkling of what the conversation would sound like.

"You did what?" Frank Leishman would scream.

"Wait till you see the footage Frank. Holy shit. His career is through Frank, and in the morning everyone in the country will know that it was the *Mosquito Lakes Daily News* who did it."

"That's fucking great. But you never told me about this understand. You did it all on your own. And throw that fucking phone of yours in the ocean. I don't want any record of this call. I'm deleting it from my phone as soon as I hang up."

"Don't worry Frank. I am using some piece of shit phone that can't be traced to anyone."

Kellogg leaned back in his chair, his eyes glued to the wide monitor in front of him. *I hit this button, and Carl Tucker is finished. Should I? Aww, Fuck it.*

Kellogg hit the upload button and watched the video and story shoot to the top of the paper's website, Twitter feed and Facebook page. The @SenatorCarlTucker handle attached made sure that the 655,000 people who followed the Senator on Twitter would see it within minutes.

The first to hear the notification on his phone was Tucker staffer Zach Nolen, who was in room 422 in the same hotel watching Kansas City and Seattle on ESPN.

"Holy shit. Holy shit," he yelled.

Nolen got his gear on and ran to the elevator. It was there. He got in, punched in floor three, pressed the door close button and when the door opened ran to room 309.

Three hotel staffers were in the room getting an earful from Tucker, who was dressed in a robe. "Don't you fuckers have any security," he screamed. Nolen looked for Erica and Sophie, but they had bolted the moment the door was opened.

"I need to speak with you Senator."

"Hold on Zach."

Nolen hustled the three hotel staffers out of the room.

"What the fuck are you doing Zach? Those fuckers are going to pay for this."

Nolen handed his phone to Tucker, who watched the clip in disbelief and threw it at the window. A small crack appeared in the window, the iphone did not have a mark on it.

Tucker sank into a chair on the far side of the room and started to sob. “I was set-up Zach. I bet it’s that fucking congressman from California who is behind this. They’ll do anything to discredit a candidate when they don’t have a record to stand on, especially when he’s the front runner.”

Nolen rolled his eyes. Tucker’s campaign for the presidency was over. He was likely going to be censored by his colleagues in the Senate. He was up for re-election in two years. Voters can be forgiving, but would his wife of 25 years feel the same way? Not to mention their three kids.

“There’s only one way out of this Senator. You must go back home, hold a press conference with your wife and kids by your side, admit that you are human, made a mistake and ask The Lord for forgiveness.”

Tucker picked his head up and wiped a lone tear from his eye. “Do you think that will work Zach?”

“If it is done properly, it could.”

“Get that worthless chief of staff of mine on the phone right away and tell him to set it all up. I’ll have to call Janice, tell her what’s going on and confess to everything. I don’t want her to see this on the news before I talk to her. Shit. Why the fuck did I come down here?”

SB YOKUM won another dozen races before Saratoga closed its doors for the summer and everyone travelled back down the Northway for the two-month long rich fall meeting at Belmont Park.

Yokum drove himself and Laura to their place in Long Island, just a 10-minute drive to Belmont Park, where the third leg of the Triple Crown, The Belmont Stakes, is run each June. He had less than six weeks to prepare his best horses for the two-day Breeders Cup Championships, which this year was being held at Del Mar Turf Club outside San Diego, where he owned a million-dollar home on a golf course. His main residence was back in Texas, but Yokum only spent about six weeks there every year, usually from Thanksgiving through until New Years. He was too busy chasing the big purses on offer in New York, Kentucky, Florida and California.

A week after SB arrived back on Long Island, he went to a highly recommended oral surgeon in Manhattan to get his wired jaw checked. "It's your lucky day SB," Dr Louis Franklin said after checking a batch of X-rays. "That doctor in Saratoga did a top job. And whoever has been preparing your meals deserves some credit. The bone has healed nicely. One of the nurses will escort you into the examination room where I'll remove the wires."

A middle-aged nurse had SB lay flat on his back. She set up several instruments for Dr Franklin, who entered the room two minutes later.

Shit I hope this doesn't hurt, Yokum thought.

"Just relax SB. This won't be too bad," Dr Franklin said.

Yokum shut his eyes and grimaced several times as fixation wires and elastics were cut and removed. A smile appeared on his face as he slowly moved his jaw for the first time in six weeks.

"The nurse will give you an important pamphlet on your way out on what to eat when you go back home," Dr Franklin said. "We've got to keep you on a soft diet since your jaw muscles will be quite stiff. No steaks or anything that involves a lot of chewing. Casseroles, pasta, soft-cooked vegetables; that's going to be your diet for another few weeks."

That same afternoon, SB Yokum got a call from a private investigator he hired after the Saratoga Police Department was unable to find out who assaulted and set him up.

"I've got some photos I want you to have a close look at and examine a timeline I've drawn up," former New York City detective Stu DeGrassi said.

DeGrassi had spent nearly a week in Saratoga, interviewing the few bar and restaurant staff who remained in town after the busy summer season ended. He had a thorough look at the Saratoga Police Department's notes on the case and was stunned at how little they had come up with. DeGrassi chatted with security guard Carl Ford at his rundown Jackson Heights apartment who added nothing while his two kids wailed like drunken opera singers in the background.

The breakthrough came from former jockey and exercise rider Joey "Tums" Kewarra, who worked for rival trainer Jordan Scavuzzo.

Kewarra always had a pack of Tums on him for the severe acid reflux he suffered from after years of starving himself half to death to try and make weight to keep his rides. When he finally got tired of eating a handful of grapes for lunch and a tasteless boiled piece of fish for dinner, Kewarra retired from race riding and started to eat and eat and eat. Pizza, lasagne, chicken parmas, veal parmas. Anything with cheese and sauce on it was gobbled down like it was his last meal.

Kewarra put on 20 pounds in five weeks. It was too much for his stomach to handle. The acid reflux kicked in and to ease the sour taste in his mouth and the pain in his chest, Kewarra, 44, started popping Tums like chicklets after seeing an ad for them on TV.

"They work," Kewarra told Scavuzzo, who hired him as an exercise rider after his riding career ended.

In late September, two weeks after the Saratoga meeting ended, DeGrassi started visiting the Belmont Park backstretch searching for information on Yokum's assailant.

He started with Yokum's rivals, figuring they would benefit from having the country's leading trainer out of commission.

DeGrassi visited several leading stables and came up with nothing until he showed up at Scavuzzo's stables on a crisp Thursday morning just after sunrise. Horses left, right and centre were being hosed down and walked after their workouts, then put back in their stalls to have a feed. The high-priced horses were well looked after and ate better than a lot of people DeGrassi dealt with. He had never seen a meth addict carrying a few extra pounds.

He struck up a conversation with Kewarra, who was munching on a bacon and egg roll as he hosed down promising two-year-old colt Safety Guide.

"You're looking good Joey. Must be nice to be able to have a decent feed in the morning."

"It is, and who would you be? You don't strike me as an owner," Kewarra said.

"I'm not Joey. I prefer to flush what little money I have down the toilet. I'm doing some investigative work and trying to find out what happened to SB Yokum."

Kewarra took a bite out of his roll and motioned for a stable hand to take Safety Guide back to his stall. "You on the job?" he asked.

"Not anymore. I work privately now."

"Yokum paying you?"

"He is."

Kewarra finished his roll and wiped his mouth on the sleeve of the purple jacket he had on. The handsome Breeder's Cup logo was prominently displayed on the back.

"SB gave me a couple of rides for a few years when my weight was getting out of hand. I could only ride at 124 or 126 pounds. He tossed me a few extra bucks when I won a Grade 3 at Gulfstream. Good fellow. A shame what happened to him."

"You hear any gossip around the track?" DeGrassi asked. His notebook was tucked away in his back pocket.

"Nah, just a lot of speculation. But nothing concrete."

Kewarra turned and walked away, headed to the kitchen on the backstretch. "I need another cup of coffee."

DeGrassi followed. "It's on me," he said, ordering two coffees.

"You were at Saratoga, weren't you Joey? Degrassi asked as he stirred his coffee. He pointed to an empty table. The pair sat down.

"I was. Scavuzzo had a pretty good run and I rode a lot of trackwork for him. I love that place. There's nothing like it."

"Were you there the whole summer?"

"Yup. All six weeks."

"Mind if I take a few notes? Degrassi asked, taking his notebook from his back pocket.

"Nope. Just keep my name out of this or you get nothing."

Degrassi nodded.

"See or hear anything out of the ordinary?"

Kewarra blew on his coffee and took a long sip.

"You didn't hear this from me, understand? I'm just telling you cause SB done right by me.

"I saw this group of guys at Harvey's one night. I was there by myself having a feed. The steaks there are freaking delicious. There were four of them I remember, and they were getting very chummy with a group of ladies. Oner of them was SB's wife Laura."

"You ever see these guys before?

"One of them is a sports agent; Stemkowksi his name is. I've seen his photo in the newspapers a few times. The other three? I have no idea."

Now we're getting somewhere, DeGrassi thought. He wrote Stemkowski's name in his notebook.

"Harvey's is the name of the joint?"

"Yup. Been there forever. Was only in the last couple of years, after I stopped riding, that I was able to have a meal there. Damn good food. Worth every penny."

Kewarra downed the last of his coffee, wiped his mouth with a thin napkin, got up and tossed the styrofoam cup into a nearby bin.

"I've got horses to look after. Didn't catch your name."

DeGrassi handed him a card. "Stu DeGrassi. Give me a ring if you hear anything."

Kewarra studied the plain looking card and stuffed it in his shirt pocket. "Thanks for the coffee," he said.

DeGrassi stayed seated and looked at the name in his notebook.

Stemkowski. He took out his phone and Googled the name.

In less than twenty seconds he had a first name, the address of an office in Manhattan and a phone number, all of which he wrote down. Now he had to find the names of the blokes Stemkowski was with in Saratoga.

"Hey Siri," he jokingly said into his iphone. "What are the names of the guys Dominick "Subway" Stemkowski hung around with in Saratoga over the summer?"

"How the fuck do I know?" was the response. "Get off your ass and find out yourself you lazy bastard."

DeGrassi looked at his half empty cup of coffee which had cooled and carefully placed it in the same bin where Kewarra deposited his empty cup.

I'll get a proper cup of coffee back in town, he thought.

Later that morning, in an office in the paid-off ranch-style house he shared with his wife of 27 years in Massapequa on the south shore of Long Island, DeGrassi got to work.

Up until three weeks ago the office was the bedroom of his son, Thomas. The 18-year-old had just begun his freshman year at Syracuse University in upstate New York where the temperature dipped below zero and snow came down by the foot during winter.

DeGrassi and his wife Emily had tried to talk their eldest son into going somewhere out-of-state, preferably one with a better climate, but Thomas had made up his mind and wouldn't budge. The would-be sportscaster had an academic scholarship in the school's communications department and fancied himself as the next Marv Albert or Al Michaels. After a six-hour drive on a perfect late summer afternoon a month earlier, the Degrassi's arrived at the campus of Syracuse University. They were directed to the dormitory where Thomas would spend the next nine-and-a-half months. His roommate had not yet arrived. Someone from New Jersey he had been told. Thomas threw his bags on one of the two single beds of the medium sized room and took a seat at what would be his desk. His dad placed a 32-inch smart TV on the desk and checked out the amenities. There was a bar fridge, two dressers and a decent-sized closet.

"What do you think? Thomas asked. "Not bad, eh?"

It was better than Stu and Emily DeGrassi expected.

"Well," Stu said. "We'll let you get settled in. Our motel is a couple of miles down the road." He looked at his watch. It was 3.30pm. "We'll pick you up around six for dinner. Okay?"

Thomas merely nodded. He was busy programming the TV, making sure the cable package he ordered included Sportschannel New York and the MSG network and Yes.

"Shit, I hope he doesn't spend all his spare time in that room watching ballgames," Stu said to Emily as they walked to their two-year-old Toyota SUV. "He needs to have a bit of fun, don't you agree?"

"Up to a point hun. Speaking of fun," she said, grabbing her husband's hand. "Let's get back to the room and have some fun ourselves."

Stu smiled and suddenly sprinted to the car like a teenager. Despite his head start, Emily passed him and got there before he did.

"I never could outrun you," he said.

DeGrassi fired up his laptop and gazed out his office window. The grass needed cutting. *Okay. Four guys, probably from the city. They must have rented a house for the week.*

He Googled real estate agents in Saratoga and found three which dealt with summer rentals. His first call came up empty. He struck paydirt with the second.

"Yes, I rented a house to a Mr Stemkowski, but that's all the information you're going to get from me," realtor Blanche White said. "How do I know you're really a cop or a private investigator or whatever you told me you do."

"I can take some photos of my identification and send them to you," Degrassi said.

"Nope. Champion Real Estate deals with the top end of town Mr DeGrassi. If you want any more information you'll have to come to our office and make a formal enquiry."

Oh for goodness sakes, DeGrassi thought. *Just what I need, another fucking road trip.*

"When's the best time to come by"? DeGrassi asked. "I'm in Long Island. It's a heck of a long drive."

"That it is,' Blanche White said. "I can meet with you on Friday afternoon, but no later than 3pm."

"Okay. I'll see you in three days. Thank you for all your help, Miss White," DeGrassi said. The line went dead before he even put down the phone.

Shit. Well at least it's not my money. That lawyer of Yokum's is taking care of my expenses.

With his belly full of French toast, Degrassi set out from home just after 8am. "You sure you don't want to come along for the drive?" he asked Emily. "We can spend the night in town, have a nice meal."

"Not this time hun. I've got things to do today."

She gave her husband a kiss. "Call me when you get up there. I'll see you tonight."

"I will love. I'm hoping to be back no later than nine. Ten at the latest."

DeGrassi walked into the garage, used the remote to open the door and backed his white SUV into the driveway. With another click the door closed. He turned on the radio, found Howard Stern's show and drove off. "Don't let there be much traffic. Please. Just once, give me a break," he pleaded.

Five hours later, which included two pit stops – a pee, and a pee and petrol – De Grassi arrived in Saratoga. A month ago the town had been buzzing from sun-up to sundown. But with the six-week race meeting over, and all the trainers, jockeys, horses, media men, gamblers and shop owners having scattered back to the city, the town was practically empty. Some of the locals, particularly the old-timers, were happy with the mass exodus. They had their town back.

Others, such as the owners of the bars and restaurants opened their doors just on weekends. They scrapped by thanks to the patronage of the town's well-to-do, which included Blanche White and her husband Geoffrey, owners of Champion Real Estate, and passing tourists.

The trotters were still racing at Saratoga Raceway but saw a big drop-off in crowds and turnover. Just a few hundred die-hards turned up each evening instead of the few thousand who jammed the course during summer.

DeGrassi grabbed a quick bite to eat at a deli and called Emily from a picnic table at one of the town's parks. It was just after 1.30pm. The autumnal sunshine felt good on his face. He looked around. He was the only one in the park. The leaves on the trees were still green. In another month they would start to turn shades of brilliant red, gold, and brown. Hundreds of tourists descended on the town each weekend to view the fall foliage giving the town's businesses their last fill-up of the year. Once the trees were bare, bitter cold and snow set in and stayed till the spring.

Just before 2pm, DeGrassi parked his SUV across the road from Champion Real Estate and walked into its office. A young receptionist manned the front counter. "Hi. I'm Stu DeGrassi. I have an appointment with Blanche White."

"I'll tell Mrs White you're here," Brittney Goulding said.

DeGrassi took notice of all the plaques hanging on the walls. Number one in sales 2015, 2016, 2017, 2018, 2019, 2022 and 2024. Another was from a local Little League team thanking their sponsor.

"Small town USA," DeGrassi said to himself with a smile. "Where did it go?"

"Excuse me, Mr DeGrassi, Mrs White will see you now," Brittney said.

"Yes, thank you."

Blanche White stood up to meet her visitor and extended her hand.

DeGrassi gently shook the realtor's hand. She was casually dressed and wore her brown hair cut short. He guessed she was in her early 50s.

"Thank you for meeting me Mrs White."

"My pleasure. Please sit down."

DeGrassi took a seat in the comfortable chair across from her desk. He removed his wallet from his jacket pocket and handed her his business card and identification.

"Interesting line of work," Mr DeGrassi.

"It can be. Every day is different."

"I suppose it would be. Now then, what exactly are you looking for?" she asked.

"You mentioned on the phone that you rented a house to a Mr Stemkowski over the summer. He and his guests stayed for a week? Or was it two weeks."

Blanche White opened a folder on her desk. "I prefer using folders instead of putting everything online. My niece Brittney is our IT whiz and handles all our social media."

"Nice girl."

"Mr Stemkowski rented a house on the lake for two weeks," Blanche White said. "Six thousand a week which is the going rate in summer for a house in a prime location."

DeGrassi took out his notepad and a pen. "You don't mind, do you?" he asked pointing to his notepad.

"Not at all."

"Do you have the names of those who stayed in the house with Mr Stemkowski?"

"We vet all of our renters for character etc.," she said avoiding the question. "Mr Stemkowski has been a client of ours for years. We totally trust him. I do know that he had three guests staying with him the second week."

"Is there anybody at the house now?"

"Yes, the owners. "They go to Europe every summer. Renting out their house pays for their trip."

"Smart. I'd do the same if I had a house like that. Mrs White, are you aware of the incident involving the racehorse trainer SB Slocum?"

"Word travels fast in a small town. The whole town knows."

"You wouldn't have any information that the police don't, do you?"

Blanche White leaned back in her chair and closed the folder on her desk.

"What sort of information Mr DeGrassi?"

"Like who was hanging around with his wife on the night he got assaulted?"

"I might."

"Did the police ever ask you about it?"

"Nope. All they know is that Champion Real Estate rented the house to Mr Stemkowski.

"You could save me a lot of time if you have any information on Slocum's assault."

"And why should I give it to you Mr DeGrassi?

"Because it is the decent thing to do. Anything you say goes no further than this room You have my word."

Blanche White picked up a pen on her desk and lightly tapped it on her diary. She motioned for DeGrassi to come closer.

"'I'll tell you under one condition."

"Go on."

"My niece."

"What about her?"

"She wants to do what you do."

"What I do? What I do is spend half my time on the road drinking coffee that tastes like it was brewed in a shoe and the other half trying not to get shot or beaten up."

"Are you through Mr DeGrassi?"

"Yeah."

"You show her the ropes down in Massapequa for a few months ..."

"Hold on. How the heck do you know where I live?"

"Brittney found out. Took her all of five minutes."

"Ahh, beginner's luck."

"Do we have a deal Mr DeGrassi?"

"Sort of."

"Meaning?"

"She can't go out on jobs with me. First of all, she isn't licensed, there are liability issues, and it can be dangerous. If she's interested in a career in law enforcement, I can call in a favour or two and get her into the next class the Long Island Police Academy runs. If she passes the physical, she is in. And I get the names of Stemkowski's housemates. Do we have a deal?"

Mrs White nodded and DeGrassi handed her his notebook.

"Write the names down for me please."

"I'll circle the name of the fellow who broke Mr. Slocum's jaw. I'm not sure if Mrs Slocum slept with any of them."

DeGrassi looked at the name Blanche White circled. Duke Carlisle. *That name sounds familiar.*

"Brittney? Come here love," Blanche White called out. "There is someone I want to introduce you too."

Unlike the old days, DeGrassi never had to leave his desk now to do his detective work. He made some calls and punched the name of Duke Carlisle into the Google machine which spit out more crap than a bear going into hibernation.

What used to take weeks to put together now took just an afternoon and a couple of hours work in the evening. DeGrassi put the SB Yokum puzzle together and wrote a full report on Stemkowski and his three mates, one which made for some very interesting reading, by the fifth inning of the game between the New York Stars and Nashville Notes. Despite their .500 records, both clubs were battling for the last National League wild card spot in the expanded Major League play-offs. Scores were level at two when DeGrassi turned the TV on in the living area. His wife, Gina, was upstairs watching the Real Housewives of Kathmandu.

Gina left a plate of pasta in the fridge which DeGrassi heated up and consumed in the top of the sixth when the Notes took a 4-3 lead on an infield hit with two outs and two runners on.

He fell asleep during the seventh inning stretch and missed a ninth inning Stars rally which tied the game and sent it into extra innings. Nashville won the game in the 12th inning on a bases loaded walk when half of the city and surrounding suburbs were fast asleep.

"If these sons of bitches ever learn how to close out a ballgame, we might actually grab that last wild card spot," Stars' manager Darren Betts told his coaching staff behind closed doors before he faced the media at 12.10am.

"The losses and these long nights are fucking killing me," he said to himself before taking questions.

The Stars fell two games short of making the play-offs in Betts' first year as New York manager, and well after the bats and balls were put away for the winter, Brittney Short graduated from the Long Island Police Academy.

Instead of emailing his report to Yokum's attorney, DeGrassi personally handed his report to RG Gaines less than 36 hours after he completed it.

"It's all there," DeGrassi said as he handed over the folder in the parking lot of a vast shopping centre near Belmont Park.

"I'm sure it is," Gaines said as he tucked it under his shoulder. "The rest of your fee will be transferred to your account by the end of the day."

When he returned to his car, Gaines eyeballed the report.

Holy shit. Duke Carlisle cold-cocked SB? I'd hate to be in his shoes once SB finds out.

Chapter 24

IT'S THE last weekend of September, and the New York Stars are playing their final three games of the season against play-off bound Philadelphia at Stars Field.

If the Stars sweep the three-game series – and they just might since Philly is resting several of its regulars – they will finish over the .500 mark at 82-80, a very respectable finish in Betts's first year at the helm of the club. It's a pass mark considering how far the club has come in 12 months. The media is behind Betts and so are the fans; callers to talk-back shows on WRBI have nothing but praise for the skipper. And with the talent the Stars have in their farm system – specifically Kennedy, Jenkins, Stokes and Cole – it is just a matter of another season or two until the Stars are playing post-season baseball themselves.

Tears of joy nearly ran down the faces of Carlisle, McLain and Betts and the club's supporters a week earlier when scans of Patrick Kennedy's injured knee revealed that the promising Aussie left-hander had torn the posterior cruciate ligament (PCL) and suffered a tear of the meniscus ligament and not a possible career-threatening ACL tear.

A week after the diagnosis, after the swelling in Kennedy's knee had gone down, Kennedy went under the knife at a Manhattan hospital.

"A routine operation," head orthopaedic surgeon Timothy Stevenson told McLain, Carlisle and Kennedy's parents after the two-hour procedure. Kennedy's parents had flown in from Australia within days of their son's injury.

"His ACL is fine. If his rehab goes as well as I think it will, there is no reason why he shouldn't be right to go come spring training in February."

"You're going to be fine son," Bruce Kennedy told his son when he woke from the anaesthesia.

The smile on Patrick Kennedy's face spoke volumes. His dream of making it to the bigs had been derailed but was still very much alive.

Meanwhile Duke Carlisle was struggling, struggling to find some female companionship.

No matter if he was at home or on the road, Carlisle liked to start his day with a brisk walk. A couple of kilometres, maybe more. It all depends on the weather. Even if rain is falling Carlisle goes for a stroll. Shorts, sneakers, Stars cap and a pull-over sweatshirt. If the morning is warm, he leaves the sweatshirt upstairs.

Carlisle could use the treadmill in the hotel gym, but what would be the point he tells anybody who asks. "Yeah, we're in the middle of Queens right next to the airport, but I want to smell the air no matter how polluted it is, not look at myself in a damn full-length mirror in some gym that stinks of sweat, liniment and testosterone."

After his walks, Carlisle relaxed in the hotel lobby with a cup of coffee and had a read of the morning paper, and not just the sports pages. Carlisle glanced at every page starting from the back and working his way to the front. Then he went outside and smoked a couple of cancer sticks. He's down to a pack a day and pretty much stayed away from the sauce all season long. "I feel better, look better. Shit, it's time I meet someone, get laid. It'll do me a world of good."

Finding some female companionship however was difficult. Any woman who worked for the Stars organisation – and there were some major league lovelies in the front office – was strictly off-limits.

His options were to give on-line dating a go or try and meet someone the old-fashioned way: at the supermarket, at church or through friends. Carlisle barely went to a supermarket: all his meals were eaten at the hotel restaurant or at the ballpark. He avoided church religiously. His friends were either married or divorced, or in the case of his brother Clive in Atlanta, diddling the family babysitter.

Carlisle joined a dating website and uploaded a recent photo which was a requirement. In between reading scouting reports and looking at tape of high school and college players from all over the US, he managed to find a few prospects in his age group he was willing to meet. More importantly, they were willing to meet him.

"I hope they don't want autographed baseballs or tickets. Thank goodness the season is nearly over. The only tickets are for next year and they won't go on sale for months.

Carlisle, 53, and his date, a lady named Doris Campbell, was 52, or so she said. They briefly talked on the phone and exchanged several text messages before they agreed to meet for coffee at a café they each occasionally frequented.

"Who the fuck are you?" Carlisle wanted to ask when they laid eyes on each other. Doris looked nothing like her photo. Carlisle guessed she was somewhere between 50 and 100.

The picture Carlisle posted of himself had been taken three weeks ago. The photo Doris posted was likely shot on film and sent off to some out-of-state photo lab to be developed.

He soon found out she was a major-league complainer. She all but put him to sleep within 10 minutes.

They were seated outdoors at a café in one of the few up-scale neighbourhoods in Queens. While Brooklyn had undergone a major transformation, turning it into a desirable place to live while displacing the poor, Queens was still known as the borough of the working class where any one of 100 different languages could be heard within a 10-mile radius.

Carlisle felt his eyes start to glaze over as he listened to the dark-haired woman sitting across from him – a nurse's assistant – meaning she emptied bedpans and colostomy bags day and night – babble on and on about her shitty hours and her even shittier supervisor.

What the fuck am I doing here? he wondered. *Why don't I just get up and walk away. The coffees have been paid for.*

But he sat there out of kindness on the sunny Saturday morning, nodding his head and smiling half-heartedly when necessary. He was able to get a word in only when Doris took a sip of her flat white.

Carlisle had finished his coffee several minutes earlier and was not about to order another. It would only prolong his misery.

Holy shit. Is this what I have to look forward to? Carlisle asked himself while Doris rattled on.

"She wanted me to come in on my day off, so you know what I did?" Doris asked Carlisle. "Do you know what I did?" Doris asked again.

"No, what did you do?" Carlisle calmly asked.

"I told her to fuck off, ha ha ha."

"Interesting."

"What's that supposed to mean? Interesting."

"Well, you work in the health care system. It's to be expected. People get sick and need care.

"That's right, take her side."

"I'm not taking anyone's side," a bewildered Carlisle said.

Carlisle rose to his feet. "I've had enough Doris. I'm going to take off. Good luck to you."

"You can't leave. We just got here."

"I can't? Watch me."

Carlisle raced from the crowded café and sprinted the 100 metres to where he had parked. He backed his SUV from the tight spot, looked both ways and drove off. Within 10 seconds, someone else pulled in. The only thing harder to find in New York than a quality left-hander was a parking spot.

Carlisle pulled over a few kilometres down the road, took his phone from his pocket and deleted the singles website he had installed several weeks ago. "What a fucking nightmare. I'd rather pay for female companionship than go on another one of these dates," he said. "Now to erase her details and block her."

With two swipes of his index finger, it was done.

Returning from one of his morning walks, Carlisle spotted a young dog in the parking lot of his hotel. The black and white mix, likely a border collie, was shaking in the morning cold. Carlisle slowly approached it. It couldn't have been more than a year old. It had no collar and had likely been abandoned. The scared animal barked at Carlisle as he bent down to pet it.

I've got to earn its trust first, he thought. "Don't you move. Stay right here," Carlisle said. "I'll be right back."

Carlisle went to the hotel bar/coffee shop where he was known by name and asked for a bowl and any scraps left over from breakfast.

One of the waiters handed him a bowl and several pieces of bacon. Carlisle filled the bowl with water and went outside to where the dog was sitting.

"Good boy," he said. "You stayed."

Carlisle put the water down in front of the dog and held out a piece of bacon. "C'mon pal. You must be hungry. You'll like this. It's good."

The dog didn't move but didn't bark either. It was still trembling, half due to the cold and half out of fear.

Carlisle moved the piece of bacon closer. The dog sniffed it, then gently took it in its mouth and ate it. "I've got more. Want another piece?"

When the bacon was gone, Carlisle tried to pet the whimpering animal. It let him.

"That's a good boy," Carlisle said. "Now, what are we going to do with you?"

Carlisle took out his phone, opened Google and searched for the nearest SPCA. There was one five miles away.

"Stay here boy, okay? Stay right here. I'll be right back."

Carlisle walked a couple of hundred metres to where his SUV was parked in a secure area for long-term hotel guests.

He slowly drove back to where he had left the pooch and with a half empty bag of potato chips was able to lure the dog to its feet. Carlisle bent down, picked up the dog and deposited it onto an old blanket in the back of his SUV.

"We're going for a little ride mate. To the SPCA, okay? They'll check for a microchip, give you an examination, give you a bath. Sound good?"

As Carlisle drove onto the Van Wyck Expressway, he heard the dog snoring away.

Carlisle carried the dog into the SPCA building and carefully set him down. One of the attendants, a young woman, distracted the dog with a few treats and put a leash on the pooch while Carlisle told her how he had found it not even an hour ago.

Another woman came around from behind a large counter with a hand-held device and checked the dog for a microchip. There wasn't one.

"I guess he's been abandoned. It happens more than you think," the young woman told Carlisle.

"What now?"

"We'll give him a check-up, a bath, take his photo for our website and see if someone wants to adopt him. He's a young dog and if he is healthy, he has a good chance of finding a new home. Would you like to adopt him"? the woman asked.

"Me? I don't think the hotel I'm staying at would approve. He needs a yard to run around in anyways."

Carlisle bent down to say goodbye to the dog. "You need a name mate," he told it as he stroked its face. "That's it. We'll name you Mate. And one day I'll tell you all about my trip to Australia."

The dog licked Carlisle's face.

"Until he finds a new home, would it be okay if I came around every morning and took Mate for a walk? It'll do us both a world of good."

Paula Rodriguez looked at the woman who had checked Mate for a microchip. She nodded.

"Sure," Paula said. "We feed the dogs when we arrive, around seven. We open the doors to the public at nine, so any time after nine would be fine."

"Great. Thank you so much. I'll be in town for another couple of weeks. Can I come by tomorrow and take him for a walk?"

"You sure can," Paula Rodriquez said.

"Some company, good company – finally," Carlisle said as he walked to his SUV.

UNBEKNOWNST TO Carlisle, he had been under surveillance by one of trainer SB Yokum's investigators, a shadowy mug named Dwight Young, who had been dismissed from the NYPD for using excessive force on several men of colour he had arrested several months earlier.

"Nice work," Yokum told Young at his Belmont Park stables one morning as he looked at a couple of photos Young had taken of the unsuspecting Carlisle.

"He's the head scout for the NY Stars and is staying at that fancy hotel next to Stars Field," Young told Yokum. "He's one of the four who entertained your wife and her friends. I'm not sure if Carlisle slept with Laura, but he is most definitely the one who broke your jaw.

Yokum was preparing several of his charges for November's Breeders Cup races at Del Mar Racetrack just outside of San Diego.

"Where'd you shoot these?" Yokum asked, "and who is the pooch?"

"On the beach near LaGuardia. Carlisle walks the mutt there every morning. It's not his. He picks it up and drops it off at the SPCA building right off the Van Wyck."

"He's a fucking dogwalker?"

Yokum howled, nearly doubling over with laughter.

"By the time I am through with him he'll need someone to walk him or at least push his wheelchair. Because of that fucker I was eating meals through a fucking straw for six fucking weeks. Nobody fucks with SB Slocum and gets away with it. Nobody.

Round him up and bring him to me. Rough him up a bit of you have to, but don't hurt him. That's my job. Understand?"

"Bring him back here?" Young asked.

"No. Too many damn cameras around here. Take him to that backyard shed on that property with the for sale sign on it near my house and tie him to a chair. And make sure you blindfold him first."

"Didn't I see that on an episode of *The Sopranos*?"

"Just do what I tell ya, okay?"

"As long as I get the 10 grand when I drop him off."

"You'll get it. SB Yokum never welches on an agreement. Now get the hell out of here."

Several mornings later Carlisle was walking Mate on what passed for a beach near LaGuardia Airport, sidestepping empty cans, bottles, tyres and seaweed when four burly blokes dressed in black emerged from two dark sedans and walked towards Carlisle.

"Uh oh. I don't like the look of this boy."

Carlisle turned around, picked up the pace and starting to run the half mile to where he had left his car.

He didn't get very far.

One bloke grabbed him under his left arm, the other under his right and lifted Carlisle off his feet. There was a foot between the bottom of his sneakers and the sand.

The dog was left chewing on his leash while Yokum's goons hustled Carlisle into one of the two cars. They tossed him into the back seat and sped off.

"Where are you taking me?" he yelled.

"To see our boss. He wants to have a word with you."

"Who's your boss?"

"You'll find out soon enough wise guy. For now, just keep your mouth shut."

Carlisle did as he was told.

Only one person saw what unfolded. Dutch Nussbaum was sitting in seat 16F on a Delta flight from Miami to New York, which was making its final approach to LaGuardia Airport. Planes come in so low that people driving by on the Van Wyck can see the faces of the pilots and co-pilots. How there had never been a crash was a damn miracle. Dutch, a forty something paralegal from Pelham Parkway in The Bronx, was coming home after visiting his elderly mother in a nursing home outside Fort Lauderdale. Rose Nussbaum liked to brag to her friends and the staff which looked after her that her son was a high-profile lawyer for a Manhattan law firm. In reality, he was a paralegal who had failed the New York bar exam the past half-dozen years.

Perhaps if he had studied more and spent less time filming planes taking off and landing with his GoPro and putting the clips on YouTube he would be a lawyer, not a partner, but at least a lawyer not doing the job of a first-year law student. Dutch though was very good at his job; meticulous was what some his colleagues used to describe him. Others, like Benjamin Katz, called him odd.

"A single forty-year-old guy posting clips on YouTube? Really?" Katz said when Nussbaum's name came up. "I don't get it. He's a good-looking guy, smart too. What's the fascination with YouTube? Wouldn't he rather be out chasing women?"

No.

After his fiancée dumped him 10 years earlier, for a friend of his no less, Nussbaum decided that was the last time he was going to let himself be hurt. He retreated into a shell. The likes his videos received on YouTube gave him pleasure and never any pain.

And the likes were in the hundreds of thousands, particularly the videos of take-offs and landing of flights coming into and out of LaGuardia and JFK. There is nothing like the New York skyline and Nussbaum's videos captured it all – from the Statue of Liberty in New York Harbour – to the new Freedom Tower in downtown Manhattan, Central Park and Stars

Field, which was just a long home run from LaGuardia.

On this morning his camera caught the exact moment Duke Carlisle was separated from his buddy Mate, tossed into a car and driven away. So clear was the vision of the GoPro that it captured the licence plates of the two vehicles involved. It wasn't until he got home to his apartment in the Bronx and had a look at the footage on his monitor that he realised what he had filmed.

"Holy Shit. It's a freaking abduction, like something out of *Goodfellas.* They even left the guy's dog there."

By the time Nussbaum called the cops and they had a look at his footage, Carlisle was in rough shape. He'd been slapped around a bit and had bits of dried blood around his nose. Several punches to his midsection caused him to barf up his breakfast on the concrete floor of the metal shed he was being held in and that was before SB Yokum got his mitts on him.

When Yokum walked into the shed several hours later and spotted Carlisle tied to a chair with duct tape over his mouth, his smile was as wide as a hyena's.

"Well look at who we have here," Yokum said.

It was only when Carlisle saw Yokum enter the shed that he put two and two together. "Uh oh. Unless that dog I was walking can talk I am fucked."

BACK AT Stars Field on the last day of the season, Dan McLain was asking if anyone had seen or heard from Duke Carlisle.

"He's not answering his phone, he's not at his hotel. His SUV is not in the lot. It's been three days. It's not like him not to check in or stop by. Even when he was in Melbourne, he emailed us every day. Think it's time we called the police?" McLain asked assistant GM Ryan Maloney.

"I think we should."

Maloney rang the local precinct and was asked by the desk sergeant to come down as quickly as possible.

"Uh oh. The coppers want us down there as soon as we can," Maloney told McLain. "You don't think?"

"No. It's probably routine. Shit, I hope he didn't fall off the wagon. If he did and the press finds out about it will be the lead story on every newscast. And once social media gets a hold of it ..."

Maloney punched Duke Carlisle into his Twitter feed and into Google. Nothing recent came up. "So far so good."

McLain asked Maloney to go down to the precinct and to call him as soon as he found out what was going on. "Don't text me Ryan, call. I'd go down there with you, but I don't want anyone to see the GM of the NY Stars at a police station. And take your own car. We've got to keep this between us and the cops for as long as we can. If it's bad news, we'll get our PR department on it."

When Maloney arrived at the local precinct which served the Flushing area, he was quickly steered into a conference room where he was met by precinct captain Gil Richardson. Two detectives were already seated. One was working on a laptop, the other going through paperwork.

"Take a seat Mr Maloney, please," Richardson said.

"Anyone else know you are here?"

"Just Dan McLain, the Stars GM."

"Good. Let's keep it that way. We are right in the middle of an ongoing operation. We have a pretty good idea where Duke Carlisle is. Detectives from the Nassau County PD are on their way to the scene."

"The scene? A crime scene?"

"Yes. We believe Carlisle is being held at a shed on a property about 10 miles from Belmont Park and that he was forcibly taken there about 36 hours ago."

"Forcibly? What the hell for? What is he mixed up in?"

"We're not 100 percent sure, but the property we're about to raid belongs to racehorse trainer SB Slocum. Carlisle isn't a horseplayer, is he?"

"Not that I know of. He scouts baseball players, not horses. What is going on?"

"Let me ask you something Mr Maloney. Is Carlisle privy to any inside information the Stars have? You know, things that the club would not ordinarily release to the media or Major League Baseball?"

"I guess he knows just about as much as anyone in the front office."

"Does Carlisle have a sports betting account?"

"A betting account? Shit, I hope not. It's illegal for any member of the organisation to bet on baseball. And we dissuade our employees not to bet on any sporting event."

"What about the horses?"

"Well, I guess there wouldn't be anything wrong with Carlisle or any other member of the organisation going to Belmont Park and putting a few dollars down on a nag."

"We're just wondering if Carlisle might have been trading information on the Stars in exchange for a tip or two from the Yokum operation."

"I seriously doubt that Captain. Carlisle is on good coin. He doesn't need the money that a winning bet or two would give him."

Richardson took a moment and then asked the detective with the laptop to show Maloney a copy of the video that Dutch Nussbaum had shot.

Maloney look on in disbelief as Duke Carlisle was tossed into a car and driven off.

"Is that Duke Carlisle?" Richardson asked.

"Holy shit. What the fuck did I just see? When did this happen?"

"Is that Duke Carlisle?"

"It is. He always wears shorts, sneakers and a ballcap when he goes for a walk. When did this happen?" Maloney asked again.

"Apparently yesterday morning, a bit after 9am. A passenger on an incoming flight to LaGuardia, who shoots take-offs and landings for his YouTube channel, happened to film this as his flight from Florida was about to touch down at LaGuardia.

The guy notified us as soon as he found out what he had. As you can see, the quality of the video is exceptional. So good in fact you can see the licence plates of the cars involved. The cars were stolen, but some good old-fashioned police work led us to a shed on a property not too far from Yokum's spread."

There was a knock on the conference room door and a uniformed officer came in and handed a cell phone to Richardson. "You better take this captain," he said before exiting."

Richardson listened and then screamed into the phone. "What do you mean he's not there? Was he there?"

Ten seconds passed, maybe 20.

"So you're pretty sure he was there? In the shed? Have forensics get back to me as soon as they know for sure."

In disgust, Richardson tossed the cell phone onto the conference table. "Fuck," he screamed.

"What? What?" Maloney asked.

Richardson sat down and took a drink from a bottle of water.

"The Nassau County PD is pretty sure Carlisle was at the property. Yokum or someone close to him, like one of those goons of his, must have gotten word that we were coming for them and got the heck out of there."

"Is Carlisle alive?" Maloney asked.

"I'll stake my career on it. Abduction is one thing, but murder? That is a whole different ballgame. We've got fifty men across two departments working on the case non-stop. We'll find Carlisle."

And Mr Maloney, not a word of this to anyone but McLain. If this gets out it could be strike three for Carlisle. Understand?"

"Yes sir."

"Write down your number. If we need anything or find out more, we'll be in touch. Does Carlisle have a family?"

"As far as I know he has a brother in Atlanta and two ex-wives. He was living with a woman before he came to New York, but they split up when he left Atlanta."

"Get me the brother's number. We'll let him know what's going on."

"Where do you think Duke could be?"

"I'm not sure Mr Maloney. But we'll find him."

Captain Richardson pointed to one of the detectives seated at the table. "Show him out will you Bill."

A BRUISED and battered Carlisle was hustled out of the shed near Yokum's home 25 minutes before the Nassau County PD arrived and taken back to Yokum's Belmont Park Stables. He was put in a horse float with two geldings, two mares and two promising fillies who were all going to be spelled at a property outside Lexington, Kentucky.

"Make sure you keep Mr Carlisle gagged and tied up," Yokum told Sid Palmer, the float's driver. "Feed and water him when you have a feed yourself."

"I don't know about this boss," Palmer said. "Who is he?"

"None of your damn business. Just do as I tell you. Deliver him safe and sound and there'll be an extra couple of grand waiting for you when you arrive. Cash."

"Cash?"

"Cash."

A former coal miner, Palmer, 42, had driven floats for Yokum's stables all over the country for the last five years. He put the float in gear and took off. It was a 12-hour drive to the farm outside Lexington. About six hours into the journey, somewhere in Western Pennsylvania, Palmer pulled off at a truck stop for a feed and a bathroom break. The sun was just about to set. It was a perfect night for a drive through picturesque West Virginia. He checked the horses – all was fine with them – and looked in on Carlisle, who was seated on a hay bale. His hands and legs were securely tied and the tape on his mouth was still in place. "I'm going for a feed and to drop a deuce. I'll bring you back a burger and a Coke. And if I'm extra nice I'll let you use the toilet instead of pissing your pants. Don't be going anywhere, like you could."

Palmer laughed and raced to the toilets.

"Shit, if I'm lucky I've got twenty minutes to get the fuck out of here," Carlisle said to himself. Carlisle had not wasted the past six hours. He had continuously been rubbing the rope holding his hands together against a taut chain attached to the side of the horse float. The rope had loosened considerably, and it was just a matter of time till it gave way. Like a 16-year-old kid jerkin' the gherkin, Carlisle rubbed hard and fast. Finally, he felt the rope give way. Palmer had been gone 10 minutes. Carlisle flexed his arms and wrists to get the blood flowing into them and untied the rope around his ankles. It took him a few moments to stand up. His wrists were sore, his ankles were sore, his ribs were hurting from being punched and he was pretty sure his nose had been broken. Carefully he took the tape off his mouth. Whiskers came off with it. He was dying for a drink, anything. He had two choices, drink out of one of the buckets the horses were using or from the water bottle on Palmer's seat. He took the bottle, checked its contents for any splashback, wiped it thoroughly and poured the contents down his mouth all without having his lips touch the bottle.

Dying for a piss, Carlisle looked around and carefully positioned himself into the passenger seat of the float. He slowly opened the door, walked down two stairs, carefully closed the door behind him and sprinted off into a wooded area. He took a massive piss and before Palmer returned to the float ran to the back of the truck stop where several drivers were having a smoke and knocking back a few beers.

"Excuse me fellas, any of you headed east? As you can see. I can desperately use a ride. I don't have any cash on me, but I'll pay any of you handsomely if you get me the hell out of here and quick too."

Four long-haul truckers looked at the sad sap standing in front of them; ripped and dirty clothes, a broken nose, two black eyes and dried blood scattered over his face.

"What the fuck happened to you mister?" one asked between puffs of a cigarette.

"I don't know where to start but if I don't get out of here in the next couple of minutes I am fucked. Can one of you help me?"

The biggest of the four truckers, with arms the size of logs and a belt buckle so big it caught the light of the moon, stared at Carlisle.

"Holy shit," Bert Reddington said. "Aren't you Carlisle? The baseball scout?"

Carlisle nodded.

"I thought that was you." He stuck his hand out.

"Bert Reddington, Charleston, West Virginia. You signed me when you was with the Braves. I only made it to A ball, but the Braves gave me a $10,000 signing bonus. What the fuck happened to you Duke?"

Carlisle looked around for Palmer, who would be noticing about now that he was short a passenger. "I'll fill you in if you get me the fuck out of here now. And I mean now."

"Follow me," Reddington said.

The former first baseman for Eastern Hancock High School quickly walked to his rig. Carlisle followed. Reddington opened the passenger side door, hoisted Carlisle into the cab and closed the door. Two minutes later they were safely on interstate 86 headed east.

"What are you hauling?" Carlisle asked.

"A bit of everything. Mainly farming and livestock supplies."

"How far you headed"?

"Upstate New York."

"That'll do just fine. You wouldn't have anything to eat or drink would you? I've got a heck of a story to tell, but it is best told on a full stomach."

Redding pointed a small fridge behind him. "There's water, apples and a couple of sandwiches in it. Take whatever you need."

"Thanks Bert. You say the Braves gave you a $10,000 bonus? I'll give you another $10,000 if you get me to New York in one piece."

After filling Reddington in, Carlisle asked if he could use his cell phone as they approached Pittsburgh where there was much better coverage than the country areas they had riding through.

Carlisle tried to remember McLain's number.

"Shit, who memorises numbers anymore, you press the name of who you want to call, and the phone does the rest. Think Duke, think." He tried but could not remember so he simply rang the Stars office. He followed the voice prompts and was put through to McLain's office. Despite the late hour, well after 10pm, McClain picked up the phone.

"Duke? Is it really you? You're alive. Thank Christ. Half of the police force in Queens and Long Island is looking for you. Where the hell are you?"

"I'm a bit knocked around, but I'm okay. Really. I'm in the cab of a long-haul trucker just outside of Pittsburgh and headed for Albany. I'll be there in six hours."

"A truck? Pittsburgh? Albany? What the fuck happened Duke?"

Carlisle told McLain just what he had told Reddington; that it was SB Yokum, who took him. That he had busted his jaw in Saratoga six weeks earlier and that Yokum wanted to get even."

"Holy crap. Did you fuck his wife, Duke?"

"Nope, never had the chance. I was simply defending myself that morning in Saratoga."

"As long as you are safe Duke, that's all that matters. We've all been worried sick about you. I'll have Maloney meet you in Albany, okay? He'll take you back home."

"Thanks Dan. Hey, have Maloney go to my hotel suite and bring me some clothes; pants, shoes, shirt, jacket, undies, socks – the works. I've been in the same damn shorts and tee shirt for two days."

"Done mate. Listen Duke, I'll ring the cops to tell them that you are safe. They'll be wanting to talk to you ASAP, so be prepared. The fuckers who did this to you will get what's coming to them."

Back at the truck stop, Sid Palmer nearly choked on his cheeseburger when he saw that Carlisle had escaped.

"Fuck," he screamed. "Yokum will have me gelded once he finds out. Think Sid, think."

I can either get back in the float and drive it to Lexington or do a runner.

Having a soft spot for the welfare of the horses he was transporting, Palmer climbed back aboard the float and drove it to Lexington. He got to his destination well before sunrise. He turned off the float's lights, steered it to the front gate, turned off the engine and left the truck and its million-dollar plus cargo sitting alongside the white fences of *Triple Crown Farms.*

Making sure he was not spotted, and aided by the light of his cell phone, Palmer jogged the four miles to the centre of town to the Greyhound bus station he had passed on the way in.

He checked the departure board, Chicago, Milwaukee, Detroit, Memphis, San Antonio, Charleston, Pittsburgh, New York.

"Fuck. I can't go back to New York. Yokum will find me in less time than it takes to run the Kentucky Derby."

He decided to let fate decide. He'd board the next departing bus no matter where it was headed. Twenty minutes later, at 5.50 am, a bus pulled in. Omaha, Nebraska was its destination. Palmer hopped aboard, paid the driver for a ticket, and slumped into one of the many empty seats at the rear of the bus. He was asleep before the bus reached the interstate.

THERE WERE more trucks than cars headed east on Interstate 80 in the wee hours of the morning as Bert Reddington's five-year-old rig made its way across rural Pennsylvania. He was used to long overnight road trips as a minor league ballplayer. Driving alone, or in this case with Carlisle, was a heck of a lot better than being crammed onto an aging bus with 24 other players and half a dozen coaches sharing the one bathroom at the rear of the bus. "If anyone drops a deuce back there, so help me God, you'll be benched for the next week," manager Randy Okerland bellowed at the start of every journey. Not once did Okerland have to scratch someone from the line-up.

Reddington preferred driving after sunset and before sunrise before every arsehole on the planet got out of bed and started clogging up the roadways. They never signalled, drove too slow or too fast, tailgated and took unnecessary risks – especially in the rain and snow – all to get to a job they would leave in two seconds if something better popped up. Come 5pm, it started all over again, just in the other direction, the exodus out of the cities to the suburbs, the workers back to their wives or husbands, and kids and pets.

"I'll tell you one thing," Reddington said to his mates back at the truck stop before Carlisle appeared out of nowhere. "Women are much better drivers than men; present company excluded. Men turn into freaking NASCAR drivers when they put that key in the ignition. Every day is Sunday at Daytona."

Reddington was making excellent time as he made his way towards Albany, New York and his rendezvous with NY Stars assistant GM Ryan Maloney. Duke Carlisle was asleep in the passenger seat of Reddington's rig, a jacket of Reddington's draped over him.

The capitol of New York State was located about three hours north of New York City. The Adirondack Mountains and a bunch of small cities, towns and farming communities dotted the countryside clear up to the US/Canadian border, some five hours north of Albany. Reddington was going as far as Lake Placid which hosted the Winter Olympics in 1980, the games which became known for "The Miracle on Ice", when a bunch of US college kids defeated the mighty Soviet Union before going on to win the gold medal in ice hockey.

Reddington gave Carlisle a nudge as he reached the outskirts of Albany.

"Hey Duke, we're nearly there."

Carlisle stirred and adjusted his eyes to the streaks of daylight coming into the cabin.

"How long have I been asleep?"

"More than four hours."

"Shit, really?"

"Yup. That fellow from the Stars is meeting you at the Hilton in town, right?"

"Who? Oh yeah, yeah. Maloney, the assistant GM. I can't wait to take a shower, toss these clothes in the garbage, have a decent breakfast and a smoke. Write down your details when we stop, and I'll get that 10 grand to you in the next 48 hours. You're a lifesaver, Bert. A damn lifesaver. Lord knows what would have happened to me if I hadn't gotten the fuck out of that truck."

There was plenty of space in the Hilton's parking lot for Reddington to safely pull into. Just a few room lights of the four-storey building were on; those with early flights out of town or aides of state politicians, who used their generous per-diem payments to rent hotel rooms when the state assembly was in session. The 24-hour news cycle meant that aides were on call 24 hours a day, seven days a week. The morning news shows were on the TV, while phones and laptops were engaged with Twitter and Facebook.

"What a shit show," veteran print journalist Eugene Harden said to anyone who walked past his small cubby-hole like workstation in the press room at the capitol building.

"I have to file stories three times a fucking day, three fucking times. I'm handing in shit that happened in my dreams and the damn editors don't even know the difference. All they ever tell me is to keep up with the news cycle, to keep the crap coming so they can get it online. I hate the fucking internet, fucking hate it. And my doctor wonders why I smoke and drink."

Maloney was leaning against his Lexus which was parked under a bright streetlight in the hotel's parking lot when Reddington pulled in.

He briskly walked to the rig with a NY Stars jacket in one hand and a ball cap in the other.

"Duke," he hollered when he spotted the Stars head scout.

"Holy shit, Duke. What the fuck happened to you? You look like shit."

"It's nice to see you too Ryan. Did you bring my stuff?"

"It's in the car mate. And I booked a room so you can take a hot shower and get cleaned up."

"Cheers."

Carlisle introduced Maloney and Reddington. The two briefly shook hands. Reddington was nearly twice the size of the pencil pusher.

"Thanks for looking after him. The NY Stars organisation is grateful. Anytime you want to go to a game next year, give me a ring and we'll set you up. A tour of the clubhouse, the best seats in the house. Shit, you can even take batting practice if you want.

Is it true? Duke signed you out of high school?"

"Yup. The Braves gave me $10,000. Never made it past A ball, but I had a blast."

Reddington gave Carlisle a pat on the back, hopped back into his rig and took off. After his deliveries were made, he headed to a nearby truck stop where he had a late breakfast/early lunch and got a few hours of sleep on a rather comfortable cot set up behind the driver's seat of his rig. He was due at a massive distribution centre outside Albany at 4pm where a well-choreographed bunch of forklift drivers went to work, filling his truck with pallets and pallets full of goods bound for stores in the Charleston area. Reddington would be back home 12 hours later, get a text with information on where he was headed next and start the process all over again. As long as the price of petrol stayed stable and there were no major repair bills, he was able to make a decent living.

Maloney waited in the hotel lobby while Carlisle showered, cleaned up and got changed. He scanned his Twitter feed and then flipped through the Albany Times Union and a couple of the NY tabloids. There was not a single word on Carlisle's abduction.

"Thank goodness everybody kept their mouths shut," Maloney said. "We'll have plenty of time to respond if and when the cops make an arrest and charge someone."

Dan McLain spoke to Police Captain Gil Richardson as soon as he got off the phone with Carlisle the night before.

"He's just a bit beat up, but he sounded okay. Yeah, I'll have him come and see you the day after tomorrow, make a formal statement and all."

"Will he file a complaint? I'm not sure to tell you the truth. Duke may want to put all of this behind him. We'll talk to our legal team here and see how they want to proceed."

"Yes, 10am Friday morning. He'll be there."

CARLISLE FELT better after a long shower – the warm water helped ease the pain around both sides of his ribcage – but he still looked like a fighter who had gotten into the ring one time too many.

"I'm going to need a doctor to look at this nose," he said as he examined himself in the bathroom mirror. "The black eyes will heal by themselves although I'll need to wear a pair of sunnies for a couple of weeks. Fuck Duke, you are getting too old for this sort of shit, too damn old."

Carlisle donned what Maloney had grabbed from his hotel closet – button-downed shirt, chinos, and boat shoes – and ordered breakfast from room service. A stack of pancakes covered in strawberries, toast, water, and coffee. *Bloody delicious and in Albany of all places, go figure.* Dessert was a couple of ciggies which he smoked on the balcony. *Good of Maloney to bring these,* he thought.

Carlisle took the elevator down to the lobby and tried not to look at himself in the full-length mirror. He spotted Maloney sitting on one of several sofas when it hit him.

The dog. What happened to the dog? And my bloody SUV. I've been gone for over two days. A car left unattended in New York won't last for two hours, and it's been out there for two days.

"You're looking better Duke, much better," Maloney said as Carlisle walked towards him. "Feel alright? And put these on," Maloney said as he handed him a pair of sunnies.

"I'm okay Ryan. Listen, the dog I was walking when those thugs took me, do you know what happened to him? Is he okay?"

"I don't know. I didn't ask."

"Shit. I'll call the SPCA from the car. Maybe someone found him and turned him in."

"And my car?"

"McLain mentioned that the police had it towed from the beach. Evidence they said. And the police found your phone on the beach."

"At least I'll get those back. But the damn dog. Fuck, I'll never forgive myself if something happened to him."

Unbeknownst to Carlisle or Maloney, police who raced to the beach near LaGuardia after seeing Nussbaum's video found Mate asleep against one of the tires of Carlisle's Ford Explorer. They took him to the same SPCA Carlisle signed him out of each morning.

"He's safe? Thank Christ," Carlisle said when he rang the SPCA as he and Maloney started the long drive back to the city. His joy turned to sadness a moment later. "He was adopted? So soon? How is that possible?"

Paula Rodriquez explained what happened. "He was brought back to us that same day. He was a little dehydrated and hungry but otherwise was fine. Yesterday afternoon, just before we closed, a family came by and adopted him right on the spot.

"I'm sorry. I can't give you the family's details. But I can tell you Mate will be going to a loving home out on the Island with a nice yard for him to run around in."

"As long as he has a good home, I guess that's the most important thing," Carlisle said as he put down Maloney's phone.

"Sorry Duke."

"Yeah."

Carlisle didn't say much for the next hour or so as they sped down Route 87. Traffic started building as they approached Kingston, New Paltz and Newburgh. What was once farmland barely 20 years ago was now housing estates. As they approached the Tappan Zee Bridge, an hour or so north of New York City which spanned the Hudson River, traffic started to build, slowed to a crawl, and then stopped.

"I don't know how our fans from out here drive to the ballpark and then back," Maloney said. "And we have plenty of fans from this area. It's going to take another two hours to get to the ballpark and your hotel so sit back and have a snooze if you need one."

Carlisle did just that. He slept for the next two hours and was nudged awake when Maloney stopped in front of Carlisle's hotel.

"I wish the bar had something to make me forget the last 48 hours," Carlisle said as he got out of the passenger seat and stretched his legs. Before he closed the door, he asked Maloney to check and see if his car and phone had been returned.

"And ask the team doctor to come to my room and look at this nose of mine. It's throbbing. Thanks for coming to get me and for the sunnies. I appreciate it Ryan, I really do."

"You're welcome, Duke. Get some rest. Dan and I will come by later. We'll grab some dinner."

Team doctor Ralph Suarez made a rare house call to Carlisle's suite later that afternoon.

Dr Suarez was well liked within the organisation. He helped several players overcome their drug and alcohol addictions, knew the top specialists in the city and never once asked for autographs for his kids or for extra game tickets.

After a thorough examination, including a tweaking of Carlisle's nose, Dr Suarez told Carlisle that nothing was broken. His ribs were bruised, and his eye sockets were intact.

"Take some Tylenol for the pain and in 10 days, when the swelling in your nose has gone down, I'd like you to see an ear, nose and throat man to check for any cartilage damage. Just to be on the safe side."

During dinner at the hotel bar/restaurant – steaks all around – Carlisle was told about his appointment with the Flushing PD the next morning.

"Aww, prairie shit. Might as well get it all over with as soon as possible, eh?"

McLain and Maloney nodded.

"Ryan will take you down there and bring you back," McLain added. "I've spoken to our legal team and it's best that you have someone with you while you are being interviewed."

"It's not that asshole Cal Brenley, is it? He never shuts up. Yack, yack, yack."

"No mate. Alfred Newberry will be there with you."

"Good. He wouldn't have a thing to say at his own execution."

Carlisle went back to his suite that night and tried to watch the first game of the National League divisional series between Pittsburgh and Philadelphia. He was asleep before 11pm, just as the seventh inning began. The game finally ended at 12.26am.

"Is anyone watching these games?" Carlisle asked the next morning as he watched the highlights on YouTube over breakfast. "Start the damn games at 7.10 just like we do during the regular season. Fuck that TV money. Baseball games starting at 8.20 and ending after midnight is bullshit."

Carlisle had cooled down by the time he was introduced to Captain Gil Richardson at the Flushing precinct. Carlisle and Newberry were ushered into a conference room where they were joined by two detectives. Richardson introduced them so quickly that Carlisle could not even remember their names. Newberry though, was on the case, listening to every word and scribbling away on a yellow legal pad.

"The Nassau County Police have made two arrests and can connect the thugs to SB Yokum. They are two career criminals with records longer than a Louisville Slugger. The question," Richardson asked, "is do you want to press charges against Yokum?"

Carlisle looked at Newberry for guidance, but all Newbery did was raise an eyebrow. "I'm not sure. If I press charges and Yokum is brought in, charged, and arrested, the press will have a field day with it. To tell you the truth captain. I don't want to be trending on Twitter."

Richardson leaned back in his chair; a bit disheartened. He absolutely hated to see anyone walk.

"I have a suggestion," Newberry said.

"Let's hear it."

"Bring Yokum in for questioning," Newberry said as he took off his reading glasses. "That will scare the crap out of him. Racing stewards are one thing, but to be brought in by the NYPD is serious business. Grill the bastard and later tell him that Carlisle has decided not to press charges but that the NYPD and Nassau County PD will be watching his every move. One slip-up and he's toast."

Newberry turned to Carlisle. "That may square things with you and Yokum, a gentleman's agreement one might call it. What do you think Duke?"

"That could work."

"And you captain? Thoughts?"

"I'm not crazy about the idea, but if it is okay with Carlisle, I'll sign off on it. I still want those two thugs charged and put away. They'll deny even knowing Slocum cause if they ever talk, Yokum himself would dig a hole on the Belmont backstretch and bury the two at the half-mile pole."

The two detectives sitting next to Richardson each closed their notepads and put down their pens.

Newberry continued. "One of our guys knows Yokum's attorney – RG Gaines. We'll set up a meeting after you question Yokum. Agree to sweep everything under the rug. Just scare the shit out of him, first."

Yokum was furious when told he'd have to turn himself in for questioning. But, he had no choice. Either he went in quietly or he would be taken into custody at his stables or at home in front of a flood of TV cameras and reporters.

The next morning, in the same conference room, Richardson got straight to the point and got right in Yokum's face.

"How the fuck do I know why those two brought that fellow – what's his name? Carlisle? – to that shed. I don't know who those guys are," Yokum said.

Richardson slid a couple of photos across the table to Yokum and Gaines.

"You don't know these men?" Richardson asked.

"Never seen them before."

"You didn't assault Duke Carlisle in that shed? Break his nose, blacken his eyes and put him on a float bound for a farm in Kentucky."

"Are you making this stuff up as you go along?" Yokum asked Richardson.

Gaines stuck his left arm out and told Yokum to stay seated and be quiet.

"I'll ask you again Mr Yokum. Did you assault or order the assault on Mr Carlisle?" Richardson said in a much stronger voice.

"I never saw the bloke, never laid a hand on anyone. You're questioning the wrong guy. Who knows what this fucker is involved in?"

"That's enough Mr Yokum," Richardson yelled.

Gaines leaned in and whispered in Yokum's ear. "You better pipe down SB. These guys are not fucking around. They have enough to indict you and remand you as well."

For the first time in his colourful life, Yokum turned whiter than a picket fence. "Fix this RG, fix it," he pleaded.

"My client has nothing else to add," Gaines told Richardson.

"He might once he is charged and booked. Take him downstairs detectives and have Mr Yokum fingerprinted and held until he is brought before a judge."

As Yokum was led away in handcuffs, he broke down and cried like a baby.

"Sit down Mr Gaines. We're not finished here," Richardson told the dapper attorney.

Richardson told Gaines about the meeting which was being organised between himself and the NY Stars legal team first thing the next morning.

"A gentleman's agreement Mr Newbury? And what is in this agreement?" Gaines asked just after 9am in Newbury's office on the 36th floor of a midtown Manhattan skyscraper which had a great view of the city.

"Mr Carlisle won't be pressing charges, but he retains the right to do so if any threats or action is taken against him. Furthermore, Mr Yokum or anyone associated with Mr Yokum, is not to contract Mr Carlisle in any form, whether it be by phone, mail, email, text or through any social media platform.

Is that understood?"

"Yes, it is. And Mr Yokum will be released today without any charges being filed against him?"

"As soon as you sign this document."

Newberry tossed Gaines two copies of the agreement he had already signed and dated.

"I'd like to read it first if you don't mind."

"Take all the time you need Mr Gaines. I'm sure Mr Yokum won't mind being in a cell in Flushing for another hour or two. Would you like a coffee? a pastry?

"Sure, you have missed out on several hundred billable hours if Mr Yokum went to trial but look at the bright side Mr Gaines. You can brag that the agreement was your idea. Just abide by its terms. Do we have a deal?"

"Yes."

Gaines reached for a pen in his jacket pocket, signed his name under Newberry's and tossed his copy of the signed document in his briefcase.

He looked at his Cartier watch as he left Newberry's office. It was 9.40. "If traffic is light, I can get SB out of that cell well before noon. But when is traffic in this damn city ever light?"

WHEN THE photos of Republican senator Carl Tucker frolicking in his hotel room with Mosquito Lakes College sophomores Sophie Hall and Erica Cosgrove hit the internet and every major newspaper in the US, Billy Jenkins could hardly believe what he was seeing and reading.

Erica Cosgrove was the girl he had lost his virginity to, the girl he had laid in bed with watching YouTube clips, the girl he had brought to dinner at the home of his host family, the girl he dreamed about in those crappy motels the team stayed in when it was on the road.

And there she was, pictured half naked with the senior senator from Kansas, the front runner for his party's nomination for president on the front page of the *Mosquito Lakes Daily News*. He could not believe it.

Elrod Stokes, who had been keeping company with Sophie Hall, merely shrugged his shoulders when Jenkins asked why he wasn't upset.

"It's not like we were planning on getting married. We were just hooking up, that's all. I guess things were a bit more serious between you and Erica. I'm sorry Billy, I really am. Don't let it get you down man. There's still plenty of baseball left to be played and we've got jobs to do."

Stokes took the newspaper from Billy's hand and stuffed it in a large bin in the Mozzies' clubhouse.

"Stay focused Billy. We've got a ballgame in two hours. We need your head in the game bro. We can't have you go 0-for-4 and booting balls in the infield. C'mon. We'll take some extra batting practice and get your mind back on baseball."

A few days before Erica and Sophie got kicked off the Mosquito Lakes College volleyball and softball teams and were suspended for the rest of the term, Billy caught up with Erica at the ballpark and told her they were through. He could have done it with a text like some of his friends back home did when they broke things off with someone, but he wanted to see her, to see if she really cared for him or was just as Stokesy said, "someone to hook up with."

"I need to concentrate on my career Erica. I can't be worrying about where you are or who you might be with."

"I'm sorry Billy, I really am. It was all Sophie's idea."

There was a bit of remorse, but not much.

"It doesn't matter whose idea it was. You went there to sleep with some guy whose old enough to be your dad. And for what? You've been suspended from school. Your sporting career is all but over. And you lost me too. Best of luck to you Erica. I've got a ball game to play tonight."

He gave her a half hug and quickly walked into the clubhouse to get dressed.

"Stokesy is right. We've got jobs to do."

The summer heat and humidity in Mosquito Lakes, Florida reached its peak in mid-July. After an even mix of day and night games in April, May and the first week of June, most Gulf Coast League games from then on were played at night to avoid the sauna-like conditions around the sunshine state.

First-year professionals Billy Jenkins and Elrod Stokes, two of the New York's Stars organisation's most exciting prospects, had all but run out of petrol by July 4.

Being from Texas, outfielder Stokes was more used to the sapping heat, but he too was dragging by the time the Gulf Coast League regular season ended a week later.

Being a Melbournian, Jenkins was used to playing in the cold, rain, and heat – often during the same day – but those conditions took a back seat to Florida's heat, humidity, almost daily thunderstorms, hurricane warnings and mosquitoes.

By finishing second in their division, the Mozzies qualified for the Gulf Coast League semi-finals.

They met Bradenton in a best-of-five series but ran out of pitching by the fifth and deciding game which was played in Bradenton on Florida's west coast. Stokes and Jenkins rose to the occasion and were outstanding throughout the series. However, Bradenton scored five runs in the last three innings of Game 5 to claim the series and a berth in the championship series against Daytona.

"I'm proud of you boys," Mozzies' manager Gene Short told his players in the visiting clubhouse after the final out. "You gave it your best which is all any manager can ask for. Many of you have had a long year and deserve a break. When we get back home, coach (Joe) Keneally and I will speak to each of you individually and give you your assignments for next season. Some of you will go on to play A Ball, and shoot, a handful of you may even jump up a grade. Some sadly will be released, and for a few of you, there is Class A advanced ball to close out the year."

"Got anything left?" Stokes whispered to Jenkins.

"I don't know mate."

"The bus leaves in 45 minutes," Short continued. "We'll stop off at that 24-hour McDonald's in town to have a feed. And the organisation is picking up the bill tonight so order whatever you want."

A few cheers went up. The clubhouse quickly quieted down when Short said the team bus would arrive back home around 4am.

If they wanted to keep playing ball the rest of the summer and fall, Jenkins and Stokes figured two options would be put to them; stay put and play for New York's Class A advanced team in Mosquito Lakes – one rung below AA – or play for the organisation's Arizona Fall League side.

"You think the Arizona Fall League might be a stretch for us Stokesy? It's for the top prospects in the minor leagues, right? Guys a year or two older than us, or more. I'm not sure if I'm ready for that. Are you? We've only played 70 games as professionals. We might be overmatched."

Stokes was as nervous as Jenkins had even seen him. Seated in front of his locker in the Mozzies' clubhouse, Stokes kept tossing a baseball into his mitt as he and Billy waited for their end-of-season reviews. They'd had just 48 hours to think about their future.

"Look, they might tell us to shut ourselves down the rest of the year and come back refreshed for spring training. But if we're given an option I'd rather stay here and play for the advanced team."

"I agree. We're settled here. I don't want to pick up and move to Arizona. We'll be moving anyways come the spring. I want to go home and see my family and mates, maybe play a few games with my old team – if the Stars let me."

A moment later, Short's voice pierced the quiet of the clubhouse.

"You're up next Stokes."

Stokes put his glove down and slowly walked into Short's office. Once inside, Short shut the door, walked to his ancient desk, and plunked his butt into an oversized patched-up office chair. Keneally was seated next to the Mozzie skipper, a clipboard on one knee and an iPad balanced on the other.

"You had a hell of a year Elrod. Batted .320, knocked in a shitload of runs, played well in the outfield. Coach K and I would like to see you line up for the Class A advanced side here in Mosquito Lakes. That's our recommendation. Fifty games are left in the season. You won't play every day, but it will give you a taste of the game at a higher level. No matter how you do, you'll go home to Texas when the season ends in late September and come back here in February for spring training."

It was a big decision for a still 18-year-old to make. Stokes glanced at Keneally who touched the bill of his cap, a sign which told him to accept the offer.

"Can I talk it over with my dad, let you know tomorrow?" Stokes asked.

"Of course, son," Short said rising out of his chair and extending his hand. "It's been a pleasure coaching you."

Short shuffled a few papers around on his desk. "Tell Jenkins to come on in here, will you?"

"You're up Billy," Stokes said when he reached their lockers.

"And?" Billy asked.

"Class A advanced."

Billy Jenkins smiled, and like the clean-up hitter he was, approached Short's office the same way he approached the plate from the on-deck circle: full of confidence.

"Close the door Billy and take a seat please," Short said as he made himself comfortable. He took a sip from a coffee mug, carefully placed it down on his desk and read from a sheet of paper.

"Three thirty-six. Three thirty-six," Short said with a smile. "Led the team in runs batted in and struck out only 11 times. Eleven. Remarkable Billy, just remarkable."

Short picked up another sheet of paper. "And just four errors, four – as a shortstop. Son, you are every bit as good as Duke Carlisle said you were, and more."

"Thank you, coach. Scooter Samuelson taught me so much during spring training, and of course you and coach K."

Short and Keneally each chuckled.

"We'd like you to play for our Class A advanced side here in Mosquito Lakes," Short said. "Fifty games are left in the season. You won't play every day, but it will give you a taste of the game at a higher level. It's the same offer we just gave Stokes. You and he are tight. Talk it over with him, give your family in Melbourne a call, see what they say. The advanced season ends the last week in September. Then you go home and come back here in February for spring training. Sound alright?"

"Yes coach. I'll talk to Stokesy and my folks and let you know."

"Good on you Billy," Short said as he got up to shake Billy's hand. "That is what you say, isn't it? Good on you?"

"It is."

Short smiled. "Send the next bloke in."

"You think he knows he'll be playing AA ball next season?" Short asked Keneally after Jenkins left.

"I reckon he does mate; I reckon he does."

Stokes and Jenkins exchanged high fives when Billy returned to their lockers with a massive smile on his face.

"Class A advanced. Fifty games. But not every day. Then home and back for spring training."

"That's just what they told me," Stokes said.

"Whose up next?" Jenkins asked.

"Donaldson the Unfuckable."

"Donaldson the what?"

"The unfuckable. I'll tell you about it over lunch. Your shout Billy."

After several phone calls to Melbourne and Texas, Billy Jenkins and Elrod Stokes joined the Class A advanced Mosquitoes just in time for a series with the visiting Palm Beach Fronds. Their seven-day break from baseball was just the freshen up each needed.

Neither played on the Friday night but the next afternoon Jenkins and Stokes were both in the line-up. It was common for Mozzies' manager Hugh Atherton to rest players after a night game to give everyone on the roster playing time. Jenkins and Stokes each singled in four at-bats in their Class A Advanced League debut and Jenkins easily handled the few chances he had at shortstop. Leftfielder Stokes did not have one ball hit to him in the 5-3 loss to the Fronds.

"All anyone does here is swing for the fences. They either homer or strikeout. It's crazy," Stokes told Jenkins in the Mozzies clubhouse as they took off their gear. For the record, neither struck out.

"That's not going to get them to the show. They need to go the opposite way, put the ball in play, move runners over, lay down a bunt for a change."

"Could not agree more Stokesy. I don't get it; it makes no sense. Don't the guys in the front office want a complete player when they're called up?"

WITH THE Stars failing to make the post-season play-offs the bats, balls and team equipment were put away for the winter in New York. Meanwhile, Duke Carlisle was mulling over the idea of heading south for the winter.

"I could work out of an office here at the stadium, or even out of my hotel suite, but I reckon it will be good for me to get out of New York for a while," Carlisle told Stars GM Dan McClain one particularly cold morning. "Let all this crap with Yokum settle down. He won't have any horses running at Gulfstream for another couple of months, so there's no chance of running into him or his goons."

"Good idea Duke, good idea. You can watch game tapes and go over scouting reports from anywhere. I'd like you to watch all the tape we have of Jenkins and that kids Stokes that our media department put together from the Class A advanced season.

"Short, Keneally and even Atherton – he's a hard marker for sure – could not have been any more pleased with Jenkins' progress, but I'd like to get your take on the kid. And take a good look at Stokes too. He and Jenkins are tight. It sure would be nice to see both make the jump to AA ball next year.

"Are you driving down or flying?"

"I think I'll drive, it's less stressful. I'll check out of the hotel; no sense spending $5000 a month if I am not there. I'll stop in Atlanta, visit my brother, see what he's up to. And map out some sort of schedule for the winter and spring."

"Are there any more prospects down under? Anyone with half the talent of Jenkins?"

"Not that I have heard. But if I hear something I'll let you know. I wouldn't mind going back there. But for now, I'll set up camp in Florida."

Hundreds of thousands of cars and trucks travel up and down Interstate 95 every day, from Maine to Florida – nearly every one of them going over the speed limit – and who gets pulled over somewhere in south New Jersey? – just before the turn-off to Atlantic City?

Yup, Duke Carlisle.

When Carlisle saw the flashing lights of a New Jersey State trooper in his rear-view mirror he immediately pulled over, turned the engine off and took out his licence and registration.

Carlisle watched in his side mirror as the trooper walked to the driver's side of his car.

"Is this your vehicle sir?" the youngish-looking trooper asked in a calm and measured voice.

"It is. Here is my licence and registration."

The trooper took off his dark sunnies, tucked them into his shirt pocket and glanced at the paperwork. He looked at the front licence plate and saw that it matched Carlisle's registration.

"Where you headed?" he asked, noticing the suitcases and boxes in the car.

"Florida, a working vacation."

"Uh huh," the trooper said as he adjusted his wide-brimmed hat. "I'll be back in a second. Just going to run your licence and registration. Stay put."

Where the fuck am I going to go? Carlisle thought.

One only had to read a local paper or watch the local news to know that New Jersey state troopers had been routinely pulling over Black and Hispanic drivers based on suspicion for years.

Close to half of those stopped were taken in under some trumped-up charge and released the same day.

Those who could not raise the cash bail became guests of the New Jersey Correctional Department. But why stop Carlisle? He was as white as an Englishman. End-of-the-month quotas? Perhaps.

No matter where I go, no matter what I do, trouble seems to find me Carlisle thought as he waited while the trooper punched his details into a small computer mounted on the patrol car's dashboard. Carlisle occasionally glanced into his rear-view mirror as the seconds and minutes ticked by. Cars and trucks whizzed past, most going well over the 105kph speed limit.

"Why not them? Why me?" Carlisle asked.

Finally, the trooper opened the door to his vehicle, put his sunnies back on and like a pumped-up linebacker walking back to the huddle after making a tackle, returned to Carlisle's Ford Explorer.

"Everything seems to be in order sir. Enjoy the rest of your trip."

The trooper got back into his car, carefully removed his hat and like a Formula 1 driver leaving the pits, screeched his tyres and merged back into southbound traffic.

"Jesus. Maybe I should have flown," Carlisle said as he turned the key and resumed his journey south, cutting through sections of Pennsylvania, Delaware, Maryland, and Washington DC.

Even with the unplanned stop in south Jersey, Carlisle had made excellent time on the crisp and cool, yet sunny autumn morning. He drove past the nation's capital, a place he had visited numerous times over the years, and steered his Ford Explorer into Arlington, Virginia. It was time for a piss, feed, and petrol, in that order.

Deciding to stay on Interstate 95, Carlisle's culinary choices were all the fast-food variety. Pick a chain, any chain. Every single one was represented. Burgers, pizza, tacos, chicken – all deep fried – even the pizza. Nearly every one of the fast-food outlets were tucked inside massive service stations with parking for hundreds of vehicles. Forgoing the fast-food option, Carlisle bought a pre-made chicken sandwich, an apple and a diet coke at the convenience store where one paid for petrol and found an empty table in the large dining area. The seats were unoccupied, but its previous occupants had left the remains of their meals on the table even though there were trash cans in every direction one looked.

"We've become a nation of fucking slobs," he said.

Just as Carlisle was about to clear the mess himself, a large bloke came by and scooped all the trash off the table and into a bin he was carting around. He gave the table a wipe with a damp cloth and moved on to the next garbage-covered table where he did the exact same thing.

"The poor bastard is probably on minimum wage; $7.25 an hour, a fucking disgrace."

It took Carlisle a few moments to pry his sandwich from its plastic tomb. Before he took a bite, he checked the package's label for an expiration date – three days from today. He gave the chicken, lettuce and mayo sandwich a sniff and bit into the soft roll. *That's not too bad, not too bad at all. I wouldn't want to eat this every day, but it will do.*

After polishing off the sandwich, Carlisle cleaned off the apple the best he could with a clean napkin and took a bite. It was surprisingly crunchy and juicy and replaced the taste of chicken in his mouth. He tossed his trash into a bin and his empty can of coke into a separate bin for recyclables. "Is that really that hard to do?" he asked.

Carlisle walked back to his car, steered it to one of the bowsers and went inside to pay. To avoid theft, one pays first in the US before pumping it.

A bunch of slobs and a bunch of thieves, Carlisle thought as he waited to pay. *What has happened to this country?*

"Pump 7. Sixty dollars please."

He handed over his credit card to one of two women behind a thick piece of plexiglass which for all he knew was bullet-proof. She gave him a receipt and set pump seven for $60. If it took less than $60, Carlisle would have to march back inside with his receipt for his change.

As the pump hit the $60-dollar mark, it stopped. Carlisle put the hose back, screwed his gas cap on tightly, dipped a squeegee into a pail full of soapy water by the pump, cleaned his front and back windows and put it back where he got it from. He turned the key and manoeuvred his way back onto Interstate 95, determined to get through Virginia and part of North Carolina before stopping for the night.

Cloudy skies and cooler weather greeted Carlisle the next morning as he wound his way through North Carolina. Halfway through South Carolina, he exited Interstate 95, picked up Interstate 20 and drove west towards Columbia, South Carolina's largest city, where he pulled in for a quick lunch, enjoyed a smoke and topped up his petrol tank.

While paying for his petrol, prior to pumping it of course, the attendant asked Carlisle where he was headed.

"Atlanta", Carlisle replied.

"You better look at another route, because a massive accident has shut down the highway in both directions."

"How bad?"

"A tractor jackknifed we was told. Full of chemicals, fire departments from all over the place are at the scene."

"Geez, thanks for the tip."

Carlisle got back on the road and instead of heading south, plotted a path northwest towards the city of Greenville.

"I've got plenty of time. Why not spend a couple of days in the mountains? Get a cabin somewhere, enjoy the peace and quiet. Clay loved going up there when we were kids, especially to Clayton, which he always thought was named after him."

Traffic thinned out as he drove through western South Carolina. There wasn't much to listen to on the radio – no sports talk or news shows. Right-wing talk shows filled the airwaves at night pitching their outlandish conspiracy theories when time was cheaper to buy, and listeners had a couple of beers in them.

By nightfall Carlisle figured he would be hunkered down with the essentials: smokes, coffee, groceries, and magnificent scenery. The scouting reports could wait. He had weeks to go through them all and figured internet reception in the mountains would be patchy at best. A good excuse to go for a few walks, toss a line in one of the mountain lakes and generally relax.

He stopped in Greenville where there was good phone reception and gave Clayton a ring. It went straight to his brother's voicemail. "Mate. I've decided to spend a few days relaxing in the mountains before coming to Decatur. I'll see you at the end of the week."

CARLISLE KEPT the radio on, tuned to a country station. Down south three out of every five stations played country music.

Carlisle hadn't seen Clay in over a year and wondered how he was doing. Clay and his wife Tracey had parted company a few months back. Clayton was five years younger; three years shy of birthday number 50.

"I should have called him, at least texted him. I was on the road, but I could have been a better brother to him. Shit, he must feel awful, only seeing his boys on weekends."

The country music took Carlisle back to all those years he spent in Atlanta working for the Braves.

Good times. I wonder what Cynthia is doing, Carlisle thought. Cynthia being Cindy Bartkowski, the feisty realtor he kept company with for a couple of years before he left Atlanta and moved to New York. He hadn't heard from her in well over six months. *Should I give her a ring? Send her a text, telling her I'm in town for a couple of days? Better not. She moved on and so did I.*

"Why am I listening to this shit?" Carlisle yelled. "Look at what's it's doing to me. Pining over an old girlfriend, getting all teary-eyed."

He shut the radio and drove in silence with the passenger side window open. Clean, fresh, cool mountain air filled the Ford Explorer's cabin.

The Georgia/South Carolina border was not more than 10 miles away when the first snow flurry kissed the Explorer's windscreen. Then another and another. The snow started getting heavier and was already sticking to the fields alongside the highway.

"Snow? At this time of year? No way, it's much too early for snow."

He checked the outside temperature on his dashboard. Thirty-three degrees Fahrenheit, then the dashboard clock – 4.02pm.

Ten minutes later snow started sticking to the highway. The small town of Valhalla, the last town before the state line was less than five miles away, Clayton another 20 miles west.

Carlisle slowed down, his headlights on and his wipers furiously working to keep his windscreen clear. While he and a few others had enough sense to slow down, others sped past.

"Are you all out of your fucking minds?" Carlisle screamed.

They did not get very far. Carlisle saw the wall of brake lights ahead of him, put his hazard lights on, slowed to a crawl and pulled over to the side of the road, well out of harm's way.

The highway had become a skating rink. He later learned that scores of cars and trucks had crashed into each other causing a massive pile-up. The highway was shut in both directions.

Carlisle figured he had two choices; stay with the car or walk to a motel. He checked his phone – the battery was at 85 percent, and he had one bar of coverage.

He checked Google for the nearest motel and found one less than two miles away.

He rang it.

"Do you have a room for tonight? You do? I'll take it. How much? $200. I'll take it anyways. Make it two nights just in case this mess isn't cleared by tomorrow."

He locked his car and left a note on the inside of the windshield with his cell phone number. "Please don't tow. Call me. I'm at the motel just up the road."

Carlisle took stock of what he had; a couple of bottles of water, three apples, a thermos half-full of lukewarm coffee and one pack of cigarettes.

"Don't I have a Stars sweatshirt in here somewhere? I'll freeze my ass off before I even get to that motel."

He dug it out from a box in the back seat, put it on and with his carry-on bag on his shoulder and ankle deep in ice and snow, started walking west, sticking to the side of the highway.

He wasn't the only one on the move. Several others were walking in the same direction looking for shelter. Several ambulances and fire trucks – all fitted with snow chains – weaved in and out of cars littering the roadway trying to get as close to the accident site as they could.

Covered in snow, Carlisle and the other walkers crossed a large hill and then spotted the glowing signs of a service station, a KFC and the motel.

Well at least I can get some coffee, maybe a loaf of bread and if need be, some chicken.

Carlisle briskly walked to the motel, stomped the snow and mud off his shoes at the office entrance and walked in.

"Hi, I have a reservation. The name is Carlisle."

"Yes, yes. Here it is. I hope you do not mind sharing"

Carlisle recognised the voice. It was the same fellow he had spoken to.

"Huh?"

"Sharing. A nice couple got stuck in the storm just like you did. I couldn't tell them no and leave people to sit in their cars and freeze. You got to double up."

"With strangers?"

"That's right."

"And let me guess, you are still going to charge me $200 a night?"

"No sir. Two hundred and fifty dollars."

"Hold on a second mate. Two hundred and fifty dollars to share a room with people I do not even know?"

"You want the room or not? You see all those people out there? They'll pay $300. You're getting a bargain."

"Yeah, I'll take it. For two nights. And who am I sharing a room with?"

The thirty-something-year-old clerk looked at several cards on the counter, picked one up and slowly read from it.

"Mr and Mrs Steven Cummings of Norman, Oklahoma. They're headed to Florida and got caught in the storm just like you did.

"How old are they if I can ask?"

"I'd say in their late 70s, early 80s."

"Two Queen beds?"

"Yes, but from what I overheard they do not sleep in the same bed anymore."

"Well tonight and tomorrow they will. I'm not sleeping on a damn army cot.

"We've got cots, $50 a night if you need one."

"What kind of a racket are you running here for fuck's sake?"

"I'm just trying to make a buck, give the kids a nice Christmas. Maybe this year even get a tree if it keeps on coming down."

Holy shit, Carlisle thought. *What fucking planet have I landed on?*

Carlisle filled in a guest card, paid the $500 bill and in return was given a room key.

"Four doors down on your right sir. Enjoy your stay," the clerk said. "Next in line please."

Carlisle knocked on the door of room 112 before gradually opening it. The room's lights were on as was the TV. Mr and Mrs Cummings were seated at the end of the bed closest to the TV, glued to some sort of game show. The split system heater/AC was cranked up so high he thought he was in Miami.

"Excuse me folks, it looks like I am your roommate tonight," Carlisle said.

Gladys Cumming got up and introduced herself while her husband Stephen, looked up, nodded and re-focused his attention on two singing hillbilly types dressed in overalls who were effectively proving that America, in fact, did not have any talent whatsoever.

Gladys and Carlisle shook hands and made small talk about the storm, where they were each headed and how many nights they had booked.

"Is that your car parked in front?" Carlisle asked.

"Yes," Gladys Cumming said. "We heard about the storm on the radio and decided to get off the road. Isn't that right Stephen?"

"Big storm," Stephen Cumming muttered.

"You'll have to excuse my husband. I can't tear him away from the TV when his favourite shows are on. Maybe the power will go out and we'll be spared," Gladys joked.

For the first time that day Carlisle laughed.

"I better charge my phone then and see about getting something to eat at the service station."

Carlisle put his bag on the empty bed, found his phone charger, plugged it in and sat down, marking it as his.

Fuck that guy and his $50 army cot. This will do just fine, he thought.

"Can I get you guys anything from KFC or the service station?" Carlisle asked.

"We've already eaten dear. Stephen loves his KFC."

Carlisle looked around the room for any empty boxes or bags or buckets or whatever the fuck they packed that excuse for chicken in. He didn't spot a thing.

Thank Christ. They must have eaten it there.

"Do you guys want a cup of coffee or anything? My treat."

"Would you like a coffee, Stephen? Mr Carlisle is going out."

"No thank you," Stephen Cumming said without taking his eyes off the TV.

"Be back shortly," Carlisle said.

He opened the door and left it open a bit longer than usual to let some cool air into the room. The snow was coming down thicker than ticker tape. People were still lined up outside the motel office hoping to get a room for the night or to share one. He carefully watched his footing on the snowy and icy walkway leading to the service station. KFC was chockers.

"Would you look at all those porkers? Would it kill them to miss a meal?"

Carlisle entered the service station's convenience store, took one of two remaining loaves of bread off a shelf and stuffed it under his arm like an NFL running back carrying a football. He dodged several people blocking his path, grabbed a packet of pre-packaged ham, a bottle of mustard, a small bag of chips, two cans of Diet Coke and waited in a long line to pay.

"Can I have a cup of coffee please? Light, one sugar, and a pack of cigarettes. Any brand will do as long as it has tobacco," he told the attendant, a chunky sized woman with a pleasant enough smile.

She rang him up, put his stuff in a plastic bag and retrieved the cup of coffee.

"That's 64.50," she said.

"I beg your pardon."

"Sixty-four, fifty. Will that be cash or card?" she asked.

"Are you and the guy running the motel working in cahoots? That's a lot of money."

"If you don't want this stuff someone else will gladly take it off your hands."

Carlisle peeked over his shoulder at the growing line behind him. *They'll eat the furnishings once the food is gone*, he thought.

"I'll pay by card," he said, fishing his wallet out of his back pocket. "You and the motel guy should be wearing ski masks. This is highway robbery, literally highway robbery."

"Would you like your receipt sir?"

"Yes, I do. I'll frame this," Carlisle said waiving his receipt in the air.

With a bag of groceries in one hand and the cup of coffee in the other, Carlisle tried to trace his footsteps back to the motel room, but they were gone, covered in another inch of snow. "This is unfucking believable. And now back to my roommates. Haven't I suffered enough Lord?"

Apparently not.

He reached for the room key and watched it fall into the frozen slush at his feet. Balancing the coffee in one hand, he grabbed the key, wiped it off on his sweatshirt and opened the motel room door. The TV was on but with no sound. The only other light in the room came from the dim lamp on the table beside his bed.

Gladys and Stephen Cumming were in bed. Stephen Cumming was fast asleep under the covers, snoring as loud as a freight train. Gladys was sitting upright watching two bozos on TV making a soufflé.

Carlisle has been gone for twenty minutes at the most, maybe twenty-five.

"Hello dear. Stephen likes to turn in early."

Carlisle looked at his watch. It was five minutes to six. IN THE EVENING.

"Is your husband a farmer or does he have a paper route in the morning?" Carlisle asked.

Gladys Cumming chuckled. "He used to work on the railroad and worked all kinds of hours," she said in a whisper. "Some nights he stays up till about 8, but no later than that. He was very tired from driving and all. He'll sleep for a good 10 hours."

"Don't mind me. I'll be over here, having a couple of sandwiches. I'll try not to stay up too late."

Carlisle poured the large cup of coffee into his thermos, made two ham sandwiches with plenty of mustard and sat down to dinner.

This is the kind of crap minor leaguers eat – sandwiches, chips, and soda. What is happening to me? I'm 52 years old, sharing a motel room with Whistler's Mother and her husband, there's a foot of snow on the ground and two weeks ago I was tied up in a horse float. I've got to start making some changes.

With dinner eaten it was time for dessert, a cigarette. Carlisle went outside, lit up and watched the snow tumble down.

How much longer can it keep snowing? he wondered. *Looks pretty though.*

His phone fully charged and back inside, Carlisle checked the latest weather forecast and Twitter, in that order. Eighteen inches of snow were expected in the mountains and surrounding areas overnight, tapering off to flurries by daybreak.

If the eastbound roads are cleared by noon, maybe I can turn around and get the heck out of here. That's what I'll do. In any case, I'll walk to the car and see if it is still where I left it.

Carlisle quietly walked to the bathroom with his toiletries. He waited until he got inside before turning on the light. Scattered about were tubes and tubs of moisturiser, face cream, skin cream, whipped cream, and ice cream. Plus, make-up, tweezers, a small pair of scissors, hair products, toothbrushes, toothpaste and dental floss.

Moist towels hung on the railing near the sink.

Did they even leave me a hand towel, or did they use those too?

On the back of the door hanging from a hook were two white hand towels. Carlisle sniffed them both and decided they were clean. He brushed his teeth, washed his face, and looked at himself in the large mirror hanging over the sink.

I've aged 10 years in the last month.

He gathered his toiletries, turned off the bathroom light and walked back to his bed as quietly as possible.

In his absence, Gladys Cumming had turned off the TV and laid down next to her husband. Stephen Cumming was snoring away. Carlisle couldn't tell if Gladys was awake, asleep, or somewhere in between.

Carlisle turned down the thermostat on the heater, took off his pants, shoes and shirt and crawled under the covers. He checked his watch. It was 8pm. He checked his phone for any messages or emails. None.

First pitch of Game 6 of the National League Championship Series between Los Angeles and Philadelphia was still twenty minutes away.

I'll check the score in the morning.

Carlisle turned off the lamp on his nightstand and tried to get comfortable. He couldn't remember the last time he had gone to bed this early. The parking lot's lights bled through the room's thin curtains, so it wasn't pitch black.

After an hour or so of tossing and turning Carlisle finally fell asleep. He was having the most delightful dream; a woman was playfully kissing his neck and rubbing his shoulders. Only this was no dream.

Seventy-four-year-old Gladys Cumming had gotten out of the bed she shared with her husband and crawled into Carlisle's.

"What the fuck is going on?" Carlisle said. His voice was muffled by Gladys's hand. "What are you doing?"

"Calm down Mr Carlisle. Everything is fine."

"Fine my ass."

Carlisle sat up in bed and quietly asked Gladys Cumming what she was doing.

Dressed in an oversized nightgown, Gladys, a grandmother of four, told Carlisle she was lonely and felt unwanted.

She looked over at the bed next to them where Mr Cummings was snoring away.

"Stephen hasn't touched me in years. We usually sleep in separate beds, but tonight considering the circumstances ..."

"Please Gladys, get back in bed with your husband. If he wakes up and sees us like this who knows what he'll do."

"Trust me Mr Carlisle, he won't be up for hours. He doesn't even get up during the night to pee.

"Don't you find me attractive?" she asked, lowering her nightgown to reveal her saggy breasts.

Carlisle pulled her nightgown back up.

"You're a very attractive woman, Gladys, you really are," Carlisle said.

She's a lot better looking than many 54-year-old women, but this is fucking crazy, he thought. *I can't do this. What if the old man wakes up? Then what? This is like some episode of the Twilight Zone.*

"Well, if I'm so attractive, then why don't you want me?"

How am I going to get out of this? Think Duke, think.

Duke Carlisle tried his best to come up with an answer, any answer, which was nearly impossible while Gladys Cumming was rubbing his pecker.

Play dead boy, play dead, Carlisle pleaded. It was no use. The appendage was very much alive.

Carlisle looked at Mr Cumming and then his wife, who was cuddled up beside him. He made a note of where his things were just in case, he had to make a run for it.

"C'mon Mr Carlisle, lay down next to me. You won't regret it."

So, with 81-year-old Stephen Cumming snoring away less than 10 feet from them, Carlisle gave Mrs Cumming what she wanted; twice.

Once he got over the fact that she was 74 years old, Carlisle had to admit that it was all very satisfying. They cuddled for a while before Gladys suggested she get back into bed with her husband.

"Just in case Stephen wakes up."

Gladys Cumming gave Carlisle a kiss on his cheek, winked and returned to her husband's side.

By the time Carlisle got up the next morning, Gladys and Stephen Cumming were gone. He pulled back the curtains. The sun was shining and off in the distance he could hear traffic.

"Thank goodness. I can get out of here."

Carlisle poured the coffee from his thermos into a small kettle which sat on the same table as the TV and waited for it to heat up. Looking around the room he noticed a folded piece of paper on top of his bag and opened it.

Gladys is one heck of a fuck, isn't she?

Stephen.

"The son of a bitch was up the whole time?"

Carlisle put his shoes on, took his coffee outside, lit up a smoke and laughed.

Chapter 33

AFTER A quick shower – he used the two hand towels to dry himself off – Carlisle gathered his things and walked back to the front desk to return the room key.

He asked the same clerk from the night before if he could have a refund for the second night which he would not be needing.

The clerk pointed to a chipped and worn-out sign hanging on the wall behind him. "No Refunds," it said.

"How about you make an exception my friend? You already made a small fortune off me and the couple I had to spend the night with."

Instead of responding, the clerk picked up a pen and shuffled some papers and cards sitting on the counter in front of him.

"C'mon mate, stop ignoring me. Do the right thing. I'm a working man just like you, on the road hustling to make a buck. Two hundred and fifty dollars is a lot of money."

"It is company policy," the clerk said, once again pointing to the no refunds sign.

"Is it also company policy to price gouge customers during an emergency? One phone call to the state consumer affairs department might be all they need to fine you or shut you down. You can kiss that Christmas tree and those gifts for your kids goodbye."

The clerk looked Carlisle square in the eye.

"I'm serious mate. I get that refund – in cash, now – or I start dialling.

Realising Carlisle meant business, the clerk lowered his head, opened the cash draw, and handed over $250.

"That wasn't so hard, was it mate?"

Carlisle stuffed the wad of bills in his pocket, picked up his bag and started the long trek back to where he left his car.

"Please be there, please be there," he said as he got closer to the rows of vehicles parked on the side of the highway. It took a while to find his SUV since they were all buried under a foot and a half of melting snow.

"Yes", Carlisle yelled when he found his Ford Explorer. He opened the passenger side door, threw his bag into the back seat, and wiped all the snow off the SUV with his thermos and bare hands.

He wiped his wet hands on his pants, got in the car and started it up. "Now," he said, "how the heck do I get out of here?"

Several vehicles had already left so Carlisle slowly followed their tracks. His tyres had trouble gripping the snow and grass, but he eventually made it back onto the highway.

"That's one divot I am not replacing."

With no cars headed westbound due to the pile-up the previous afternoon, which was still being cleared, Carlisle made a U-turn and headed east.

"So much for a few relaxing days in the mountains. Next stop: Decatur."

Carlisle pulled over to send his brother a text message.

"Got caught up in that snowstorm up north. Back on the road. I'll be at your place this afternoon."

At Greenville, Carlisle exited Interstate 385, followed the signs to Interstate 185 and headed south to Atlanta, some 150 miles away.

With plenty of time on his hands, Carlisle drove leisurely and thought about the last 24 hours; the snowstorm, sharing that motel room, sleeping with the older bird with her husband 10 feet away, the hassle of getting his refund.

"Somebody should make a movie out of this. But who in their right mind would believe it?" he asked.

About halfway to Decatur, Carlisle spotted a sign for a joint called Smitty's Family Restaurant and decided it was time for an early lunch since coffee had been the extent of his breakfast.

"It's a family place, in a small town, what could possibly go wrong?"

He parked his trusty Ford Explorer close enough to the restaurant so he could keep an eye on it, yet far away from the other cars in the lot, which were mostly pickup trucks.

"That's how you know you're in the deep south, pickup trucks outnumber SUVs."

Several had mini confederate flags mounted on the doors and Trump stickers on their bumpers. Every pickup had a gun rack.

This would not be a place to talk politics.

Carlisle took off his sunnies and walked into Smitty's, a nice enough place which he guessed would be full by noon, 40 minutes from now.

A waitress gave him a menu and directed him to a booth.

"Just you hun?"

"Just me. Still serving breakfast?"

"Depends on what you would like."

Carlisle scanned the menu. "Either French toast or pancakes will do, and some coffee please."

"We always make plenty of each, I'm sure we can fix you a nice plate."

"Thank you. I appreciate that."

Carlisle checked his emails, Twitter, and CNN to see what was making news. *Those three letters would not be welcome in a town like this.*

Ten minutes after his coffee arrived, the waitress set a large plate of French toast and pancakes in front of Carlisle and a tin of maple syrup.

"Enjoy hun. If you need anything else, let me know."

"Thank you, I shall."

Carlisle washed everything down with another cup of coffee and a glass of water, left a $10 note as a tip, made a visit to the gents, and paid his check at the front counter.

"Was everything to your liking?" the cashier asked.

"Yes, it was. I enjoyed every bit of it."

"That's what we like to hear."

Carlisle placed the change from his twenty – two singles and 53 cents in coins – in a Red Cross tin on the counter, said good day and walked back into the sunshine with his belly full.

He lit up a smoke and leaned against his truck, soaking up the sunshine on what was now a beautiful, if cool, afternoon.

He was 90 minutes from Decatur. He thought about making a side trip to Athens, Georgia, the home of the University of Georgia and one of the prettiest college campuses in the country but decided against it.

"It's been an uneventful day. Let's keep it that way."

Carlisle turned the Explorer's key, checked the gas gauge – it was half full – backed out of Smitty's parking lot and got back on Interstate 85.

"Next stop, Decatur."

Daylight saving time would not be ending for another month, so there was still plenty of daylight left when Carlisle arrived at his brother's house in the well-to-do suburb some 20 miles east of Atlanta.

He parked his Explorer next to Clay's Ford Ranger pickup truck in the driveway of the modest house he was renting. Tracey and their two boys, Dan, 16, and Ed,14, lived in the family home about 10 miles away.

Clay came out to meet his older brother. They exchanged a warm hug, patted each other on the back, backed off and looked at each other.

Clay was about 10 pounds thinner, Duke about 10 pounds heavier.

Carlisle patted his expanding girth. "Too many meals on the road brother. And you?"

"Not enough home-cooked meals. Tracey sure knows how to cook."

Carlisle took an overnight bag from his SUV, locked it, and followed Clay inside.

"Nice place," Carlisle said as he looked around the ranch-style home. "You buy all this?"

"Nah, it came fully furnished. I signed a two-year lease on the spot. Seventeen hundred a month. I doubt there is anything cheaper in Decatur. And it is in good nick too. I haven't had to do a bit of work on it.

"The building business has been good so I'm able to keep my head above water – for now. Tracey got the house. That's all she wanted. I give her a couple of hundred a month for the boys and we're square."

"Any chance of you too getting back together?"

"I reckon there's a better chance of that ballclub of yours in New York winning the World Series."

Carlisle laughed, but he could tell his brother was still hurting. Seventeen years of marriage down the drain due to what they both said were irreconcilable differences.

"Let me show you to your room Duke. You even have your own bathroom."

"You're spoiling me little brother. Next thing you'll tell me is we're having steaks, baked potatoes and a few cold ones for dinner."

"Spot on. Cooked to perfection on the barbeque. Still another couple of hours till I fire it up. That okay with you?"

"Sure is. Oh, I picked up a home-made cherry pie from that bakery outside of town. Let me get it out of the bloody car."

Over dinner Duke filled Clay in on his trip to Australia but didn't say a word about his run-in with SB Yokum. Duke's black eyes had healed relative quickly and his nose had been given the all-clear by an ear, nose, and throat man before he left New York.

Duke talked about the previous day's snowstorm and how he had to walk in the snow to a motel. He left out the bit about sharing a room with Mr and Mrs Cumming of Norman, Oklahoma.

The two watched about half of the seventh and deciding game of the American League Championship Series between Boston and Kansas City before calling it a night.

"I've got a job on the other side of town Duke, so I'll make some coffee and breakfast and be out of here by 6.30. Take whatever you need and shut the door behind you when you leave. Was great to see you again. Take care of yourself."

"You too little brother. Give my regards to Tracey and the boys. Maybe we can catch up over Thanksgiving or Christmas."

"We should."

The brothers smiled, wished each other good night, and retreated to their bedrooms. Clay set the alarm on his iPhone for 5.45am. Duke set his for 7am, just in case he overslept.

CARLISLE WAS up just before 7am. He showered, packed his bag, finished off the eggs Clay had cooked, had some toast, and topped up his thermos with what was left of the coffee. He cut what was left of the cherry pie in half, wrapped his half in aluminium foil and returned the rest of the pie to the fridge.

Before leaving Duke checked the Atlanta area forecast and the radar on his iPhone. Overcast with a 50 percent chance of rain and a top of 45 degrees Fahrenheit. Any rain was to the west and north. He was headed southeast. Not the best day for construction work but a decent enough one for travel.

He collected his things, being careful not to forget his thermos and slice of cherry pie, made sure the front door was locked and closed it behind him. It was just before 8am. There'd be some traffic, but nothing like what he had to endure in New York.

Due to road works, lower speed limits and detours, it took Duke Carlisle nearly four hours to reach the city of Macon – two hours longer than usual.

It was 12 noon, but the sky was so dark most drivers had their head-lights on.

Then it started – seemingly out of nowhere. A heavy shower. Rain, rain, and more rain. So heavy that cars and even truckers were pulling over to the side of the road waiting for it to let-up. The road was gradually turning into a pond. Thinking quickly, Carlisle got back on the road before it became impassable. With his wipers working overtime, he got off at the next exit, drove to higher ground and waited until the storm passed.

"First the snow, now rain? What's next? Locusts? What in the wide, wide world of sports is going on here?"

Carlisle checked the radar on his phone; the rain was moving west to east. He was headed south.

Finally, the rain tapered off and stopped. Carlisle got back on Interstate 75 and followed the long conga line of cars and trucks inching forward. Eventually traffic started to flow smoothly, and pedals got pushed to the floorboards in a bid to make up for lost time. Without a clock to punch or a deadline to make, Carlisle took his time, driving more like an old timer than the head scout for the New York Stars.

The southeast Florida coastal town of Mosquito Lakes and its minor league baseball complex, the winter home of the New York Stars, was an eight-hour drive away.

Carlisle's goal was to make it to Valdosta right on the Georgia/Florida border by late afternoon. As he continued his drive south, gazing at road signs for the small towns of southern Georgia just a few miles off Interstate 75, Carlisle suddenly wondered why he was even going to Florida.

"I could have stayed at Clay's, kept him company, watched the Series with him."

A loud trucker's horn suddenly snapped him out of his stupor. He looked in his rear-view mirror and saw a trucker right on his arse.

"What the fuck? Back off mate."

The loud horn pierced Carlisle's eardrums again, and then for a third time. Carlisle looked at his dashboard and saw that he was only travelling 40 miles an hour. The speed limit was 60.

"No wonder he's pissed off."

Carlisle raised his right hand; said he was sorry and sped up. He opened the driver's side window to get some fresh air.

"Why am I going to Florida? Cause the Stars are paying me $500,000 a year to watch ballgames, that's fucking why. You know how many guys would kill to have a job like mine? So, let's get our shit together and focus, okay? Focus."

He did.

"I'll stay at the hotel at the minor league complex, set myself up in an office, watch all that game tape, go over scouting reports, make some calls, check on some prospects. I'll have a good two months to myself before the snowbirds arrive and start clogging up the roads, shops, and restaurants.

"I wonder if there is anyone worth looking at in Australia. Shit, I'd like to go down there again. Sydney must have its share of good players and Major League Baseball has an academy set up on the Gold Coast, wherever the hell that is."

NEITHER SNOW, nor sleet, nor rain, nor traffic, nor roadworks nor several enterprising individuals could stop Duke Carlisle from reaching his destination, Mosquito Lakes, on Florida's east coast and the home of the New York Stars minor league operation.

It was a set-up that few major league clubs could match, but it hadn't brought the parent club a championship in more than 20 years. The Stars' billionaire owners had made it abundantly clear to the club's top management that they wanted a pennant, any pennant, flying next to old glory on the flagpole in centerfield of Stars Field within three years. The Stars were more than competitive in their first year under skipper Darren Betts. Reaching the play-offs was the goal of season two of the Betts/McClain regime.

Around the organisation Billy Jenkins, Elrod Stokes and Patrick Kennedy were called Carlisle's kids. Those three signings along with number one draft pick Chris Cole and rapist turned born again Christian Logan Kenworthy were being counted on to bring a championship to New York. But first, they had to reach the big leagues.

Carlisle checked into the upscale hotel adjacent to the complex on a late autumn afternoon and unpacked his things for a planned two-month stay. The suite he requested set him back $4,500 a month and included laundry and daily maid service.

The next morning, coffee in one hand and briefcase in another, Carlisle was led to a well-appointed office at the ballpark by a Stars official. From his spot atop the 10,000-seat grandstand, Carlisle had a perfect view of the main playing field. Groundskeepers kept it in pristine condition even during the off-season. The Atlantic Ocean was several miles behind the right field fence and when the wind was blowing in, the sea breeze made summers bearable.

"All those tapes and paperwork I requested back in New York. Have they arrived?" Carlisle asked the fellow who showed him to his office and who held down the fort in Mosquito Lakes during the winter.

"Came in yesterday. I'll have someone bring them straight over."

I'm sorry, I didn't catch your name," Carlisle said.

"Kline, Jerry Kline."

"With a name like that you have got to be a native New Yorker?"

"Bronx bred."

"How are you enjoying living down here?"

"It's not too bad for a fellow my age, there's plenty to do but when those damn mosquitoes start biting in summer, look out. No one is safe, and I mean no one."

"Well Kline, it looks like I have picked a good time of year then."

"You'll be with us for a couple of months before getting back on the road?"

"That's the plan Kline. But I've found things don't always go according to plan."

"Whatever I can do to help, just let me know."

"Do these windows open up or am I going to have to go outside for a smoke?"

"They do; however, club policy forbids smoking in any of our offices."

"Shit. Rules are made to be broken, eh Kline?"

"Not this one. Sorry."

"Geez, when I started in this caper we used to smoke in the dugout, chew tobacco."

"It's all sunflower seeds now Mr Carlisle."

"Cut out the Mr Carlisle bullshit and we'll get along fine Kline. And get me some of those seeds. I might as well give them a try. These damn cigarettes will cost me a lung if I don't start cutting back."

Kline laughed.

"The hotel restaurant is where most of us wind up having lunch. Feel free to join us. About 12.30."

"How many are working here this time of year?"

"About 20-25. A mixture of front office personnel from our minor league clubs and the ground staff."

"Any fillies?"

"Only at Gulfstream Park. Some of us head down there on the occasional Saturday. It's a 90-minute drive but a good day out."

I'll check the entries first, make sure Yokum hasn't set up shop down here. That's one fucker I do not want to run into again, Carlisle thought.

"I'll leave you to it then Duke. There's a fridge behind you stocked with water and soft drinks. Ring me if you need anything. All our numbers are by the phone as is the internet password. I'll say this about Mosquito Lakes, it has outstanding internet service. It never goes down."

Carlisle glanced at the phone on the right-hand side of the desk where he had set his briefcase down. A printer sat on a table to the right. A large flatscreen TV adorned the wall behind him.

"All right, I reckon this will do just fine. Thanks Kline. I'll get set up and maybe you can introduce me to everyone over lunch."

EXCEPT FOR a break for the Thanksgiving holiday, which Carlisle spent at his brother Clayton's house in Decatur watching football and eating turkey, Duke worked six days a week. He looked at game tape and scouting reports until his eyelids shut.

The more he saw of Jenkins and Stokes, the more he was sure the two were going to make it to the big leagues. Jenkins had put on 20 pounds of muscle since he had seen him in Australia, always made contact at the plate, and never showboated. He ran hard all the time no matter if his side was 10 runs up or 10 runs behind. His defence was impeccable.

"If he doesn't win a Gold Glove award in his first five years in the league or a batting title, I'd be shocked."

Leftfielder Stokes did not have the same natural ability that Jenkins had but was a fine ballplayer in his own right and like Jenkins played hard all the time. He had a knack for driving in runs and had a superb throwing arm which kept many sure doubles to singles.

As expected, cocky number one draft pick Chris Cole came as advertised.

"Is there anything this kid can't do?" Carlisle asked as he watched hours of tape. "Even when he moved up to AA ball, nothing fazed him. He's like a young DiMaggio. He hits, he covers more ground in centerfield than anyone I've seen in years and the fans and press love him to bits. A year of AAA ball and he'll be ready for New York."

As for Logan Kenworthy, Carlisle could not believe the northern Californian's transformation. He turned from a kid you wanted to beat the crap out of into a model citizen in just over a year. Carlisle read all the clippings on Kenworthy he could find, including several on how he had turned his life around by finding God.

If Kenworthy had indeed turned his life around by finding God, Carlisle was sure he had found New York's future right-fielder.

"He hits with power from both sides of the plate, runs like an Olympic sprinter and has a better than average throwing arm. All he must do is stay out of trouble, which is a lot to ask of a 21-year-old."

After a few phone calls, Carlisle managed to get a bit closer to the truth. Yes, Kenworthy had become a born again Christian but only after his Class A manager in Columbia, South Carolina, one Zach Anderson, heard that Kenworthy had taken a liking to Anderson's 17-year-old daughter.

Anderson, a champion in the discus and a thrower of the shot put in high school, in addition to being an All-State catcher, told Kenworthy in no uncertain terms that he would toss his ass clear onto Main St if he even looked at his daughter again. And to prove he was serious. Anderson picked up Kenworthy by the seat of his pants during batting practice one afternoon and tossed him on top of the batting cage which stood some nine feet tall.

"Anybody who helps that motherfucker down gets fined $100," Anderson yelled.

Batting practice continued with Kenworthy perched on top of the cage. It was only after batting practice was completed and the cage taken down that Kenworthy's feet again touched the dirt near home plate.

"You get the one warning and that's it. Understood?" Anderson told Kenworthy in his office an hour after the incident. "Fuck you and your signing bonus. If it wasn't for your well-connected father you'd be in jail. And I guarantee you that a jail in South Carolina ain't going to be a picnic like the ones in California. So, you have one choice. You concentrate on baseball and keep that dick of yours well clear of the ladies or we'll release you. That comes from New York. One fuck-up and you are finished. Got it?"

Kenworthy nodded.

"Good, now get the fuck out of my office."

Kenworthy took a seat at his locker and vowed then and there to turn his life around. When asked by a local reporter several weeks later about his change in character, Kenworthy blurted out the first thing that came into his head.

"I found God mate. I'm a born-again Christian."

His teammates burst out laughing when they read the story in the local paper.

"Born-again Christian? Who the heck is he kidding? He ain't never been to church since he's been here," first baseman Charlie Hanneberry said.

"Where did he find God? On top of the batting cage skip threw him on?"

Whether it was God or fear, Kenworthy kept his nose clean and wound up leading the team in hitting and runs batted in. He got promoted to Class AA Binghamton in upstate New York, replacing the promoted Chris Cole. New York also shifted Anderson to Binghamton to keep tabs on Kenworthy.

"If he needs a damn babysitter, I'm not fully sold on him," Carlisle said before he gave his tick of approval. He noted that his approval was based purely on Kenworthy's on-field ability.

The Stars minor league complex was set to shut down over the rapidly approaching Christmas – New Year's holiday which left Carlisle in a bit of a pickle.

He had been in touch with several contacts in Australia who reported that while there were several good ballplayers worth taking a punt on, none were in the class of Billy Jenkins or Patrick Kennedy.

"To be honest Duke, I think you'd be wasting your time coming down here," Simon Taylor of Baseball Australia told him in an early morning phone call. "But, if you want the best holiday of your life, come on down. Air fares are cheap, the beer is cold, and the women are bloody beautiful."

"They are indeed mate, even the one that gave me the clap."

Taylor laughed. "Give me a ring or shoot me an email if you decide to visit. Shit, any town here has got to be better than a place called Mosquito Lakes."

Taylor has a point, a very good one, but a five hour-flight to LA, and another 15 hours to Sydney? I think I am going to pass, Carlisle thought. *But what am I going to do? Clayton is trying to patch things up with his wife and kids so a trip to Decatur is out. I may as well stay here. The weather is perfect this time of year. I'll play some golf, do some fishing, go to the races. It won't be so bad.*

Carlisle's mates in New York – Pete Giacomin, Subway Stemkowski, and Saul Bernstein – all had family commitments they couldn't get out of which left Carlisle on his own.

He paid for another month at the hotel which took him to mid-January. By then it would be time to hit the road, starting in Florida and working his way north in search of the next Jenkins, Stokes or Kennedy.

BILLY JENKINS and a recuperating Patrick Kennedy spent their off seasons back to Melbourne. Jenkins showed up at the Aspendale Aces home ground occasionally, where he was treated like royalty, but was asked by New York GM Dan McLain not to play any competitive games.

"You can take some batting practice and field a few ground balls but nothing more. We don't want an injured Billy Jenkins showing up at spring training," McLain said in a video conference call a few days before Jenkins flew home.

Jenkins gave McLain his word and to his credit stuck to it despite being hounded by several of his former Aces' teammates to suit up.

Kennedy had a much more difficult post-season. He spent several days a week in the gym with a physio and a personal trainer building up his injured knee. It was gruelling work, but it had to be done. He didn't pick up a baseball until the middle of January and even then, just played soft toss in the backyard of the family home in Williamstown with his dad.

Kennedy was given the all-clear to resume light jogging and cycling in late January. His physio and personal trainer were more than happy with his progress which was relayed to McLain in New York.

"Hey Ryan," McLain yelled to assistant GM Ryan Maloney one morning while a light blanket of snow began to cover the Stars Field outfield.

"Figure out the damn time difference in New York and Melbourne this time of year and see if you can get Patrick Kennedy on the line for me. I want to personally invite him to spring training and give he and Jenkins, and their families first-class tickets out here. I'm telling you; those two Aussies are going to take us to the top. What a great story that will be. Just wait and see. And we owe it all to Duke Carlisle. He's a bloody legend mate, a bloody legend."

Down in Mosquito Lakes, a rested and relaxed Duke Carlisle and young Jerry Kline ventured to Gulfstream Park one Saturday afternoon.

It was a perfect winter's day – a chamber of commerce day the Yanks called it. The sky was clear, the temperature mild but not hot thanks to a slight sea breeze coming from the east. The track was listed as fast and the turf course firm for the 10-race program. Carlisle had picked up a copy of the *Daily Racing Form* the previous afternoon and scanned the entries to see if SB Yokum had any horses entered. If he had, Carlisle would have stayed back at his hotel and watched the races on TV.

Wearing a ballcap, sunnies and a three-day growth of beard just to stay on the safe side, Carlisle did see someone who looked familiar prior to the second race, a 1600 metre affair on the main dirt track for fillies and mares. Leading the number four horse into the mounting yard was someone who looked just like the driver of the float which Yokum had tossed Carlisle on – the one headed to Kentucky.

What the fuck is his name? Think Duke, think. Palmer, that's it. Sid Palmer. Oh, how I would like to get my hands on that fucker, tie him up and throw him onto a horse float. See how he likes it.

"You seem a bit agitated Duke. Anything up"? Kline asked.

"See the grey horse, the number four? She reminds me of a sure thing I had in Saratoga last summer. Four lengths in front with 200 metres to go and she laid down like a $200 hooker. Got beat by a nose, cost me a small fortune."

"I've had a few tough beats of my own, I know the feeling."

"An old coach of mine once told me to keep my dick in my pants and my money far away from the betting windows."

"If you ask me, that's no way to go through life," Kline replied.

"Agreed."

Once the horses had been led onto the track for the second race, Carlisle told Kline he'd meet him back at their seats in the grandstand. "Gonna water the horses and put a bet on."

Carlisle kept an eye on Palmer, who unsurprisingly was walking to the betting windows. Carlisle followed him.

"Putting a bet on your horse mate?"

"Just a couple of dollars," Palmer said while studying his form guide. "Who are you backing?"

Carlisle turned Palmer around, so they were standing face-to-face. A voice boomed from the track public address system. "Five minutes to post time."

"Remember me you fucking cunt?" Carlisle asked.

"Excuse me?"

Carlisle took off his ballcap and sunnies and looked right in Palmer's weathered face.

"I was a bit worse for wear last time we met. I had a couple of black eyes, a bloodied mouth and nose, sore ribs and was tied up in a horse float. Remember now?"

"That was you?" Palmer asked, taking a step back. Carlisle had about four inches and 40 pounds on him.

"Look pal, I was just doing what I was told."

"Were you?"

"Yeah. You know, you cost me a job running off the way you did," a now angry Palmer said. "If you're pissed take it up with Yokum. Leave me out of it."

"Just as soon as we even things up."

Carlisle snatched the strapping chain from Palmer's hands, quickly tied Palmer's hands behind his back with it and led him from the ground floor betting windows.

"The horses have reached the starting gate for the second race of the afternoon," the track announcer said.

With everyone's eyes glued to the starting gate on the Gulfstream Park backstretch, no one noticed as Carlisle paraded Palmer to the tie-up stalls behind the grandstand.

He stopped at the first pile of manure he spotted, knocked Palmer to the ground and with a knee in Palmer's back pushed his face into the steaming pile of shit and held it there.

"If you mention this to anyone, and I mean anyone, so help me I'll feed you your balls for breakfast.

"Don't you dare get up until you finish counting to 100. Understand?"

Carlisle lifted Palmer's face out of the manure to hear his response.

Satisfied with the answer, Carlisle shoved Palmer's face back into the mound of shit.

"Start counting now, slowly."

Carlisle returned to his seat in the grandstand just as the field for the second race crossed the finish line.

"How'd you do, back the winner?" Kline asked.

"I evened a score," Carlisle said.

"Huh?"

"I broke even."

Carlisle flipped the page in his Racing Form to race three.

"Who do you like in the next?"

Behind the grandstand trainer Cash Walker was leading a colt from his float to the tie-up stalls when he noticed someone laying face first in a pile of manure with his hands tied behind his back.

"What the heck is this all about?" he asked.

With his feet, Walker flipped Palmer onto his back. "Is he breathing? If he ain't, there's no way anyone is going to give him mouth-to-mouth."

Walker took his phone from his pocket and rang track security.

Two fellows on minimum wage masquerading as cops showed up moments later, untied Palmer and with a hose used to wash down horses after their runs, cleaned him up the best they could.

"You alright pal?" Enrique Rojas asked.

Palmer glared at him and partner Jose Alomar, got to his feet, cleared his mouth and nose, and began walking to the track exit some 200 yards away leaving a trail of foul-smelling water in his wake.

"I don't know who that son of a bitch was but I'm through with this fucking game," he said.

A long-shot winner in the seventh race on the card made the day a profitable one for Carlisle and Kline. As he brought $24 winner Value For Money back to the winner's enclosure jockey Jacinto Baez told anyone within earshot they should have listened to him in a pre-race television interview he did with racing channel TVG.

"He had nowhere to go last start in a large field and I had tons of horse under me. All I need to do today is give him clear running room and he'll do the rest."

Carlisle and Kline listened, collected well north of $1500 each and decided to get an early jump on the Federal Highway traffic back to Mosquito Lakes.

As they exited, others were streaming in, drawn by the waiving of the $10 general admission fee after race six and eager to have a bet on the last three races on the card. Carlisle handed a fellow horseplayer his *Daily Racing Form* and wished him good luck.

Kline and Carlisle walked to where Kline had parked his year-old Mazda four hours earlier but instead found an empty space.

"I'm sure this is where we parked, isn't it Duke?"

"I think so, but let's have a look around. Maybe we're wrong."

"I cannot fucking believe this," Kline said after their fruitless search. "I grew up in New York for fuck's sake and never had anything stolen. I'm here for not even two years and my car is stolen? In broad fucking daylight? That's what happens when you put a damn casino next to a racetrack. A horseplayer would never steal from another even if he was down to his last two bucks. There's a code Duke – a fucking code."

"It's not the end of the world Jerry," Carlisle said as he put an arm around the 30-year-old.

"Look, we'll report the car stolen, then get a cab back home. I'll pay for it. Your insurance company will have a loaner ready for you by Monday. It's just a small inconvenience."

"But what about all my gear in the car? – CDs, my spare pair of sunnies, clothes?"

"It can all be replaced."

"I guess. But you know, I liked that car and now it's probably being cut into pieces at a Hialeah chop shop."

As they walked back to the main entrance gate looking for a cop or a security officer, Carlisle grabbed Kline by the arm and ducked behind a tree.

"Don't say anything, just look straight ahead."

"My car," Kline yelled out.

Carlisle put his hand over Kline's mouth and told him to pipe down.

"What the hell is going on?"

"I reckon your car was pinched minutes before we got there and the bozo behind the wheel is picking someone up. I'll take the driver's side; you take the passenger side. Unlock the car with your remote and we'll grab the scumbag and toss him out of there."

Carlisle and Kline briskly walked to where Kline's Mazda was idling and on Carlisle's command sprang into action. Kline unlocked the car with his remote and distracted the driver while Carlisle got him in a bearhug, pulled him out of the vehicle and flung him onto the asphalt. Two of Hallandale, Florida's finest responded to the fracas and once they were told what was happening handcuffed the thief and waited for back-up to arrive.

Officers O'Halloran and Davidson took statements from Carlisle and Kline and once it as established that Kline was the legal owner of the vehicle, allowed Kline to drive it home.

The suspect, a twenty something punk, was arrested for theft and drug possession. "Yeah, I pinched the car," Rafael Barraga told O'Halloran and Davidson, "but the meth ain't mine. Those guys planted it on me. You gotta believe me."

"Of course, we believe you," O'Halloran said. "Don't we Davo?" "One hundred percent," Davidson said trying not to laugh. When back-up arrived, they placed him in the back seat of a patrol car and went back to their posts.

"That took a lot of guts Duke, thank you," Kline said on the drive home.

"Not really, just a good eye."

"I don't know what it is," Carlisle continued, "but trouble just seems to find me."

"What do you mean?"

"Well, when I was down under my pecker turned a kaleidoscope of colours and was nearly amputated, and I saw a carjacker turned into guacamole by an eighteen-wheeler. A few months ago, a leading trainer kidnapped and nearly killed me, and recently I was forcefully fucked by a 74-year-old woman while her husband feigned sleep and listened in."

A stunned Kline stared at Carlisle, speechless.

"But I've also discovered the backbone of a team that will win a World Series in five years."

"You could have told me all of that this morning."

"Well now you know, consider yourself warned. By the way, there's this combination steakhouse/strip joint in Fort Lauderdale I've heard good things about. Up for a little surf and turf?"

"Not really, but that's where we're going, isn't it?"

"Yup."

"Oy vey."

Acknowledgements

Special thanks to Kerry Russell, Simon McEvoy, David Turner, Chris Tatman, Glenn Best, Professor Quincy Adams Wagstaff, Dr Hugo Z Hackenbush, Rex the kelpie, Bernie, the 40kg labrador/chicken parma cross and the Forty South team of Lucinda Sharp, Kent Whitmore and Rayne Allinson for their support, suggestions and encouragement.

—Marty Shevelove

Tasmania, June 2025

OTHER BOOKS BY MARTY SHEVELOVE

The Gary Delaney series

Too Hard Wrong Spot

Great Barrier Grief

Driving Miss Crazy

Available by emailing martymelbourne@gmail.com
or through Forty South Publishing at fortysouth.com.au

TOO HARD WRONG SPOT

Shouts of "Stop the Presses" are being replaced by the cry of "Put it Online, Mate" and after 25 colourful years as a newspaper reporter and editor, Gary Delaney is having a hard time adjusting to the new digital age. A share in a promising overseas stayer with Melbourne Cup aspirations could erase the memories of a disastrous Mongolian mining investment. But two gamblers recently released from prison have a large cup wager of their own and threaten to derail Delaney's dream in the most unusual and amusing Spring Carnival Melbourne has even seen.

GREAT BARRIER GRIEF

After getting tapped on the shoulder, veteran sports journalist and racehorse owner Gary Delaney is faced with a dilemma; regroup and look for work in Melbourne or make a fresh start in another city; preferably one with palm trees, warm sunshine and lovelies sunning themselves by the pool. He chooses the latter.

While ex-cons Johnny Pastrami and Frankie "Fingers" Tannenbaum pull off a massive betting plunge, Delaney hits it off with one of his new neighbours but falls for a stunning financial advisor who promptly separates him from his life savings and disappears. Can Delaney track her down and recover his lost loot or is he doomed to spend the rest of his days dancing for gold coins on the Cairns Esplanade?

DRIVING MISS CRAZY

Former sports journalist and racehorse owner Gary Delaney makes a welcome return, while other somewhat dubious characters – we all know one or two – seemingly jump right off the page in this amusing collection of short stories that take readers from Tasmania to far north Queensland, with stops in The Lone Star State of Texas and the manicured fairways and greens of Augusta National Golf Course, the home of The Masters Tournament.

Along the way there are car chases, gambling, fistfights, food fights, dates that go sour, whisky sours, risky racehorses, women with legs as long as the Bruce Highway, more gambling, sex workers, plane crashes, medical procedures, and golf outings on crocodile-free courses.

www.ingramcontent.com/pod-product-compliance
Lightning Source LLC
Chambersburg PA
CBHW050606190726
48283CB00007B/2307

* 9 7 8 1 7 6 4 2 0 1 1 0 0 *